To Danielle Naji-Allah.

From Dr Sarkar

THE
UNDERCURRENT

T.A. Sarkar

THE
UNDERCURRENT

T.A. SANKAR

ISBN: 978-1-4834-7969-9 (sc)
ISBN: 978-1-4834-7968-2 (e)

Library of Congress Control Number: 2017919727

Lulu Publishing Services rev. date: 12/27/2017

Visit the author's website at www.tasankar.com.

To the health care workers who worked in the dark days
of AIDS.

To my family.

SOUTH CARIBBEAN

1

THE WHIP CRACKED!

Paul felt the sting then the numbing pain.

Another crack!

The whip wrapped itself around his waist.

Another jolt!

Again!

The tip came all the way to his lower chest.

Again and again!

He tried hard not to scream. He didn't want to appear cowardly, but his mouth opened without his permission. He covered it with his hands.

He heard Ramon's voice. "You lying bastard! Do you know how much those drugs are worth?" Without waiting for an answer, he said, "You tell me where you hid them or I kill you."

Paul tried to look over his shoulder. Ramon sounded distant as if he were in another room. But there he stood, half-smiling about eight feet away. His two thugs stood on either side of him. All three seemed to be enjoying Paul's pain.

"I will kill you slowly," Ramon continued.

"I don't know anything about any drugs." The feeble voice came out of Paul's dry lips. He barely recognized it as his own.

Ramon nodded to one of his thugs, who then raised the whip. Paul closed his eyes. Paul barely felt the pain before multicolored lights flashed in his brain. The whip hit the bare skin of Paul's back. He felt nauseated. He thought he would vomit. His right hand covered his mouth.

Again, another crack!

Paul felt this one biting through his skin. He felt the whip wrapping itself on his bone. Right down to his vertebrae. This time, he reached for his back. He felt the huge welts crisscrossing his back. Somewhere in his consciousness, he was surprised that his skin was not cut through.

And yet again!

This time, Paul screamed. He couldn't hold it in any longer. The gush of his breath spurted out. It didn't sound like a scream to his ears. It wasn't noiseless either. It sounded like a hoarse, high-pitched shriek that ended abruptly with a choking sound. More like someone suffocating than in pain.

His brain registered everything in slow motion as if it were happening to someone else and he was the witness.

Paul Karan was stripped to his underwear. His knees were wobbly. He absorbed blow after blow and still tried to stand. He leaned against the once-white wall of his cell. He tried to support his weakened body. Without the wall, he would topple over.

His cell was large by prison cell standards. About twelve feet by fourteen. There was a mattress in one corner. A crude toilet with a bucket of water at the other end. His three captors, Paul, and the whip.

Paul deduced that he was about fifty miles from Caracas. It was under an hour's drive from his real prison cell in Caracas. It could be closer, but he was blindfolded. He had estimated based on the speed of the vehicle. They were on a highway for a bit. Other than that, he knew little. He had tried to put pieces of information together. The pain was too great now. He couldn't think any longer.

Ramon's voice came thundering down at him. Ramon moved closer. Paul tried not to cower. Instinctively, he flinched.

"Tell me," Ramon hissed angrily.

"I don't know him," Paul pleaded.

"He is dead now, you know."

Paul's eyes flickered in comprehension. He digested the information.

"Nobody double-crosses Ramon. *Comprende?*"

Paul nodded without meaning to.

Ramon motioned to his other thug, the larger one. He took the whip from the first one. He raised it in the air and swung. It knocked Paul off his feet again. Something was different this time. The pain was raw. Paul didn't try to get up.

"Tell me!" Ramon shouted.

No answer from Paul.

The whip stuck again.

Again and again. Paul was on the verge of unconsciousness. He knew his skin has been cut through now. He didn't have to feel his back. He felt wet as blood dripped down his sides. He prayed to lose consciousness, but some powerful god denied him. The pain burned bright red waves in his brain.

The whip moved to his legs. Paul curled up on the floor. He felt the fingers of his left hand break as he tried to protect his right shoulder. It was almost impossible to describe his feeling. It wasn't only agony. It was agony swallowed by despair. Despair at being completely helpless.

Just before he slipped into unconsciousness, he heard Ramon's voice. "Stop."

A minute passed before he heard Ramon again. "If we kill him now, we get nothing. We come back tomorrow."

Paul heard the door of his cell close. He allowed himself to slip into a deep blackness. The deep blackness of unconsciousness. Peaceful and quiet.

He wanted to stay there and never wake up.

2

It was April 10, 1988. Less than a week before his capture, Paul Karan's life was going according to his general plan.

Paul had awoken early that morning. He didn't appear excited. But inwardly he was. He was heading to Washington, DC, where he had a job interview. This was going to be his step into the big outside world.

His fiancée dropped him off at the airport just outside Port of Spain, Trinidad. As she bade him goodbye, she said matter-of-factly, "See you in a few days."

"I promise," he said with a quick kiss.

At the airport terminal, Paul thought something was wrong. The security appeared tighter than usual. There were two separate checks on their baggage. He quickly dismissed it as the new norm. He didn't fly often enough to know for sure.

He was about to board the massive Pan Am jet when he knew for sure that something was amiss. As they walked across the open tarmac to the aircraft, every passenger was asked to identify his or her luggage. The luggage was lined up in neat rows. He identified his and proceeded to board the aircraft.

He quickly took his window seat in economy class. He wondered if his luggage was going to make his connection. He had chosen to fly to JFK via Caracas and then connect with Piedmont to Washington, DC. He knew, from a previous visit to New York, the chaos at JFK. He shrugged. Not much he could do about it now.

Paul's choices from Port of Spain to DC were limited. He could have gone to Miami with American Airlines and then to DC. For some reason, that was much more expensive. He didn't mind going through New York. That would allow him to make a quick visit to his cousins.

Paul peered out the window. Instead of the crew scurrying to pack the luggage into the belly of the airplane, he noticed a dog sniffing at the suitcases. They were still lined up on the tarmac. He sighed inwardly. Despite his careful planning, he would probably miss his connecting flight. He should be okay, he reassured himself. His interview was the following day.

Conveniently, his row had only two seats. There were eight across, but four were in the middle with two aisles. A young, brown-skinned man took the seat next to Paul. He appeared slightly older than Paul. He mumbled pleasantly, then stared straight ahead.

Paul glanced over but didn't pursue a conversation. The man looked somewhat unkempt. He had a short beard and black hair. He was probably of Indian ancestry, Paul thought, but he wasn't sure. He could have been Hispanic or multiracial. Paul didn't stare. That would have been rude. He figured everyone was frazzled due to the early-morning flight and the added hassles.

They waited on the ground for another half hour. After what seemed like ages, the plane took finally off. It headed southwest toward Caracas. It was the short leg of the flight. In an hour, they would pick up more passengers and then continue on to New York.

Paul tried to snooze without success. The light from his window was bright. He hesitated to pull down the shutters. There were a couple of readers close by. Instead, he decided to stare outside. The aircraft gathered height and then leveled off. They did not seem to be flying very high. Probably because it was a short flight, Paul thought. He finally closed his eyes.

Minutes later, Paul was woken from his nap. Someone was tapping his arm. It was the guy sitting next to him. His eyes were protruding. He looked anxious. His hand was clutching his chest.

The doctor instinct in Paul quickly took over. "Are you having chest pain?" he asked.

The swarthy, bearded man nodded. He continued pleading with his eyes.

Paul quickly stood up and pressed the call button. A flight attendant appeared almost before the chime ended. Paul identified himself as a doctor.

"Is the chest pain pressing or burning?" Paul asked.

The man continued to point to his heart.

"How old are you?" Paul asked.

"Twenty-eight," he replied softly.

"It's very unusual to have a heart attack at your age," Paul said aloud, for the benefit of both the passenger and the flight attendant.

The man remained silent.

Paul's brain was working overtime. "Did you have heart disease as a child?"

No answer.

"Did you have rheumatic fever as a child?" Paul persisted.

This time, the man nodded. He made a noise that sounded like a yes.

By now, two other flight attendants had joined the first. With Paul and his newfound patient, there was a small crowd in the tight aisle. Paul was too engrossed to notice the gawking of the other passengers. Paul nodded to the flight attendants. Their puzzled looks indicated that he needed to elaborate.

"He is kind of young to have a heart attack. But with his history of rheumatic fever, it is certainly possible," Paul explained.

"Great!" the head flight attendant exclaimed. The annoyance in her voice was apparent.

"Can he make it to New York?" another asked.

"I wouldn't take that chance," Paul said.

"So he would have to get off in Caracas?" the head flight attendant asked, looking for confirmation.

"That would be the safest option," Paul opined.

Paul knew that they had already gone more than half the way to Caracas. Turning the flight around to get help would take longer than going forward.

"What can we do now?" the third and most concerned of the flight attendants asked.

Paul had already been thinking about it. He also knew the medical resources of most flights were limited. "I will give him some oxygen. Oxygen and two aspirins until we get to Caracas."

"Aspirin?"

"Yes, that can help in chest pain and heart attacks," Paul explained.

"Let's take him to first class," the third flight attendant offered.

The other two looked questioningly at her.

"There is more space there. We can lie him down and give him the oxygen," she explained.

"Let me help you," Paul offered.

"No, no. We can handle it," the head flight attendant said.

Before Paul could protest, they half-lifted and half-dragged his new patient up the aisle. The rest of the passengers looked on with curiosity and horror.

Paul finally sat down again. He exhaled. He tried to make sense of what just happened. He hoped they would get his patient to a hospital in time.

3

THE DOOR OF HIS CELL OPENED. JUST AS HE HAD PROMISED, Ramon returned with his two thugs. Paul's heart skipped several beats. The terror that flooded into him paralyzed him instantly. His brain was like an erupting volcano, but his body was frozen.

Ramon just stood there. He looked at Paul with cold eyes. Paul wanted to run. There was nowhere to go. With a smile, one of Ramon's stooges waved the whip at him. The big one. The same way he did twenty-four hours earlier.

A few hours earlier, pain had woken Paul up. Scorching pain from all his wounds. Deep pain in his body. He had the mother of all headaches. He felt his temporal arteries pulsating.

When he woke up, Paul had no idea of the time. From his counting, it was Monday or Tuesday. In this dungeon, he couldn't tell night from day. There were no windows. There was a dim bulb overhead behind a metal frame. No switch, no wires. He couldn't electrocute himself if he wanted to. The only way in or out was the door. It was locked from the outside.

Paul must have had a visitor when he was unconscious. They had placed some food, a cup of water, and some clothes near the door. Paul saw it but didn't have the energy to get it.

Finally, his cerebral functions forced him to. He knew he needed some strength. He needed to be able to think if he were to leave this place alive. He knew they would kill him without a second thought. All they wanted was information about the missing cocaine.

Paul dragged himself over to the food. The bread was hard. The thick soup-like liquid was cold. It must have been there for hours, he thought. He dipped the bread into the bowl of broth. He consumed all of it. His stomach stopped grumbling. He felt a bit stronger as the glucose coursed through his veins.

The cell was hot. There was no need for clothes. They had brought him a pair of pants and a T-shirt. That would just cause him to sweat and lose more fluid, he reasoned. In addition to bruising his wounds. Modesty was long gone. He remained in his underwear.

Paul drank half of the large cup of water. With the other half, he wet the T-shirt and began to clean his wounds. First his trunk, then his arms. Finally, his legs. The pain was intense. When the shirt was no longer moist, he stopped.

He didn't want to use the water from the bucket by the toilet. That would be as good as introducing infection in his wounds. He was glad that his clinical mind was still functioning. It allowed him to somewhat remove himself from his present predicament.

Ramon's voice brought him back to the present. "Where are my drugs?" he asked. His tone was conversational, as if he was inquiring about the weather.

Paul didn't answer.

"Where are my drugs?" Ramon asked again, with more intensity.

Paul knew the whip was coming soon. "I do *not* know that man," he replied.

"You lie," Ramon hissed

No answer from Paul.

"Sooner or later, you will tell me," Ramon bellowed.

He stared at Paul with snakelike eyes.

"Better now than later."

Paul knew that they wouldn't believe him, whatever he said. He wanted to make up an answer. But he knew if he gave them a fake location, they would soon discover his lie. He decided to remain silent.

Ramon nodded to the man with the whip.

He raised it, and the whip cracked. The sting around Paul's raw back was savage.

Again and again.

Flashes of white pain erupted in Paul's brain. He screamed. This time, it was soundless. No air crossed his vocal cords.

Yet again.

Paul prayed to lose consciousness. No luck this time.

Instead, a strange thought crossed his mind. He was becoming detached from his body. He was thinking what a mess they were making of his wounds. The careful cleaning he had done earlier.

Blood dripped down to the band of his underwear. It stalled there for a moment before it overflowed. Like a shallow dam blocking water.

Another crack! Paul lost count. He had no energy to resist.

They were breaking him. Bit by bit.

Then it stopped as suddenly as it had started.

"Are you ready to talk now?"

Paul tried to answer but failed. A croak came from his throat.

The other thug without the whip walked over. He picked up the bucket of water meant for the toilet. He threw it over Paul. The sudden jolt of cold hit Paul, momentarily clearing his mind.

"Go ahead," Ramon urged.

"I told you, I am a doctor."

Ramon waited.

"I did not know your man."

"You lie," Ramon said calmly.

Paul didn't answer.

"I will pull your fingernails out. One by one until you tell me."

Silence.

"When I am done, I will start on your eyeballs."

With that, he left. His cronies followed him. They locked the door behind them.

Paul curled up on the wet floor.

4

PAUL FORCED HIMSELF TO RESETTLE IN HIS SEAT. HE WOULD have preferred to be tending to the patient with the chest pain. He was pensive for less than five minutes before the head flight attendant returned.

She took the seat, just vacated, next to him. She introduced herself as Patty. Her attitude had shifted. She appeared less annoyed and more apprehensive. Paul didn't greet her.

"You realize we had a slow start this morning?" Patty half-asked, half- stated.

"Yes," Paul answered, still staring straight ahead.

"We are well behind schedule," Patty said.

"I am sure."

"Almost two hours."

"I think I will miss my connection to Washington," Paul said.

"Don't worry, we'll get you on a later flight," she said.

"We'll see."

"Hopefully your connection is with Pan Am."

"It's not."

"It might cost you a bit more, but you will get there today."

Paul switched gears. "How's the patient?"

"He seems to be doing okay. The other flight attendants are with him."

"That's good."

A break in the conversation ensued. After a few moments, Patty leaned over and whispered to Paul, "We had a bomb scare this morning."

That caught Paul's attention. His questioning eyes asked Patty to go on.

"Someone called the airlines this morning. They said that there would be a bomb on the airplane," Patty explained.

13

"This flight?"

"Yes, they specified this flight."

The thought registered in Paul's brain that they could go up in flames at any moment. However, the denier in him responded, "Probably somebody's idea of a joke."

"I really hope so," Patty responded nervously.

Paul realized that Patty and the rest of the flight crew were on edge. Now that he had been given information that he didn't ask for, he was joining their ranks. He was certain he would have been better off not knowing.

"Does this happen often?" Paul asked, trying to defuse the subject.

"No."

His probe for reassurance fell flat.

Patty kept on talking. "You noticed the extra security this morning?

"How could I not?"

"The bomb-sniffing dogs?"

"It's the reason we're running late, isn't it?" Paul asked with more than a hint of sarcasm.

"Delayed start wasn't a big problem. We thought we could make up the time from Caracas to New York."

Paul noticed her use the past tense. "And now?"

"To start with, we are not going at normal speed. You might have noticed that we have been flying low."

Paul's expression again asked the question.

"Eight thousand feet. Cabin not pressurized."

"That's it!" Paul exclaimed.

"What?" Patty asked.

"The low oxygen pressure. That's what precipitated his chest pain."

"Oh."

Paul realized that she wasn't following. Inwardly, he was patting himself on the back for his correct diagnosis. He went on to explain to Patty, "He must have had a borderline heart condition. With the low oxygen tension, it tipped him over, and he developed symptoms."

"I see," Patty said, not nearly as excited or convinced as Paul.

"Now I'm sure. We have to get him off in Caracas."

"Your friend, you mean?"

"He's not my friend. I just met him."

"We will get him off in Caracas. But we have to get every piece of his luggage off the airplane."

As Paul raised his eyebrows to ask, he realized the answer to his question. *The bomb scare!*

Patty continued, "He checked multiple pieces of luggage to New York. We have to find each one and remove them before we take off again."

"You investigated him?"

"We did," Patty replied.

"I suppose," Paul reluctantly agreed.

Patty resumed. "He goes by the name Joseph Laala. He has flown several times in the past with us. Always to New York via Caracas. Our security people think that Joseph Laala is one of his names. His records are completely clean."

"I see," Paul said, not knowing what to make of all this new information.

"We are ten minutes from Caracas," Patty stated.

Paul nodded. Patty got up and left.

Paul was left sitting there. His anxiety rose steadily. Waiting for a jolt. Praying that it was an air pocket.

5

It had taken hours for Paul to pass out after Ramon's last visit. When he finally did, he couldn't call it sleep. It was more like semicomatose state. He was aware that his wounds were throbbing. He was dreaming but could still feel his body. He was floating in the sky, but his legs were taut. They were weighed down with bags of cement.

His mattress was still wet from the water they had dumped on him. His cell stank. He could ignore the stench. But the pain continued.

It was hot in this dungeon. He could tolerate it. But his wounds festered.

Paul knew that he was being watched. There were no mirrors in the cells' walls. The cameras were probably in the ceiling. More than likely, in the light fixtures. He briefly entertained the idea of ripping it out. He discarded the thought, as he needed the light.

Paul was awake this time when one of Ramon's men brought him food. He opened the door and left the food on the floor. He didn't utter a word. He quickly locked the door and left. A menacing glare, and he was gone.

A few minutes later, Paul crawled over. He ate all the food. He drank some water and crept back to the mattress. He placed his pants on the mattress, hoping to cover up some wets areas. He tried to sleep.

The pain wouldn't let him. He tried to not think about Ramon and his threat. He found it difficult to not to look at his fingernails. Eventually, he pushed that thought away. He tried not to think about his predicament. That was near impossible.

Paul looked at his body. He examined his arms and legs. A yellow crusting had appeared on his wounds. Particularly, those on his torso. He didn't bother to clean them. He had nothing to work with. What was the point anyway? he thought.

They would kill him before they let him go. He had no knowledge of their missing cocaine. He briefly contemplated taking matters in his own hands. Even as a doctor, he had little to work with. The cell was barren. He dismissed the idea.

He drew on all his mental reserves. He tried to meditate. Desperately, he attempted to push the pain. Multiple times, he failed. He kept trying. Eventually, he either fell asleep or passed out. He didn't care. Either way, he welcomed the blackness.

The peaceful blackness of his brain shutting down. For the moment, it protected him. He knew it would be temporary. Still, it was the best option he had available. When he awoke, the nightmare might disappear. He hoped.

Ramon's voice woke him.

"Ready to talk?"

Reality returned instantaneously. He was still in the cell. He was still a prisoner.

Paul's eyed widened. He stared at his captors.

"Ready to talk now?" Ramon prodded.

Ramon kept a tight schedule. He arrived like clockwork at Paul's cell. His cronies were at his side. Thugs were a better description. Paul noticed that neither had a whip today.

"My friend, how are you?" Ramon mocked.

Paul didn't answer. He felt apprehension building in him.

"I am sure today is the day," Ramon said.

His tone was different.

"Today you tell us everything."

The tone of Ramon's voice sent Paul's blood pressure to rocket upward. It wasn't apprehension Paul was feeling. It was terror.

"I do not know anything. I don't know about your cocaine."

"Your English is excellent, senor," Ramon stated matter-of-factly. "But you lie!"

"Please believe me. I am a doctor," Paul pleaded.

"Senor Doctor, you will die slowly unless you tell us the truth," Ramon continued.

"I am telling the truth," Paul yelled, surprised at his own tone.

"You lie," Ramon scowled, showing his teeth in a menacing grin.

Paul didn't know what took hold of him. With a sudden fury, he lunged toward Ramon. He swung his fist. One of Ramon's bodyguards calmly intercepted him.

Paul swung again. He caught the bodyguard squarely on his jaw. He let out a surprised snarl. He quickly reacted with a fist to Paul's jaw. He followed with an elbow to Paul's midsection then a knee to his groin. Within seconds of his unplanned retaliation, Paul was doubled up on the floor. He was bleeding from his mouth. His testicles felt as if they had receded to his abdomen.

They waited. They didn't say a word. They just stood there and watched him. Paul finally sat up. For some reason, he finally noticed the size of Ramon's bodyguards. They were much larger than Ramon. Taller and better built than Paul.

"Ready now?" Ramon asked.

Paul didn't answer.

"Do you know how much those bags are worth?" Ramon asked.

He wasn't expecting an answer. Paul didn't know the answer.

"Every one of those bags had thirty-two kilos of coke. Every one is worth more than one million American dollars," Ramon said slowly.

Paul digested this information.

Ramon slowly spelled it out for him. "Now you know, you talk or we kill you."

Paul knew he meant it.

"Where are the drugs?" Ramon hissed, the intensity building in his voice.

"I ... I ... don't know," Paul muttered, almost unintelligibly.

Ramon nodded to his thugs. They jumped on Paul. They pinned him to the floor. Then they pinned both of his arms to his sides with their knees. They reached into their pockets. Slowly, they each took out a pair of pliers.

Paul tried detaching himself from his body. He knew what was coming. They appeared to be well-versed in their actions.

They started with the little finger of his left hand. They wrenched the nail completely off its bed.

Blood squirted. Paul howled in pain.

He was still howling when they moved over to his other hand. They pinned it first. The pliers closed on the little finger of his right hand. The massive hand of his torturer yanked. Paul screamed louder—the screams of a wounded animal.

Their faces were close to his. Paul looked into their eyes. Right there and then, Paul knew he would live. His purpose for survival was to personally kill these animals.

They eventually got off him. They stood on either side of Ramon.

Ramon was completely unperturbed. Calmly, he said, "Every day, we take two nails."

His men nodded.

"Then the eyeballs."

His men nodded again.

"I promise," Ramon said.

His men smiled.

"If you want, we can take the eyeballs first."

Paul winced.

"Remember that Ramon always keeps his promise."

With that, they locked the door and left.

6

PAUL HELD HIS BREATH AS THE HUGE PAN AM JET TOUCHED down. If it was going to explode, it would be now.

The back wheels hit the ground.

Nothing.

The aircraft leveled off. The front wheels touched. A small bump.

Nothing happened.

The screeching of the brakes sounded louder than normal. The squeaking of the wing flaps was magnified. Nothing happened.

The pilot took his time. He taxied to the edge of the airfield before slowly returning to the terminal. Paul, armed with his extra knowledge, remained tense.

Still, no explosion. Paul let out a partial breath.

A few of the passengers began to disembark. The majority stayed on, as they were headed to New York. Paul remained in his seat and stared through the window.

He saw an ambulance pulling up to the plane. He didn't see them taking the infirmed passenger. He presumed it was the reason for the ambulance. He nestled himself for the wait. He had been forewarned warned by Patty that it could be a long wait.

Ten minutes passed. Fifteen. Then thirty. It appeared to be longer, but he knew that time moved slowly when waiting. He invoked his hunter's patience and waited.

Suddenly, there was commotion ahead of him. Paul looked up. He saw four uniformed officers coming down the aisle quickly. Two of them had guns drawn. Necks were craning to look at them. They stopped at the row where Paul sat.

They pointed the guns at him.

"You are under arrest!"

Paul was stunned. He couldn't speak.

"Come with us!" one of the uniformed men, with a drawn gun, said.

Paul finally found his voice.

"For what?" he asked.

"You are under arrest for smuggling drugs!"

"I don't know what you're talking about," Paul protested.

"I am sure you don't."

"Reach your hands out in front of you."

Paul complied. It would have been foolish not to. These were uniformed officers with guns drawn. Before Paul's brain could figure out what was happening, one of the officers had efficiently handcuffed him.

"Get up."

Paul stumbled to a standing position. With his hands cuffed in front of him, they dragged him off the airplane. The stunned passengers craned their necks as he was pulled down the aisle.

No one said a word.

†

Paul was taken to a police station some distance from the airport. They placed him in an interview room. The officers took turns questioning him.

They asked him the same questions. Over and over again. He had no answers. None of his answers pleased them. They didn't believe him. He got tired and frustrated.

They interrogated him all day. No food. He asked for a glass of water. He must have said the same thing a dozen times. No, he did not know the passenger who sat next to him. Not even his name. He was told his name by the flight attendant. No, they had not colluded to feign an illness to get him off the plane. No, Paul was not a drug smuggler.

Paul spoke in English. Most of the officers spoke accented English. He also tried his limited Spanish. Same result. But he tried anyway. It wasn't that they didn't understand him. They just did not believe him.

Paul put bits and pieces together since his arrest. They had found

21

cocaine in the luggage of Joseph Laala, the passenger who sat next to him. Laala was probably a drug smuggler, based on what Patty told him. With all the extra security of the bomb threat that day, Laala felt like a cat on a hot tin roof. He wanted to get off the plane, fearing that his cargo would be unmasked.

Laala had faked an illness. By sheer coincidence, Paul had been assigned the seat next to him. Good luck for Laala, as Paul was the one who had called the flight attendants. His testimony enabled Laala to get off the plane. Now the authorities believed that it was all part of a preconceived plan. No amount of explaining, no amount of pleading would convince them otherwise.

It was gift wrapped for them. Now they wanted Paul's confession. Even some inconsistency in his story would do. They could nail it to him. And kill two birds with one stone.

Paul had not seen Laala since his chest pain. He didn't know if they had taken him to hospital or if they had jailed him. It was certainly possible that Laala was in this same building. Paul had no way of knowing. He didn't want to ask.

"So, you claim to be a doctor, eh?" the officer sneered at him.

"Yes," Paul said.

Paul's voice carried no conviction now. Why would this one believe him when all the others didn't?

"How convenient for you and Laala," the officer said. "That was one sure way to get him off the flight."

"You can check my medical certificates. I had them in my carry-on bag."

"You take those with you every time you travel?"

"No."

"Why do you have them now?'

"I had them because I was going for a job interview. In Washington, DC," Paul pleaded.

"Even more convenient," the officer said.

Paul didn't answer. He was tired. It must be night by now, he thought. The room had no windows.

He had long given up his earlier hope. He had hoped that they would clear him and put him on the next flight to New York. They showed no inclination of believing him. Paul didn't dare to contemplate how long they would detain him.

About this time, another officer entered the room. This one looked different from the others. He was probably the chief from the way he gave orders. He had the same black pants and hat as the others. He didn't wear the same type of shirt. Instead, he wore a dark blue shirt. He had holsters on both hips.

He also had something in his hand. A ragged-looking piece of paper. He waved it at Paul. "You mean *this*?"

Paul's heart skipped a beat. It was his medical school diploma.

"Yes!" Paul exclaimed. "You found it!"

The police chief motioned with his chin to the other officer in the room. He left noiselessly.

"I told you, I'm a doctor," Paul said, relief in his voice.

"You really expect us to believe this?" the police chief said.

Paul was confused. It was the original certificate with the Latin words and all. It was the one he had worked so hard for. The one he treasured.

"You really underestimate us," the police chief said, not concealing his annoyance.

"It's real," Paul replied. There was intensity and defiance in his voice.

"I could forge one better than this," the chief responded.

Paul was speechless.

"Doesn't matter. You fetch a good price," he said evenly.

The police chief calmly tore his certificate into small pieces.

"No!" Paul cried.

His hopes of release had risen dramatically in the last few minutes. Now, they fell even more precipitously.

Before Paul could protest any further, the police chief made a hand signal. Three men burst into the room. They grabbed Paul and quickly blindfolded him. They put him back in handcuffs and dragged him out of the room.

Paul heard one of them say, "Ramon will take care of everything."

"Give him my regards," the chief replied.

Paul's feet barely touch the ground as they half-carried and half-dragged him outside. They tossed him into a waiting vehicle.

He heard the engines roar. He lurched forward as the vehicle accelerated. He was too stunned to react.

7

PAUL SAT WITH HIS BACK TO THE CELL DOOR. IT WAS TWEN-
ty-four hours since he had lost the first two of his fingernails. He now
knew the real meaning of the word *torture*. He waited.

He waited for Ramon and his men. He stared at his hands. There was
still dry, crusted blood. He refused to wash it off. The cuts on his trunk
and legs were definitely infected now. A raised yellow layer had formed
over all the wounds.

Paul sat in the same spot for hours. Suddenly the door opened. He
felt an electric shock move through his body. He didn't look. He waited.
No footsteps. He finally turned his head to the side and looked. He was
trying to make sense of the sudden silence. To decipher what Ramon and
his men were up to.

He stared. He rubbed his eyes. Standing at the doorway to his cell was
an attractive woman. She was in her early to mid-twenties, he deduced.
Quite beautiful, he thought.

This must be some cruel hallucination, he thought. His brain was trying
to escape from his present reality. A well-described medical phenomena,
he knew. He closed his eyes and opened them. She was still there.

"Hello, Paul."

He didn't answer. She knew his name.

"My name is Andreina," she said softly.

Still no answer from Paul. He was trying to make sense of it. Was
this another tactic by Ramon to get information from him? he wondered.

"Can I come closer?" she asked.

Her voice was kind.

He nodded.

She moved toward him. She had a small case in her right hand. "I brought some medicines for you," she said.

The questions in Paul's head were many. He was expecting to lose at least another two fingernails today, and here was someone bringing medicines for him! *What twisted humor*, he thought.

"Who are you?" Paul finally found his voice.

"I told you. My name is Andreina," she said hesitantly.

Her English was very good. Much less accented than Ramon's and his thugs'.

"I mean, who *are* you?"

Her expression showed incomprehension. This was quickly followed by clarity. She now understood what he meant.

"I live here. I am part of the family."

"Where is here? Whose family?" Paul asked.

"This is San Tome. A small town just outside Caracas," she replied clearly.

Paul was alert now. "Whose family?" he asked again.

"This is the family of Luis. Brother of Ramon."

Paul digested this for a moment. Luis was a new name to him. Ramon was not.

"Where is Luis?" Paul asked.

"Luis does not live here. This is the Casa de Ramon."

Paul spoke slowly, in a measured voice. "I do not want anything to do with Ramon."

"Ramon is not here right now," she replied evenly.

"Where is he?"

"He has gone to do business with Luis."

"Where is Luis?"

"Luis lives in Colombia."

Paul was silent for a moment. He had just quadrupled his knowledge about his situation. He still had to piece together the big picture.

"How did you get here?"

"One of the guards owed me a favor. He allowed me to enter this part of the building."

"Why?"

"Can you please hold off on the questions?"

"Why?"

"I need to get you taken care off. Before Ramon comes back."

"You said he went to Colombia."

"He took a private plane. He can come back at any time."

Paul froze.

"If he finds me here, I am dead."

Paul suddenly realized she was taking a huge risk.

"Okay," he replied.

She sat next to him on the hard concrete, the floor of his cell. She pulled out a few white pills from the case she had. "Here, take these," she said. "It will help the pain."

"What are they?" Paul couldn't help himself.

"They are plain Tylenol. We don't have anything stronger here."

"Why?"

"The druggies in the family will clean them out," she explained.

She gave him three pills. He took it with a gulp of water. Paul was putting a lot of faith in Andreina. A little voice in his head reminded him that he was following his gut. His intellect advised him to be wary. His gut overrode his intellect.

"Keep these for later," Andreina said.

"Thanks."

"Please hide them."

She provided him with a small zip-locked plastic bag. There were about twenty white pills in it.

"Now, please stay still."

She moved closer to him. She held his arm. She removed a small bottle from her case, along with some gauze swabs. Before he could ask, she said, "It is antiseptic lotion."

It smelled like it, Paul thought.

She began to clean his wounds, starting with his arms. It burned. Paul bit his lip and kept silent.

"You're a doctor?" Paul asked, trying to take the focus away from his smarting wounds.

"No, a nurse," Andreina replied, without looking up. She moved meticulously from cut to cut.

"How did you know I was here?" Paul asked.

"I saw you on the monitor."

Paul looked questioningly at her.

"Ramon has a camera in this cell. The monitor is in his office."

"Why did you come?"

"You looked badly hurt."

Paul was quiet.

"I cannot tell you everything, Paul. Just know that it is very dangerous for me to be here."

She completed her cleaning of the infected areas. She took out a tube of ointment. "This is antibiotic ointment," she said. She began applying it to his wounds.

Paul's mind was active. Did she know he was a doctor? Or was she just explaining what she was doing as she would with any patient? *One quick way to find out*, he thought. "Do you know that I am a doctor?"

She didn't answer. Her touch was gentle, and her manner exuded care. Yet she was professional enough as she sat in close proximity to him.

"Yes," Andreina finally said.

Paul noted that she deliberated before she answered. He wasn't sure why, but he reminded himself to not to let his guard down. She was the first person who had shown him any kindness in a long time. He knew he was vulnerable.

"How did you know?" Paul asked.

Another long pause.

"Ramon told me."

Paul tightened at the mention of the name. She felt his change of feelings. Whether it was a reciprocal response, he couldn't be sure. She became quickly more guarded. She was almost finished.

"I have to go now," Andreina said.

"What is your connection with Ramon?"

She didn't answer.

"Why do you live here?"

She looked at him with those kind eyes again.

"In time, Paul. I hope to tell you everything. In time."

"When?"

"Depends on when Ramon returns."

He looked at her.

"If he comes back today, the next time he leaves."

She got up and quickly slipped out the door. He thought of rushing out behind her. Before he could finish the thought, the door locked.

She did say she had to get past the guard to visit him, he rationalized.

8

EDUARDO STARED AT THE THICK JUNGLE BELOW HIM. IT WAS pitch-dark. Less than half an hour earlier, it was bright. Sunset was quite sudden in these parts. This was how he had planned it. Fly over Venezuelan territory in the daylight and into Colombia after it got dark. His current location was about one hundred miles northeast of Cucuta.

His three passengers were playing a game of cards. They paid him little attention. He had done this trip with Ramon and his two bodyguards dozens of times. Alonso and Felipe never appeared to be concerned. They left the work and worrying to Eduardo.

Eduardo circled the small plane above the clearing. He didn't see the flashes of light from the men below to guide him. He knew the landing strip well. Yet it was always a test of his skills to land in this small area of jungle. He could have used the help from below.

Eduardo felt his heart rate climbing. He told himself for the umpteenth time that this would be his last trip. He would let Ramon know when they got back. He had promised himself to quit several times before. He never followed through.

His reasons were simple. Firstly, he was afraid of how Ramon would react. But what was more important was the money. The pay was excellent. He knew that only too well. There was a six-month period when additional US security caused them to lie low. He had practically gone broke. He couldn't do without the women and the booze. He had gotten used to the high life.

He pointed the nose of the plane down for landing. He decided to touch down in the opposite direction. Away from the shacks that they usually pulled up to. It was just a short walk. He set down the small bird lightly. He decelerated quickly over the bumpy strip. As he slowed to a stop, Eduardo exhaled.

Ramon got up and peered outside. Alonso and Felipe quickly followed. It took Ramon a few moments to realize that they had to walk back to their usual pickup point.

"Cabeza de Guevo!" Ramon exclaimed.

"Sorry, boss. Was easier to land this way," Eduardo explained.

Without another word, Ramon, Alonso, and Eduardo jumped off the small plane. They headed for the shacks. Eduardo was still digesting his compliment when the silence was shattered. Machine-gunfire erupted behind him.

He snapped his head to the left to look for his passengers. He saw the big frame of Alonso fall forward. Ramon and Felipe dove to the ground. They began crawling to the edge of the jungle. Eduardo suddenly realized he was in trouble. He had to turn the plane around to take off.

He snatched the controls as the first shots hit the side of the plane. They turned their full attention to him. Eduardo deftly made a one-eighty. He accelerated hard for takeoff. His path would take him closer to the source of the gunfire. It was the only way out. He had no choice.

The small plane quickly gained speed. Eduardo heard shots bouncing off the side. More hits as the front wheel lifted off the ground. They couldn't see him. Still, a lucky shot could take him out. He held his breath.

The plane took multiple hits as he lifted off. He climbed up a couple hundred feet. He exhaled. He was thinking he had made it when another barrage hit.

The last thing Eduardo heard was a loud explosion. His fuel tank had taken a direct hit.

†

Ramon was the first one to reach the edge of the jungle. Felipe was right at his feet. They scurried under the thick undergrowth. Bullets snapped off the top of the short bushes. A few ricocheted off the larger tree trunks.

They crawled for a few minutes. Deep into the dense undergrowth. And into safety. For the moment anyway. Nothing could penetrate this.

The gunfire stopped.

Ramon pulled himself forward by his elbows. A few minutes later, he stopped to catch his breath. Felipe joined him. Their eyes had accommodated to the darkness. Ramon put his finger to his lips. He had heard something. So too did Felipe. He cocked his head to one side.

The rustling was getting louder. It was moving in their direction. Ramon drew his gun. Felipe followed suit. Ramon held his hand up. Felipe nodded in understanding. He knew they shouldn't fire unless absolutely necessary. It would give their position away.

Moonlight had sneaked through the clouds. They peered through the underbrush. They saw a large figure dragging forward. They waited a bit longer to make sure. It was Alonso.

Alonso used his arm to propel himself forward. He hauled his leg behind him. Felipe's first instinct was to rush in and help. He checked it.

He waited for his boss's order. Ramon was caught in two minds. He wanted to help Alonso. But he knew the injured man would slow them down. Alonso would be a liability. Helping him might result in them being hunted down.

Ramon didn't waste time. He made a quick a decision. They would go over and assess Alonso. If he was badly injured, they would leave him. If he could walk, they would take him to the village with them.

Alonso was surprisingly alert. He had lost a lot of blood. He had been hit in the thigh of his left leg. He had managed to get to the edge of the jungle. Like Felipe and Ramon, he had crawled to safety.

The skin of his chest and back was torn. He was shirtless. He had taken off his shirt and tied it around his leg to stop the bleeding. The makeshift tourniquet worked.

"Water," he whispered.

They had none.

Ramon nodded to Felipe. "Check the huts."

Without hesitation, Felipe headed off. Ramon stayed behind with Alonso.

Ramon calmly assessed the situation. Felipe was the one risking his life by going to the huts. For now, Ramon was safe. Ramon surveyed Alonso. Alonso was loyal but not indispensable, Ramon thought.

"Can you walk on your right leg?" Ramon whispered.

"I think so."

"One bullet?"

"Si."

Silence.

They waited.

The wait was short. They heard a faint rustle as Felipe emerged from the woods. Empty-handed.

Ramon looked at Felipe.

"All gone," Felipe stated.

"Not surprised," Ramon replied.

"Burnt to the ground," Felipe added.

"Who?"

"Don't know."

"Rivals?"

"It was recent. Still smoking."

"The authorities wouldn't plan a raid this late in the evening," Ramon said.

"Makes sense," Felipe replied.

"What happened to our men?" Alonso whispered.

"Didn't see anybody," Felipe said.

"Probably dead," Ramon replied.

"What do we do?" Alonso asked. He bravely tried to hide his pain.

"The village is five miles away. Let's move," Ramon said.

Felipe helped Alonso to his feet. Alonso was a big man. He leaned on Felipe's right shoulder. He tried to hop on his good leg. It was tough going.

Ramon watched. He didn't help. Alonso bit his lip in pain. His leg throbbed. But he moved forward.

"You can do it," Felipe urged.

"Shhh," Ramon hissed.

"Lead the way, boss," Felipe whispered.

"We can't use the trails," Ramon instructed. "Those men know the area."

Felipe took a deep breath. He forged on.

"We have to get there before daylight," Ramon grunted.

Felipe didn't know if they would get there at all. But he knew Ramon wouldn't hesitate to abandon them.

Step by step, he moved forward. His human cargo was getting heavier with each step.

9

PAUL STARED AT HIS BARE CHEST. HE HAD LOST WEIGHT. They brought him food regularly. He ate it all. Somehow, he had managed not to get sick. He knew it would happen sooner or later.

He heard a key turning. He looked up quickly. He was hoping it would be Andreina. Every time they opened the door to bring him food, his heart raced. Every time, he had been disappointed. He concluded that Ramon had returned. Yet, like a Pavlovian dog, he reacted to the door opening.

This time, it wasn't one of the regular guards. An older man, dressed in a suit, stepped through the door. He had the beginnings of gray hair at his temples. He appeared calmer. His movements were measured.

The man smiled and moved forward. He extended his hand. He spoke in near flawless English.

"Hi, Paul. I am Javier."

Paul nodded in acknowledgment. He didn't say a word.

"I am Ramon's business manager," Javier said politely.

He had no problem declaring his allegiance, Paul thought.

"I am here to make a deal with you," Javier continued.

Paul's ears pricked up. The optimist in him rose to the fore. He once again reminded himself not to let his guard down.

Paul looked at him up and down.

Finally he asked, "What deal?"

"You checked out," Javier said.

"What?"

"You checked out."

"I don't understand," Paul said.

"Our man in Trinidad said you are real," Javier said.

Paul still had a blank look in his eyes.

"Our man in Trinidad told us that you are really who you said you are," Javier said.

Paul was beginning to understand.

"He checked his sources. He also checked with the medical board. You are really a *medico*."

Paul's spirits lifted.

"Great," Paul said.

"I am glad too," Javier said.

Like a child, Paul rushed in. "Will you release me now?"

"Not so quick, Paul."

"Why not?"

"We know you are a doctor. You may be telling the truth about that. Doesn't mean that you were not involved."

"Why would I be?" Paul asked.

"Do you really want me to answer that?"

"Yes."

"Simple."

"What?"

"Money," Javier said.

Paul briefly considered what Javier said. That was a good enough reason for many, he thought. Not for him. But how would Javier know that?

"I was once a bank manager in Caracas, Paul."

"Why did you leave?" Paul asked.

"Exactly my point," Javier said.

Without prompting, Javier added, "I make more money here in one year than I would in my entire life at that job. And I still maintain my contacts."

"I see," Paul said.

It made perfect sense, Paul thought. To most people anyway.

Javier was silent. He allowed Paul to contemplate. He would draw him in with time. Paul complied.

"Tell me more about this deal."

"Ah, yes. The deal."

Paul waited.

Javier took his time. Then he got right to the point.

"We need a doctor."

"And?"

"We want you to join us," Javier said.

"Not interested," Paul replied.

"Don't be so hasty."

"I am sure," Paul said flatly.

"You might want to think about it," Javier said.

His voice was colder now. It was the voice of a man who was not accustomed to being told no. He fully expected Paul to comply.

Paul cleared his throat. He forced himself to continue the conversation.

"What do I get in this deal?" he asked cautiously.

"You will be well compensated."

"I already make a decent salary."

Javier laughed.

"Real money, Paul. Lots of money. And lots of women."

"What if I don't join you?" Paul asked.

"Paul, you are a smart fellow."

"Spell it out for me."

"Do you really think we would let you go free?"

Javier didn't wait for an answer. "With all that you saw?"

The rhetorical question chilled the blood in Paul's veins. He was dealing with a cold and calculated professional. He had to play this safe.

"How long do I have to decide?" Paul asked.

"The earlier the better."

Paul was silent. He gave the appearance as if he was considering it.

"Felipe and Alonso will soon be back," Javier reminded him.

"What have they got to do with this?"

"You still have eight fingernails left."

Paul winced. Javier made a mental note of it.

"I will return tomorrow," Javier said.

10

FIVE MILES WAS A LONG WAY IN THICK JUNGLE. AVOIDING the trails increased the difficulty tenfold. Carrying an injured man made it near impossible.

Several times, Alonso asked to be left behind. Felipe was profuse in his refusal. Ramon, not so much. Felipe soldiered on.

They covered half the distance by midnight. A rudimentary compass that Felipe kept guided them. Lack of water slowed them. It was the wee hours in the morning when they saw light from a couple of houses on the hillside. Their spirits lifted as the village came in range.

From the village, Ramon could get help. Cash did wonders in these parts. They would be able make their way to Cucuta soon enough. His brother, Luis, would take it from there. It should be easy enough to make their way to back to Venezuela. Maybe they would go overland this time, Ramon thought.

Ramon hated the idea of using roads to Caracas. They had been forced to do that in the past, when the Americans had shut off the air routes. The Americans' grand war on drugs. Business had suffered. For a period, Luis halted operations. Luis knew they were taking big risks. They had had to pay off too many people. He figured that they would outlast the Americans. He was correct.

Another mile to the village; they were exhausted. Ramon pushed on. He wanted to get there before daybreak to decrease visibility. There was a good chance their enemies were stationed there. It was a small village. Word got around quickly.

Felipe and Alonso lagged. Ramon wasn't sure that they would make it before sunrise. He took a turn to half-drag Alonso. So far, Felipe had done most of the work. Their pace was excruciatingly slow. Their lips were parched. Extreme fatigue and dehydration had taken hold.

Minutes later, the solution literally fell upon them. Alonso collapsed. They couldn't carry him any further. The rest of the way sloped upward.

"Leave me," Alonso whispered.

Ramon agreed. Felipe reluctantly continued on with his boss. He was upset, but it wasn't all for Alonso. He had left a wounded man to die. He knew the wounded man could have easily been him.

The pace picked up. Ramon seemed lighter. He was. He felt freer. He reckoned that they would raise suspicion if they brought an injured man to the village. Heading to Cucuta unnoticed would be so much more difficult.

Ramon focused on the task on hand. His plan was to find a farmer with an old pickup truck. He would pay him well. It was a simple job. Take them to the city. Keep his mouth shut.

He knew they would find a ride. A willing or unwilling driver would do.

11

PAUL KNEW THIS WASN'T A DEAL. A DEAL HAD TWO SIDES. A deal could be negotiated. In this arrangement, he had to agree or face death. Probably tortured before death. There was only one option.

He would let Javier know. There was no point dwelling on it. It was time to move on. Time to plan for the next step. If he made the decision quickly, they would probably let him out of this cell. Anywhere would be better than here. At the moment, his chances of escape were zero.

The next time a guard brought him food, he would ask to see Javier. He had no idea of the time. He had no watch. He saw no sunlight. He calculated the time from the spacing of the food they brought him. The last meal they brought him, he presumed, was dinner. So it would be around midnight now. He wasn't expecting a guard for at least another six hours.

He was still awake when he heard the key turn. The door opened slowly.

It wasn't a guard. It was Andreina. She had kept her promise.

"Hi, Paul," she said.

"Hi," Paul replied meekly.

Silence.

"Sorry I didn't come before."

Paul nodded.

"There was a problem with Ramon's plane," she explained.

More empty silence.

"Is he back?" Paul said finally.

"Not yet."

"What happened?"

"We are not sure. Luis informed us that Ramon had some trouble with the plane. That he was returning by land. That's what Javier told me."

"You know Javier?"

"Sure."

"How?"

"He lives here."

"How many people live here?"

"A lot," she said.

Understanding his question, she elaborated, "Too many for you to escape."

"How long have you known Javier?"

"Since I came here."

"And how long is that?"

"Please be patient, Paul."

Paul gently bit his upper lip.

"I came to look at your nail bed wounds."

"They are healing," Paul said matter-of-factly.

She wasn't deterred by his attitude. "I am glad."

"Painful but healing," Paul added.

"I'm sorry."

"For what?"

"For what they are doing to you," Andreina said.

"Why? You work here, don't you?" Anger and cynicism had crept into his voice.

"I live here, Paul."

"Is there a difference?"

He wasn't expecting an answer, but she said, "There is."

"Tell me?" he asked.

"One day I will."

"You keep saying that." Paul couldn't hide his exasperation.

"I mean it."

"When?"

She didn't answer.

Paul persisted. Any information he gleaned might be useful later. "Do you trust Javier?"

"He has been kind to me."

"You didn't answer my question."

"He is better than most of Ramon's savages."

"How?"

"In a weird kind of way, he is gentleman."

"What does that mean?"

"Javier is respectful."

"That makes him kind?"

"The rest of them won't touch me because if they did, Ramon would kill them. Javier is different. He has education and upbringing."

"But do you trust him?"

"He is Ramon's business manager, Paul. He *does* work for Ramon and Luis."

Paul knew this was as far as she would go on the subject. He decided to leave it for now.

Paul looked directly at her. In his loneliness, he connected. He felt she wanted to connect as well.

"Please sit down," Paul said, gently tapping the ground beside him.

She did.

He held her hand. She didn't object.

"The guards are probably asleep," Paul said.

She nodded.

"Tell me," Paul whispered.

He looked directly at her again. She was hesitant.

He waited.

✝

Andreina squeezed his hands. She began timidly.

"Just over two years ago, chance brought me in contact with Ramon," she said. "It has been a long two years. It feels more like twenty."

Paul shifted closer to her. His body language encouraged her to continue.

"I had just graduated from nursing school. I was working in the General Hospital in Caracas."

She paused. Her voice was getting stronger. Paul sensed that few people had heard this story.

"He was a patient on the private ward. I was doing the evening shifts at the time. I was a junior nurse."

Paul squeezed her hand again. It encouraged her.

"He was there for a long time. I got to know him. I was young and impressionable. I was stupid."

"What was he there for?" Paul couldn't quite get his medical mind out of a hospital situation.

"He was shot in the chest. His lung had collapsed. He had surgery, and they placed chest tubes in him. It took nearly six weeks for his lungs to re-expand."

"I see," Paul muttered.

"I was on that ward for the entire time. Ramon told me he tried to prevent an old lady from getting robbed. That was how he was shot. I believed him. I didn't know at the time."

She paused and then resumed.

"He had a lot of important-looking visitors. They were all well dressed. He told me he was a businessman. I thought he was rich."

Another pause.

"He showed me a lot of interest."

"You fell for him?"

"Sort of. I took care of him every day. I got close to him. He looked like he was accustomed to getting what he wanted. That seemed oddly attractive at the time."

Andreina stopped again. She wasn't sure how to proceed.

"Go on," Paul urged.

"When he was ready to go home, he said he had something for me. I first thought it was a gift."

Paul waited.

"He asked me to come and live with him."

Silence.

"I was surprised. But he really meant it. He was determined," Andreina continued.

"And?"

"I turned him down."

Paul looked up at her.

"I told him that I had just become a nurse. I wanted to get more working experience. I wanted to help out my family. My sister and my mother needed the help."

Andreina looked at the wall. She stared at it for a few moments before she spoke. "He said money was not a problem. He said that my family would be taken care of. He said that he would give me two weeks to decide."

"And that is how you came here?"

"Not quite. I didn't know it at the time, but while he was still in the hospital, he knew everything about my family. Their whereabouts, their lack of income, everything. His men had already checked them out. True to his word, he came back two weeks later."

This time, Paul didn't prompt her.

"My answer was the same. I turned him down."

"What?"

"I had time to think it through. I told him no."

"And?"

"That is when he told me about my choices. Come with him and enjoy the luxuries of life or refuse and never see them again. He gave me one more week to make up my mind. He told me he would meet me at my apartment in exactly seven days."

"Why didn't you go to the authorities?"

"Paul, you met them. Ramon's contacts are right at the top. They wouldn't do anything. And that would have been the end of my mother and sister," Andreina said.

"I see," Paul said slowly.

The pieces of the puzzle were falling into place. The modus operandi of Ramon had become much clearer to him.

Her voice was calm again. "Next week will be two years, Paul," she said softly, her eyes wet.

Paul pulled her head over to his chest.

She began to sob. Gently at first, then deeper. And then it all came out. The pent-up emotions of the last two years.

12

RAMON AND FELIPE CAREFULLY SURVEYED THE SMALL house at the edge of the village. They had been watching it for almost a half hour. The battered pickup truck was parked in the rear. It looked sturdy enough. It was getting brighter by the minute. They had to make a move.

Guns drawn, they forced open the back door. It was a single-bedroom house. The old farmer was still asleep when they entered. He sat up and rubbed his eyes. He stared at them.

"Quiet," Ramon hissed.

Felipe quickly looked around the rest of the house. He smiled. They finally caught a bit of luck. The old man lived by himself.

"I have no money," the farmer mumbled.

"We are not common thieves," Ramon snapped.

"What do you want?"

"Food."

The old man blinked.

"We need food and drink. And a place to rest."

The old man continued to look at them with a puzzled expression. He showed little fear.

"Are you running from the police?"

"You ask too many questions," Ramon said.

Ramon moved closer to the farmer. His gun was pointed squarely at the man's head. The old man bit his lip.

"Listen, hombre," Ramon began slowly. "We want to sleep here today. We pay well."

"How much?"

Ramon pulled a stack of money from his pocket. He waved the hundred-dollar bills in front of the farmer's face. The man's eyes widened.

"Tonight, you drive us to Cucuta," Ramon continued.

"Si, senor."

"Good."

The man nodded.

"You tell no one you ever saw us. *Comprende?*"

The man nodded again.

"Por supuesto."

13

PAUL SAT ON THE LONG, LOW TABLE. HE WAS SHIRTLESS. Stripped to his underwear, he waited. The two men were ready. One already had the long steel needle in his hand.

"I am glad you agreed to join us," Javier said.

Paul didn't answer.

The room was well lit. There was a large window on the side wall. Paul was happy to see outside again. In the distance, he saw a high wrought iron fence with pointed spikes at the top. No doubt there would be a locked and guarded gate, Paul thought. Just to be able to see outside upped his mood.

He looked at Javier. He returned to the matter at hand. "Is this really necessary, Javier?"

"Not my rules."

"Whose?"

"Luis says it is mandatory."

"Why?"

"You will have to ask him yourself when you meet him."

"What did he tell you?"

"His explanation was it helps us to bond as a family."

"Do you think that is the reason?" Paul was trying to stall as much as possible.

"Personally, I think it is to prevent us from joining rival families."

"Do you have one?"

"Yes, we all do."

"Andreina?"

"She has one too. Every member of the family has one."

Paul was silent. He didn't want to imagine Andreina's lower back and buttocks right now.

"Turn over!" The man's voice was blunt. He had a long, pointed needle in his hand. The other one held a container of ink.

"Wait a minute."

"We are ready to start," the first man insisted.

"I want to see how extensive it is."

The man holding the ink rested the container on the table. He pulled off his shirt. "I had them put a second one on my chest."

Paul stared. The man had no hair on his chest. Right down the middle of his sternum, he had a beautiful multicolored tattoo. It was in the form of a dagger.

A curved dagger with a long handle had become part of his chest wall. There was a wavy pattern on the blade of the dagger. The handle was even more elaborate. Studded with colors depicting precious stones. Something out of the Orient, it appeared. If Paul had not been facing the needle right now, he could have appreciated the beauty of it.

"Like it?" the proud owner asked.

Paul didn't answer.

"The one on your back is black ink only," the man added ruefully.

Finally Paul spoke up. He addressed the man with the needle directly. "I want you to wear gloves. And please sterilize that needle."

"I do this all the time," he protested.

Javier nodded in his direction, consenting to Paul's request.

"How do I sterilize it?" he asked, waving the needle about.

"Just put it in boiling water," Paul replied.

Paul accepted his fate. He rolled over. He lay face-down and waited.

The tattoo artist pulled his underwear band down, exposing all of his lower back and the top of his buttocks. He flinched as the needle broke his skin.

Paul gritted his teeth. He made no sound as the make-believe surgeon repeatedly pierced his skin. The sadistic ritual picked up pace. The tattoo artist intensified his carvings. Then he widened the area. The pain got progressively worse.

Paul began to sweat. He felt the trickle of water coming down the sides of his back. He bit into his folded shirt as he tried to shield himself from the raw pain. He held his breath. He refused to scream. He didn't want to show weakness in the presence of Ramon's men. He knew if he did, they would prey on him later.

It would soon be over, he consoled himself.

Soon was a long time.

14

THE NEXT FEW MONTHS BECAME ETCHED IN PAUL'S MEMORY forever. Under stress, his brain always returned to Ramon's mansion. The house he could never forget. Not much happened, yet so much happened.

He could describe specific incidents in great detail. However, what he did on a day-to-day basis often escaped him. Each day seemed to roll into the next. He later reasoned that his brain had purposely tried to shut it out.

Two days after his body was mutilated with the cartel's logo, Ramon and Felipe returned. With Javier in charge, there was hardly a break in operations. Alonso turned up a couple of weeks later. For reasons unknown to Paul, they appeared surprised to see him. Soon too, he fell back into his normal routine. That of being Ramon's personal bodyguard.

Paul had been given a room on the main level. After his dungeon cell, this was on a scale of a penthouse suite. Paul hardly spoke to Andreina. He wanted to but was warned by Javier. Javier had all but told Paul to avoid her. That if Ramon got the impression he was fond of Andreina, they would be looking for another medic.

Paul knew Andreina had deep feelings for him. He could tell by the way she looked at him. He read the yearning in her eyes. If only they could escape from this prison, her eyes said.

Paul got to know Ramon's mansion well. It was much larger than he had initially thought. It was a gated luxury home on the top of a hill. It was located on a dead-end road. To outside eyes, it was the enviable residence a millionaire businessman. It was no secret that he was fastidious about his privacy. Inside, it was so much more.

In time, Paul visited almost every corner of the house. He had more access than everyone, barring Ramon and Javier. It had become his office and his hospital ward.

He treated everything and everyone. From coughs and colds to lacerations and gunshot wounds. On rare occasions, Andreina helped. More often than not, he worked alone. He had little to work with. He lost two men to gunshot wounds to the chest. He knew they would die without major surgery in a hospital setting. Despite his pleading, Ramon refused.

The mansion had three levels. All had living quarters. The basement level was the largest. It was where Paul's cell was located. Little did he realize at the time that a dozen of Ramon's men lived down the hallway. This was also where the temporary visitors from Colombia were housed.

The basement level was by far the most active. It was the center of the operations. The goods were kept here. Several large storage areas lined the walls.

An apparent patio was the entrance. It opened into the side of the hill. Transport vehicles came directly into the basement. There, they were loaded or unloaded without the pressure of time. Under the cover of night, this was a busy hub.

The main level housed offices and more quarters. Javier lived there. So too did Alonso and Felipe. The kitchen and conference room was on this level. This was where Paul lived. His most treasured asset was a metal-framed exterior window. He had a decent view of the outside grounds. It helped to keep his sanity.

The upper level was private. Ramon and Andreina lived there. It was accessible only by a locked elevator and a locked stairway. At the foot of the stairway were the quarters of Alonso and Felipe. Ramon's offices, a private meeting room, and a swimming pool completed that level.

Paul calculated that twenty to forty people occupied the mansion at any given time. Every day, escape was on his mind. But the more he got to know the place, the less his chances appeared.

The compound was large with a fenced perimeter. Javier occasionally granted him permission to go on the grounds. He managed about once per week. He was always accompanied by an armed guard. Paul noticed a pattern. He usually got the latitude when Ramon was away.

Paul thought he could possibly escape the building one night. With some luck, he might even make it to the fence. Getting over the twelve-foot fence with spikes would be a challenge. It would be risky, but he had to try. He couldn't live here forever. As the days passed, he made up his mind. He would try and execute his low-probability plan.

By sheer coincidence, he discovered the fence was electrified. He was casually chatting with one of Ramon's injured men. His patient didn't know the voltage, but he knew of two people who had tried to escape. Both had died instantly. Since then, no one had tried.

Paul was inwardly angry for this oversight. He should have asked Andreina. She would have told him. The end result was worsening despair. The flicker of hope had been squashed.

Paul felt ill for few days. Lethargy and tiredness paralyzed him. He slept poorly. His muscles ached. He didn't care about anything.

He perked up when he began to plan anew. He knew he needed this for his day-to-day survival. He had to keep his hopes alive. It was the only thing that kept him from intractable depression.

15

PAUL STARED AT THE CEILING FROM HIS BED. ONE MORE
seemingly endless night. He closed his eyes, but sleep would not come.
The house was quiet. It was late in the night. Everyone had gone to sleep.

For the thousandth time, Paul's mind drifted to his home in Trinidad.
By now, they would believe he was dead. Missing at first, then later presumed dead. They would have no reason to believe otherwise.

The airline records could reveal that he left the plane in Caracas.
Probably not. How much information did his family get? Did his fiancée
think he abandoned her after going to the US? Unlikely. Were they still
looking for him? If so, where? Certainly, not here. Did the Trinidadian
authorities close his case?

The questions kept swirling in his mind. He had no answers.

Paul took several deep breaths and reestablished his priorities. First,
he must stay alive. He reminded himself not to do anything rash. Play
along with Ramon's men. Give them what they want. Be patient. As long
as he was alive, he had a chance. An opportunity would come one day,
he prayed.

Paul heard a slight rustling sound. His door opened silently. He didn't
move. A figure approached him.

In the dim light, he recognized the figure as Andreina. She had on a
long bathrobe. Her hair was loose. She moved toward the bed.

"Shhh, it's me," she whispered.

"I'm awake," Paul said softly.

She sat at the edge of the bed. In the dim light, he could see the outline of her breasts as one side of the robe hung loosely on her shoulders.
She took her finger and gently rubbed it against his lips. He was still lying
on his back, his head on two pillows. He held his breath.

"I've waited a long time for this night," she said.

Paul didn't answer.

"Ramon and his bodyguards are away. Javier went to visit his mistress. I gave cookie the night off," she said.

Paul understood. "How did you get in?' he asked.

"I took Ramon's master key."

Paul's heart was pounding. He wasn't sure of the reason. He didn't move.

She bent over and kissed him. Slowly in the beginning then more urgently. At first, he didn't respond. Then with eyes closed, he gradually let go. He returned her kiss. It was tantalizingly sweet.

He gently nudged her away so he could look at her. He stared directly at her. Andreina waited.

With the backdrop of the moonlight coming through the window, she was stunningly beautiful. Her long black hair was loose over her shoulders. He couldn't quite see the depth of her brown eyes, but he could picture it, having gazed at it many times. Her pearl-like earrings stood out in the dim light.

Her robe had fully fallen off her shoulders now. Her neck appeared longer than usual. Her breasts were fully exposed, staring at him. They rocked gently as she breathed.

Andreina allowed him to admire her form. Then she bent over and kissed him again. He reached behind her and felt her lower back. As his hand moved downward, he realized that she had nothing on under the robe. Her hunger for him ignited a passion in him. Paul's hands moved lower, and he felt her firm buttocks. He pulled her toward him. Months of pent-up emotion burst through as their bodies joined together.

Afterward, she lay next to him and snuggled on his shoulder. They said very little. She gently toyed with his skin. Like a baby exploring with new fingers.

Then suddenly she said, "Javier won't be back till dawn."

Paul said nothing. Again, he understood her meaning.

Andreina reached for him again. She made love to him a second time.

It was different from earlier. More demanding. More primitive. More frenzied. More selfish this time. As if she knew this was going to be the last time. And she wanted to get as much of him as possible.

In the end, they were both drained. Then she got up and put her robe on slowly. She fluffed out her hair and then sat at the edge of the bed.

She pecked his lips gently. Then she said, "Paul, I love you."

He cleared his throat.

"You don't have to say anything."

He remained silent. His let his fingers talk for him. He gently stroked her thigh.

"I will help you escape," Andreina said matter-of-factly.

Paul was taken by surprise. He was silent for a moment. Then he said, "If Ramon finds out, he will kill you."

"I know."

"Why risk it?"

"Because I love you."

Before he could find the right words, Andreina got up. She headed through the door, closing it quietly behind her.

16

THE NEXT FEW WEEKS MOVED AGONIZINGLY SLOW. THEY made many escape plans. One by one, they discarded them.

In the end, they settled on a rather simple one. Andreina would lock him in the trunk of her car. She would drive right through the front gate. They would do it the first night that Ramon and his bodyguards were away. She should be able to pull rank on the guard at the gate. She would allege that she had a family emergency.

Paul was afraid of closed spaces. He refused to be locked in the trunk of the car. He wouldn't budge. Eventually they agreed that he would lie on the floor of the rear seat. He knew the risk of being discovered was greater, but he also knew that he wouldn't die from suffocation.

Andreina had arranged the help of a cousin. If they made it out of the compound, she would take him to a rendezvous point outside Caracas. She would make a brief stop at her mother's place before returning to the mansion. She would claim that her mother had an urgent medical condition.

Paul knew that was just the initial hurdle. He had no identity. He had no documents.

"How do I get back to Trinidad without a passport or money?"

"Money is not a problem," Andreina replied calmly.

Paul looked at her questioningly.

"Papers are the hard part."

"Agreed."

"I hope you don't need them."

"How so?"

"Paul, you cannot stay around Caracas to get on a plane. Ramon's men will find you."

"I know. I've been thinking about this for months."

"And?"

"I have to go overland," Paul said.

"Yes."

"Just a little problem. Trinidad is an island!"

"Paul, don't joke. I know that."

"Sorry."

"I got some maps for you. I studied them. Trinidad is four hundred miles east, by land. You have to go through Barcelona and then to Carupano. From there, you can go by boat to Port of Spain."

Paul smiled gently. She was really trying hard. He knew much more about Venezuela then she knew about Trinidad. To get to the north of Trinidad by sea was quite a challenge. Even though it was only twenty miles from the mainland, the open sea was treacherous. Small boats rarely made it over. There was a better option.

"I will try to enter the south of the island. Lots of fishermen there."

"You think that is better?"

"Yes, I think so. Every week, I used to hear news of fishermen from Cedros getting arrested. By Venezuelan coast-guards."

"When you leave Caracas, it is all up to you, Paul. You and Dios."

Paul nodded. The odds were against him. He could use any help he got.

"Paul, I have faith in you. I know you will make it," Andreina said firmly.

She looked deep into his eyes. He stroked her face gently.

"Thank you for believing in me," he said gently.

"I do."

"God knows, I need it."

✝

The first window to escape came and went. When it was all over, Paul was still a prisoner in the mansion. Andreina had gotten the money for Paul and had alerted her cousin. Ramon and his bodyguards were away for the weekend. Andreina knew she could count on Javier visiting his mistress on Saturday nights. Unexpected events took the fore.

A white van roared through the gate. It pulled directly up to the mansion. Javier supervised the men getting out. Two were wounded. One badly. Javier was going nowhere tonight. Nor were Paul and Andreina.

The first man had deep lacerations on his arms and forearm. Down into the muscle. Paul didn't know what had caused the wounds. A machete was the likely culprit, he deduced. Some tedious suturing and antibiotics, and he should be okay. If he escaped major tendon injury, in a couple months, he would be good.

The second man had been shot in the thigh and abdomen.

"Javier, this man needs to go to the hospital," Paul stated.

"No," Javier said flatly.

"He will die here."

"Do what you can."

"I cannot open his abdomen here. And he needs blood."

"No one is going to the hospital," Javier said coldly.

Paul backed away from the bleeding man in protest.

"Do I have to hold a gun to your head, Paul?" Javier said slowly.

There was no hedging in his voice. Paul knew they were not taking the man to the hospital.

In desperation, Paul began to work. He started an IV. He pumped in fluids as quickly as he could. A temporary bump in his blood pressure was all he got. His patient continued to bleed internally.

The man's eyes were closed. He had resigned himself to his fate. His pulse was weak, and his heart tried to compensate. He was very pale. Paul had no idea of the source of the bleeding. Without anesthesia, he couldn't possibly cut open the poor fellow. If the bleeding was from a major artery, they might as well call a priest. If it was not, Paul prayed that a blood clot would form and seal off the bleeding. That was the only hope.

The gunshot wound in the man's thigh was accessible. Paul applied a rubber tourniquet proximal to the bleeding. This stemmed most of it, allowing him to work. He then opened the leg up under local anesthesia. He found the artery and tied it off. The bleeding from the leg stopped.

The internal bleeding continued unabated. The man slipped into unconsciousness. He was wet and clammy. Paul knew his hemoglobin couldn't be more than four. He basically had water in his veins carrying a few red cells.

One last time, he begged Javier. "He needs a blood transfusion."

Javier shook his head. "No one is going anywhere."

Andreina looked pleadingly at Javier.

"It is the nature of the business," he said softly. "They all know it."

A few minutes later, the man's heart gave up trying. It stopped.

Paul didn't try to resuscitate him. It had all been an exercise in futility.

Paul went and sat in the corner of the room. He pulled off his blood-stained gloves. He buried his face in his unwashed hands. He wanted to cry, but he didn't. Andreina wanted to comfort him. She didn't move either.

Javier and his men watched without a word.

Two weeks later, another opportunity came. Two long weeks!

Andreina stuffed Paul in her small car. Paul curled up on the floor, wedged between the front seats and rear seats. She tossed a bag and a coat loosely over him.

Andreina approached the guard hut. Paul was afraid to breathe. She didn't pull the car all the way up. She stopped short, avoiding the better-lit area.

The guard strolled over to the side of the car. He recognized it and her. His automatic weapon hung loosely on his side.

He spoke brusquely in Spanish. "A donde va?"

"My mother is sick," Andreina replied politely.

"At this late hour?"

"I said my mother is ill," she repeated firmly.

"Does Senor Ramon know?"

"Yes," she lied.

He looked at her suspiciously.

"I spoke to Ramon by phone tonight," Andreina added.

"Are you coming back tonight?"

"Yes," she replied politely again.

He peered into the car. Paul's heart stopped. The windows were all up except for the driver's side. He didn't ask her to roll them down. He didn't try to open the door. Paul could only guess how well he could see inside. He held his breath.

The guard returned his attention to Andreina.

"When?"

"I will be back in a few hours."

That seemed to appease him. He opened the gate to let Andreina through.

As the car picked up speed, Paul exhaled slowly.

A few moments later, Andreina said, "You can get up now."

Paul uncoiled himself and sat up. He looked out into the darkness. It was his first view of the outside world in months. He inhaled slowly.

He was free. Almost. For the moment, anyway.

With Andreina still driving, Paul crossed between the front seats. He sat next to her. She squeezed his hand. He pressed back firmly.

He was grateful. She was silent. He had no idea what she had on her mind. Maybe, their next step. She continued driving.

Forty minutes later, she pulled up to a deserted-looking shack. The street was narrow and unpaved. The area screamed of poverty. Shacks of galvanized zinc lined the hillside. The one they pulled up to was larger than most. There was a single light inside.

Andreina got out and knocked. Five slow knocks.

A well-dressed young man opened the door. Andreina gave him a hug and a peck on the cheek. She turned to Paul.

"This is my cousin, Sebastian," Andreina said, looking from him to Paul. Sebastian shook Paul's hands. His grip was firm but friendly.

61

"My car is parked at the end of the street," Sebastian said, in good English.

Paul looked at him.

"We must leave soon," Sebastian continued.

"In a minute, Sebastian," Andreina said.

"It is three hundred kilometers to Barcelona. I want to be back before daylight," Sebastian staid matter-of-factly.

"I know," Andreina said softly.

Paul looked up at her. He didn't know how to say goodbye.

She pulled Paul to her in the full view of Sebastian. She gave him a deep, long kiss. Paul hugged her tightly. He felt the wetness of her tears flowing down her cheeks. He tasted the salt from them.

When she was out of breath, she let him go.

Paul stepped away.

"Ve con Dios," she said.

17

A WEEK LATER, PAUL LICKED HIS DRY, CRACKED LIPS. HE rubbed his index finger over his lower lip. He was on his back in the hut of a fisherman. Beaten, bruised, and penniless. As he stared at the low ceiling, he rehashed the events of the last week.

Getting to Barcelona was the easy part. Sebastian dropped him off without a hitch. He had no real problems getting to Carupano. It took him two days, going through Cumana. He travelled mainly at night. He paid his way generously.

Andreina had warned him to speak as little as possible. His understanding of Spanish was quite good, but he still had a strong accent. It would be clear to the locals that he was an *extranjero*.

He had checked into a cheap motel. Cash was king, and no questions were asked. He never strayed far from his backpack and money. He slept lightly at nights. He feared that Ramon's men would pursue him. Paul reasoned that when they found out that he had escaped, they would figure he try to get back to Trinidad. This would be the probable route.

He prayed that they didn't suspect Andreina. She had been friendly to him, so he knew it was very possible. He hoped the guard at the gate would lie in an attempt to save his own skin.

After a couple of days in Carupano, Paul made his way to the smaller town of Yaguaraparo. From there, he hoped to join a fishing expedition. His plan was to get to Icacos in the southern tip of Trinidad. They would have to cross the Columbus Channel. The closest point was just ten miles from the mainland. The maps showed that the southern main road in Trinidad reached Icacos.

Paul figured a small motorboat should be able to get to Icacos. All he needed was money. He had a good amount of cash.

Paul made cautious inquiries. He deduced that many of the fishermen traded more than fish. He could guess the nature of the more valuable cargo. He wasn't put off. All he wanted to do was to cross the Gulf of Paria. He wanted to get back to his home and family.

Paul was patient. He finally got connected to a small group. He offered them five thousand bolivars. All he had. The money would be of little use to him when he got back to Trinidad. He had hidden the money in his socks.

The following night, he rendezvoused with three men. At midnight, they headed off on a motor boat. Paul's heart raced in anticipation. He felt that home was not within reach. He could smell it in the murky waters of the gulf.

The rest he pieced together later. They were more than halfway to Trinidad when they saw the coast guard. He heard the men conversing rapidly in Spanish. He understood some most of it. Their leader explained to Paul that they would take an alternate route. But they would be in Trinidad in an hour. True to their word, in an hour, they dropped him off at a deserted coastline.

They told him the village was two miles away. He could walk there and get transportation to San Fernando. Their job was done.

Paul knew he would be able to make his way around in Trinidad. It was a small country. He walked quickly along the mucky beach. He saw no lights and no one. He quickened his pace and plodded on.

He didn't realize something was wrong until he heard voices. They were in Spanish. Still, he moved toward the voices. He politely inquired about the nearest village.

The next thing Paul remembered was an older man leaning over him. He was giving Paul water from an enamel cup. The sun was high in the sky and hot. Paul must have been out for hours. He reached up and touched his head. It was pounding. He felt a lump the size of a small orange there. His backpack was gone. The money in his socks was long gone.

The man took him to his hut. His wife gave him fish broth. Very slowly, he got a bit of strength back. In conversation, he found out he was still in Venezuela. The men whom he had paid to take him to Trinidad had deposited him back on the coast of Venezuela. Close to the Isla Cotorra.

Paul could only guess as to whether they had any intentions of taking him to Trinidad. Maybe they did, and the coast guard encounter changed their plans. He would never know. Still, he was grateful to be alive. They could have easily killed him and tossed him overboard, he thought.

His host was quite gracious. Paul learned that his name was Ramsingh. He had been fishing the gulf for more than three decades. He still had his Trinidadian drawl. A dozen years ago, he had met a Venezuelan woman. He had decided to settle down on the mainland side of the gulf. He still made a living from fishing the muddy waters of the sea.

Ramsingh told Paul he had heard a groan. Someone asking for water. He found him injured on the beach. He had been mugged. He had been bleeding from his mouth and nose. His lips were dry and swollen. The harsh sun and salty air made it worse.

Paul never asked if Ramsingh was one or two names. Ramsingh quickly earned his trust. Paul told him of his predicament. Ramsingh and his wife were good listeners. They hardly interrupted.

"I will take you to Trinidad myself," Ramsingh promised.

Paul nodded his thanks. He had nothing to offer Ramsingh.

"I have friends in Cedros."

"Thanks," Paul managed.

"I will personally deliver you to their doorstep. That way, you will safe," Ramsingh said in his singsong drawl.

"How about the coast guards?" Paul asked.

"Not to worry, Paul."

Paul looked at him.

"Didn't I tell you I have been fishing here for thirty years?"

Paul's eyes flickered with incomprehension.

"The coast guard has a schedule. Three hundred and sixty-five days a year," Ramsingh explained. "Every night, they have three patrols. One just after dark, one about midnight, and one just before dawn."

Paul was beginning to understand.

"We leave after the first patrol. We will be in Trinidad when they do midnight rounds. By the time they go out in the morning, I will be sleeping in my bed again," Ramsingh said with a big smile, showing a missing tooth.

"Sounds like a plan."

"Not to worry, Paul."

"I can't thank you enough, Ramsingh."

"Then don't."

"I am very grateful. I cannot even begin to repay you."

"God gives me strength to help people. Your thanks are enough," Ramsingh said.

Paul didn't speak for a while. Then he asked, "When do you plan to go?"

"Two nights from tonight. Low tide then."

"Great."

"I have some work to do on the boat engine."

Paul nodded.

"You rest," he assured Paul. "Rest and get strong," he said, with another wide grin.

†

Two nights later, just before midnight, Ramsingh docked his boat in Cedros. With Paul right behind him, he knocked on the door of a wooden house. Ramsingh had kept his word to the hour.

The crossing of the Gulf of Paria was uneventful. Ramsingh was more than a skillful sailor. He navigated the waters easily. He did it nonchalantly, as if he could have done it in his sleep. The stiff current posed little problem for him. He crisscrossed the waves at a forty-five-degree angle. His net direction was always to toward the tip of Trinidad.

The rocking of the boat made Paul nauseous. Somehow, he managed to keep everything inside. Ramsingh hummed all the way across.

Mikey, opened the weather-beaten door of the wooden house. Ramsingh had known him since he was a boy. His father had fished the gulf with Ramsingh. Mikey greeted them like royalty. Mikey's children were still awake, since it was Friday night. Ramsingh hugged each of the three of them. They called him Uncle, but Paul knew they were not blood relatives. They welcomed Paul as if they had known him for years.

Mikey's wife brought out hot tea. She set it out on a small table draped with a plastic tablecloth.

"You not going back tonight?" Mikey asked, facing Ramsingh.

"I can't stay, Mikey. You know it's hard to travel in the day."

Mikey nodded.

"I left the ole lady alone," Ramsingh replied, changing to his friend's lilting vernacular.

Mikey gestured in Paul's direction. "You friend staying?"

"Paul staying," Ramsingh replied.

"Good."

"He just need a ride to Sando."

"No problem. I will give him a drop to Point early in the morning. From there, he could take a taxi to Sando."

"That will be great," Paul answered.

"You got to take quick one before you go," Mikey stated, returning his attention to Ramsingh.

"Awright, just one."

Mikey brought out a bottle of white rum. Ramsingh inspected it. "Good stuff," Ramsingh said.

They all poured a shot. Paul did what the other men did. They knocked it back in one gulp.

"Good for the nerves," Mikey said.

Ramsingh agreed. After a few minutes, Ramsingh got up. His intentions were clear.

"One more," Mikey said.

Ramsingh shook his head.

"One for the road," Mikey insisted.

Ramsingh smiled. "More like one for the sea."

Ramsingh took out an old thermos flask. He poured the rest of the hot tea into it. Then he carefully added the equivalent of two shots of white rum. "This should keep me warm on the way back."

Mikey heartily agreed. He hugged his friend and bade him goodbye.

Paul walked to the door with Ramsingh. He embraced him.

"I will forever be grateful. Thank you again," Paul said.

"No worries," Ramsingh said. His voice was cheerful as ever.

"Tell the ole lady hi for us," Mikey said.

"For sure."

Ramsingh flashed his big smile. With that, he headed out in the darkness. He walked quickly to the small dock.

It was the last time they saw Ramsingh.

18

PAUL DIDN'T SLEEP FOR ANY OF THE NEXT FOUR HOURS. NOT a wink. Mikey had brought out a folding cot. He opened it out in the living room. Paul had more than a comfortable bed. But sleep wouldn't come.

He couldn't believe that he was really in Trinidad. That in a few hours he would see his fiancée, Karissa. His family and friends. His old hospital. The anticipation excited him. It also scared him.

He thought of calling Karissa that night. He quickly put the idea away. Mikey's house did not have a phone.

At 4:30 a.m., the fully dressed Mikey emerged from his room.

"You ready?" he asked gently.

"Yes," Paul whispered.

"Ramsingh tell me to take you early."

Paul was overjoyed. They drove in Mikey's old Nissan to Point Fortin. Mikey dropped him off at the taxi stand. He gave him some local money for his passage. Paul knew his way from there.

He got into a route taxi to San Fernando. The driver made more stops than he had hoped. The winding Southern Main Road hugged the coast. It took him through La Brea. Across the bumpy roads of the rising pitch lake. The same one that Walter Raleigh had visited centuries earlier. Not knowing that the gold he sought was sitting at his feet.

They passed the Oropuche Swamp. Soon they were on the outskirts of San Fernando. His heart really started to thump as they passed Gulf City.

It was almost bright when Paul stood at the door of his fiancée's apartment. He raised his hand to knock. He stopped in midair. He read the name one more time. *Karissa.* In fancy lettering on the door. She was still living here, he reassured himself.

He gathered his courage. He inhaled deeply. He raised his hand again.

Paul knocked gently.

He waited.

†

A thousand thoughts went through his head as he waited. The few seconds seemed like an eternity.

Did Karissa think he was dead? What if she did? Did she move on with her life? Did she have another boyfriend? At moments like these, his irrational fears rose to the fore. A pain in his chest told him that he was scared.

A shadow pulled the curtains to one side. The face peeked cautiously at the early-morning intruder. He recognized the form of Karissa. Karissa quickly flung open the door. She grabbed him by the shoulders.

"Paul!" she cried.

Her eyes were widely dilated. She looked like she had just seen a ghost.

"Sorry," he mumbled.

She dug her nails into his arms.

"I knew you were alive," she hissed in an intense, low tone.

She dragged him though the doorway. Before he could say another word, she kissed him harshly. Then she pushed him away.

"It's really you," she said, looking at him in disbelief.

"I am back," Paul said softly.

That was all he could muster. He looked apologetic.

"We have been looking for months!" Karissa wailed.

Paul closed the door behind him.

"I am back," he repeated, as if to assure himself that he really was.

"That's it," Karissa said, her voice rising.

Paul didn't answer. He did not know what to say.

"I went to New York to look for you."

"I wasn't in New York."

"Nothing. Not a clue!"

"I didn't make it to America," Paul said feebly.

70

"Nobody knew anything. You just disappeared!" she continued.

Paul remained silent. He didn't know how to put a synopsis on his last six months.

With her small fists, she began to pound his chest. "You were gone for months, and that's it!"

It wasn't the reception he was expecting. But he understood. She was deeply hurt. Her emotions came through. His felt the blows on his chest and absorbed them. He waited for her to calm down.

Her fury gradually subsided. She finally placed her head on his chest. She began to sob.

After a few minutes, she whispered, "Everybody thought you were dead."

"I will tell you everything."

She didn't lift her head up.

"Soon," Paul said softly.

He gently played with her hair with one hand. He hugged her tightly with the other arm. She tightened her grip around his chest.

Finally, she looked at him. "We looked everywhere."

"Sorry," Paul mumbled again.

"I knew you would come back."

"I did."

"They all told me that I was crazy. That you were dead. That I should move on with my life."

"I promised I would be back, didn't I?" Paul said, trying to force a smile.

"Come," Karissa said, pulling him by the hand.

He followed her.

"You must be hungry. Let me get you something to eat."

"No, I just want to rest," Paul said, collapsing on a sofa.

His exhaustion suddenly overtook him. She sat next to him, one leg touching his. She gazed up him. She gently stroked his face. As if to convince herself that he was really there.

"You want to know what happened."

Karissa rubbed his face again. She massaged the stubble on it.

"Sure."

"Well ..." he began.

"Not now."

She rested her hand on his thigh. She squeezed his fingers.

"Just rest," she whispered.

Her voice comforted him. For the first time in months, Paul relaxed. His body went limp. He fell into a deep sleep.

His sleep had vivid dreams. He dreamt the boat with Ramsingh capsized. That he was somehow under the boat. He was looking at the boat from underneath. Like a fish in a large aquarium.

19

JAVIER STARED ACROSS THE LARGE TABLE. RAMON STROKED his beard. No one spoke.

Finally, Javier piped up. "Paul showed up in San Fernando."

Ramon nodded.

"He took two weeks," Javier continued.

Ramon didn't show much emotion.

"Somehow, he made it."

Alonso and Felipe listened. They didn't participate in the conversation. They weren't expected to. Their bosses made decisions. Their bosses gave orders. They carried out those orders.

"When did you find out?" Ramon asked.

"Our man in Trinidad was monitoring his girlfriend's apartment. I got word last night."

Another pause. Ramon glared at him.

"I didn't want to wake you for that," Javier added.

"Should we kill him?" Ramon asked.

"I think we should wait," Javier replied.

"Wait for what?"

"We watch him for a couple of weeks."

"I think we should get rid of him now. Before he goes to the police."

"I don't think he will," Javier said.

"How do you know?"

"He is a smart fellow, Ramon. He knows we can take him out if we want to. He knows the police cannot protect him and his family all the time."

"Is that a good enough reason?" Ramon asked.

"Not by itself. But we don't want things to get messy in Trinidad. We need our connections there."

"I still think we should finish him. He defied us."

"Ramon, Paul is a doctor. He has good cover. We could use him later."

"Okay, your call," Ramon conceded.

Javier nodded. "Thanks."

"At the first sign of trouble, I want him gone."

"Agreed, boss," Javier replied, with emphasis on the word boss. He knew he could still subtly guide Ramon when he had to.

"He's got balls though. I got to give him that," Ramon said.

"He is a tough one."

"Did we ever find out how he got out?"

"No," Javier said.

"The circuit wasn't broken. He must have had inside help."

"Possible."

"Who do you think?" Ramon persisted.

Javier had an idea. He kept it to himself. He had noticed Andreina's car parked in a slightly different position when he returned the next morning. He didn't know Paul went missing until later that afternoon. Javier had pieced it together. The guard at the gate vehemently denied that Andreina left the premises.

"Maybe one of the men he treated," Javier said offhandedly.

Javier knew not to mention his suspicion. If he did, it would be the end of Andreina.

"If you ever find out, let me know," Ramon said.

"I definitely will, boss," Javier assured him.

WASHINGTON, DC
SEPTEMBER 1989

1

THE MULTITUDE OF SIRENS FADED INTO THE DIN AS THE ambulances pulled into the emergency bay of the General Hospital. The alarming frequency appeared to go unnoticed. Ambulance sirens were background noise here. Only the helipad garnered any real attention. Patients, visitors, and onlookers had all become immune to the distress signals of ambulances.

It was weekend at this inner-city hospital of Washington, DC. The campus was still hectic and alive. Incessant activity was nothing unusual for a level-one trauma center. Paul had a twenty-four-hour shift ahead of him. He knew it was going to be a busy day, as the Redskins/Giants game was just across the street at RFK Stadium. Scheduled start was 1:00 p.m., but the entire area was already congested.

Paul wiped his eyes as he walked across the parking lot next to the DC jail. The medical residents' lot was close to the hospital. It wasn't close enough for him to escape the fury of the ragweed. Ragweed hung in the air like fumes from a chemistry experiment gone bad. The trees at the end of Massachusetts Avenue provided a constant supply. By the time he reached the main building of the hospital, his nose was runny, and his eyes were red. All from an allergy he didn't know he had just a few months earlier.

"Good morning, Dr. Karan."

"Good morning, Dr. Marshall."

"I want you in the main ER today. You, Dr. Anderson, and the two family practice residents."

"Yes, sir."

"Dr. Gupta is on the walk-in side. You can join her after midnight."

"Thanks, Dr. Marshall."

The walk-in side meant he could possibly squeeze in a snack or even a short break. No such luck existed in the main ER.

"Dr. Allen is handing over. You can join his rounds when we are done."

"Who's new?" Paul asked.

"An MI in bed 8. Came in, in the last half hour."

Paul raised his eyebrows questioningly.

"An early bird to the game. Weighs over three hundred and was climbing up the stadium steps," Dr. Marshall said.

"Thrombolytics?"

"Waiting on Cardiology to assess him."

"Trauma side?"

"The surgery boys are going nonstop. Seven gunshots overnight. Five dead. The other two are in the OR," Marshall stated.

"Neurosurg?"

"In house right now. A couple of bad MVAs. The EMTs brought both parties of the accident here."

"Casualties?" Paul asked.

"Three dead. Another two with serious head injuries," Marshall reported.

"Looks like you had a heck of a shift," Paul said.

"Yes, indeed! And still four hours to go."

"Go get some coffee. I'll call you if there's anything major."

"Thanks, Paul. I know I can depend on you."

"My pleasure, Dr. Marshall."

"With all these new residents around, I haven't peed yet," Marshall added.

The truth was Paul was just as new to the program. The difference was he had loads of experience before starting his residency in DC. He had had three years of intense grounding in Trinidad. It included both the ER and general surgery.

Dr. Marshall respected his maturity and trusted his judgment.

"This is the weirdest EKG I've ever seen."

Paul cocked an ear. He overheard Dr. Anderson muttering to himself.

"Somebody, please get Dr. Marshall," Dr. Anderson said.

One of the ER nurses hurried over to the break room, where Dr. Marshall was finally having his coffee. He had just poured himself a hot cup. Black coffee, no sugar. He had barely been out of the bay five minutes. They were already looking for him. Paul could guess his response.

"I don't drink cold coffee!"

"I will bring the EKG over," the nurse explained apologetically.

Twenty minutes in his shift, Paul was assessing his fourth patient. He was systematically catching up. He was working on a patient who had been brought over from the jail. Drug overdose was the tentative diagnosis.

Paul got little useful information from the accompanying officer. After a few minutes, Paul managed to gain the trust of his prisoner patient. The young black man was conscious. He had refused to give anyone information earlier. He had been held a stone throw's away at the DC jail adjacent to the hospital. Paul's apparent concern had breached his defenses.

The poor fellow wanted out at any cost. Depression or drug withdrawal was the likely culprit. He was being treated in jail for a skin infection. He had painstakingly hoarded all his pills over the course of a week. When he had collected thirty, he took them all. Then he waited to die. Unfortunately for him, the pills were Keflex, an antibiotic.

The end result was severe abdominal pain and diarrhea. Diarrhea running off the stretcher. A few days in the psyche ward, and he would be back to where he started. Paul shook his head from side to side.

Two beds away, Dr. Marshall held up the EKG in his left hand. He had returned to the main ER bay. Senior resident Dr. Anderson had filled him in on the case. Marshall nodded his head in satisfaction.

"Dr. Karan, come over here," Marshall said.

Paul headed over.

"Anderson, call the other residents," Marshall continued.

As if reminding himself that the residents were not free labor, he added, "This is still a teaching hospital."

They were all gathered around the bed. Dr. Marshall handed the EKG to Paul. "Tell us what you see."

Paul stared at the tracing for a few moments. "He has pretty marked ST elevation."

Marshall tugged his graying beard and smiled. A wry smile while waiting to see what this hotshot, Paul Karan, could come up with. He didn't want to let slip this opportunity to impress them.

"Prinzmetal angina!" he proclaimed.

He waited for them to digest it. Then he asked, "Paul, have you ever heard of it?"

"I have, Dr. Marshall," Paul responded modestly.

The term quickly stirred the information stockpile that Paul's British training had drilled into him. It was variant angina described by an American cardiologist, Dr. Myron Prinzmetal, some thirty years ago. A couple other authors laid claim to it much earlier, but no one knew their names.

"It usually occurs at rest," Marshall said.

"Correct."

"This fellow was sitting at home when he developed severe chest pain. His roommate called 911," Marshall explained.

Paul looked down at the patient. He was a young Hispanic man. Without looking at the chart, Paul estimated he was about thirty. Not exactly the age for cardiac ischemia.

"The EMTs said his roommate opened the door for them. Then the roommate disappeared," Anderson piped up.

"Odd," Marshall said.

"Probably doesn't have his papers," the nurse chimed in.

Marshall turned and looked at her without comment.

"What do you think caused it, Dr. Marshall?" One of the family practice residents had finally gotten the courage to join the conversation.

"Most likely cocaine. Vasospasm from cocaine use." Marshall's response was precise.

Marshall noticed that Paul was peering closely at the patient. His breathing was getting slower. Paul had noticed the patient had a good-sized stomach for a muscular young man.

"Let's turn him over," Paul said.

A few eyes glanced questioningly at him. Paul moved forward. Anderson and the nurse helped him. They flipped the patient over on his belly. He still had on his light blue boxers. Paul grasped the waistband of the man's underwear. He had the full attention of the team now. Using both hands, he pulled down.

There it was. Unmistakable. *The tattoo of the dagger.* With the long handle and wavy blade.

Paul's heart skipped several beats. In what he hoped was an emotionless voice, he said quickly, "A coke mule."

"What?" Marshall asked.

"A coke mule with a leaking bag," Paul said.

Comprehension dawned in Dr. Marshall's eyes.

"He needs surgery stat," Paul said in a flat tone.

Paul finished his twenty-four-hour shift without a wink of sleep. Coffee and adrenaline pushed him over the line. He was still standing. Barely. Exhaustion crept in as the adrenaline receded.

He limped to his car. He tossed his lab coat in the back seat. He drove slowly out of the parking lot. At the light, he pulled onto Mass Avenue. He made a right on Nineteenth Street and headed toward the freeway.

Normally, his biggest challenge was to stay awake on these post-call drives. This afternoon, it was quite the opposite. Paul was anxious and jumpy. No, he was downright fearful.

He almost rear-ended a cab as he caught the light at Nineteenth and

Independence Avenue. He kept seeing the tattoo of the dagger on the back of his patient. His hand reached around his back to feel his own.

The coke mule had been taken to the operating room. They recovered several bags of cocaine from his stomach. It wasn't in time to save him. He died on the table. Another one lost to the drug trade. It wouldn't even make the news in DC.

He had to tell Karissa. He knew it would be the sensible thing. He dreaded it. He vividly recalled her reaction when he had told her Javier tried to contact him in Trinidad. She was upset for days. She thought that, after his return to Trinidad, everything belonged in the past. A closed chapter. A locked box never to be opened. That drug cartels receded to movies and TV shows.

That was why he didn't tell her about the letter in the mailbox. She was certain that they were safe here. In the United Sates. Far from South America.

Paul knew she was wrong. Just like in Trinidad, they could take him out whenever they wanted. They could do things that would effectively end his medical career. He knew the only reason they had let him go was his potential usefulness. That much he had figured out.

He drove up Kenilworth Avenue and onto the BW Parkway. His brain went back to two weeks earlier. He had gotten home early that day. Unusual for him. He stopped to pick up the mail downstairs. One plain white envelope caught his eye. His name was handwritten on the front. There was no stamp or return address.

Paul opened it as soon as he got in his apartment. His heart stopped when he saw the words. It was typed on a full sheet of white paper. All uppercase letters: WE KNOW YOU LIVE HERE.

To remove any doubt of the source, there was a signature under the words. It was a stamped picture of the dagger.

When Karissa came home that evening, he didn't tell her. She knew something was amiss. Paul was jumpy all that evening. But he kept it to himself. She still thought the danger two thousand miles away. He couldn't see any upside of telling her.

Paul returned to the present as he pulled off onto Route 193. He still hadn't decided. He would get a load off his mind if he told her. Would she be safer if she knew? He doubted that. He decided to wait. For what, he wasn't sure. There was more to lose than gain by telling her, he rationalized.

2

KARISSA WORKED EVENING SHIFTS THAT WEEK. PAUL WASN'T
on call. It was a rare evening that he was home by himself. He flipped idly
through the TV channels. Channel 4, 7, and 9. Same thing.

The Berlin Wall had just fallen. East Germans were all pouring into
West Berlin, and stores were out of condoms. Joe Montana and the 49ers
were expecting to win the Super Bowl. He paused at the MTV channel
when the phone rang. Probably Karissa on break, he thought.

"Paul Karan?"

Paul didn't answer immediately. The voice at the other end was low.

"Who's calling?"

"This is Felipe."

The voice sounded vaguely familiar. Was it really him?

"I don't know any Felipe," Paul said finally.

"Felipe. Your friend from Caracas."

They told him they knew where he was. Paul was almost expecting it.
No point in any further denial.

"What do you want?"

"I need to see you."

"I don't want to see you," Paul said slowly.

"I am sure you do. Boss says so."

"When?"

"Tonight," Felipe said.

"What if I refuse?"

"Boss says to tell you we know where your fiancée works."

Paul was silent. They knew exactly which buttons to push.

"Where are you?" Paul asked.

"I am at the Howard Johnson on New York Avenue."

"You want me to meet you there?"

"Boss says you cannot come here. Too risky."

"You expect me to believe you?"

"No."

"You know the police can trace your call?"

"I am on a pay phone. You think I'm stupid?"

Paul didn't respond.

"Where do you want to meet?" he asked finally

"Two miles from where you live. The Safeway Plaza in Greenbelt."

"In the Safeway?"

"No. There is a Hunan King at the back. We can eat," Felipe said.

Paul's mind was being stretched. He couldn't help thinking how much Felipe's English had improved. He now spoke English with an American accent.

"Is Ramon coming?" Paul asked.

"No."

"Alonso?"

"No."

"If Alonso comes, I will kill that son of a bitch," Paul hissed.

He hadn't realized how much repressed emotion he had for his torturer. It just came out. Paul reflexively looked down at his fingernails.

Felipe didn't comment.

"I don't want to eat with you," Paul said.

"Your choice. We don't have to."

"I don't want to be seen with you," Paul said.

Felipe waited. As expected, Paul conceded.

"I drive a Blue Honda," Paul said.

"I know."

"At 10:00 p.m. sharp, I will pull up in front of the Peoples Drug store. Next to the Chinese restaurant. You can get into my car," Paul instructed.

"Good," Felipe said.

Paul hung up.

†

Paul made it home early the next day. He was still tense. He was glad that Karissa was working evenings. Less explanation needed.

The previous night, he had reluctantly kept his word. At 10:00 p.m., he pulled up outside the Peoples Drug store. They were waiting. Felipe and another man jumped into his car. It was a short meeting.

Paul surmised they were feeling him out. They wanted reassurance on the half a million dollars' worth of drugs they were planning to leave with him. They wanted to make sure he wouldn't turn it in to the authorities.

They demanded Paul store the goods in his apartment. He refused at first. In the end, they got their way. They threatened to ruin his new life. They reminded him that wasn't the worst thing they could do.

Paul waited. Time moved slowly. The parking lot outside his apartment was quiet. It was a weekday. Most people had turned in for the night. At 9:00 p.m., Felipe stepped out of a car. He didn't say much. They had worked out the details the night before.

Paul led the way to the basement level of his apartment building. The laundry room had a storage area that served six apartments. Barring a few boxes, a few pieces of luggage were usually present.

Felipe brought in two suitcases. Paul looked at them. These guys did their homework. The cases were not new. Felipe could have easily been a visiting relative. Paul knew the contents. It was worth more money than he would make in a lifetime.

Felipe went back to the car and returned with two more. Paul opened the storage room with his apartment key. He nodded to Felipe. Felipe placed the suitcases next to some boxes.

"Good," Felipe said.

Paul didn't answer. He knew he was breaking several laws. He consoled himself that he had no choice. He shuddered at the alternative.

"We will be in contact," Felipe continued.

"No you won't."

Felipe looked at him questioningly.

"I had these made today," Paul said.

Paul handed him two keys.

"The long one for the main door. The other for the storage room," Paul explained.

Felipe nodded in comprehension.

"You get them whenever you need to. I don't want to know."

Felipe smiled. He was starting to understand why Javier had not gone after Paul. He could be valuable asset. A low-risk one. Credible and intelligent.

Paul headed up the basement steps. Felipe was close behind. As Felipe turned for the door, he said, "Andreina asked to me tell you hello."

Paul lifted his headed in surprise. He hadn't inquired about Andreina during their conversations. He had wanted to. His concerns for her safety had forced his silence.

"Please tell her I said hello."

3

PAUL SLEPT IN THE HOSPITAL EVERY THIRD NIGHT. IT WAS the accepted routine of a medical resident. Last night was a busy night. He had eighteen admissions. He had only two interns on his team. He had to do the history and physical on a half-dozen of them himself.

Then the real work began. Getting all their tests done and addressing the results. Post-call days were often busier than on-call days. He worked quickly but meticulously. He was dog-tired. He had been on his feet for thirty-six hours straight. He had started at eight o'clock the previous morning. He plowed on. One last patient, then home and sleep.

Just as he was done, he got an overhead page. His senior resident asked him to check on an AIDS patient. She was in with respiratory distress. She was evaluated earlier in the day and needed an ICU transfer. The ICU had no empty beds.

Paul Karan's task was to reevaluate her. He had to decide if she would be stable enough to remain on the floor overnight. If she was going to require mechanical ventilation, she would have to be transferred to the ICU.

He bypassed the elevator and took the stairs. He hustled out to the fourth floor of Henry's University Hospital. He tried to remember the name he was given. Was it Cynthia Johnson or Cynthia Jones? It was a common name. Anyway, he knew the room number. It was room 25 on ward 4E.

He knocked on the door and entered the room without waiting for an answer. Peering at him from behind an oxygen mask was an African American woman. She was propped up at sixty degrees.

She was thin and wasted. Her chest heaved, and she labored to breathe. The food on her tray table was untouched. She showed no signs of fear.

"Miss Johnson?"

"Jones," she rasped.

"Sorry, Miss Jones."

"Who are you?" She managed to get it out in one breath.

"I am Dr. Paul Karan. Dr. Adams asked me to see you."

"What for?"

"I want to know how your breathing is."

"Bad."

"Is it better than this morning?"

"Same."

Paul put on the pulse oximeter. Her oxygen saturation was 87 percent.

"Not good?" she asked. It was a half question, half statement.

Paul's face must have given it away. He didn't answer her question. "Can I listen to your chest?"

She nodded. It was tough for her to speak. It took a lot of effort out of her. She nodded her head when it would suffice.

Paul took out his stethoscope. He listened. Her heart was pounding away at about 120. Her lungs had diffuse crackles.

"We need to transfer you to the ICU," Paul said.

"What for?"

"Your lungs are not working well."

She pointed to her oxygen mask. It was her way of stating that her problem had already been addressed.

"You have pneumonia. It is caused by an infection, Pneumocystis carinii. It damaged your lungs," Paul explained.

"How would … transfer … help my lungs?" She had to stop after every couple of words to get her question out.

"You are not getting enough oxygen into your bloodstream."

"I know that."

"We can put you on a ventilator. It will help with your breathing."

"No!"

Paul looked directly into her eyes.

"No machines!"

"It will help with the work of breathing. Just until your lungs heal. Then you should be able to come off it."

"Are you sure?"

Paul couldn't lie to her. The truth was there was a good possibility that she would not be able to come off the machine. She had severe pneumonia. She had advanced AIDS. Paul looked down on the floor.

She waited.

Paul shook his head slowly. "No, Miss Jones. I cannot be sure."

Cynthia appreciated his honesty. Her eyes showed it.

"Will they … give me … a different anti … biotic there?" she asked.

"No. It would be same one," Paul answered.

"I don't want … to go."

Paul was at a loss for words.

"Leave me here."

The medical thoughts formed in Paul head. But he couldn't put them into layman's words. The ventilator was the only chance she had. They could give her more medications in the ICU to make her comfortable. But the treatment for the pneumonia would be the same. He just stood there.

"Sit down, boy," Cynthia said.

Paul didn't know why, but he obeyed. He was already late. He was supposed to pick up Karissa an hour ago. Cynthia was his last patient today, but he couldn't leave her. He sat on the single chair in the room, facing her. She wanted to talk. She knew that she didn't have much time.

"How old … are you?" she asked.

"Twenty-seven."

"How old … do you … think I am?"

"I know," Paul said. "Thirty-one."

She raised her eyebrows.

"It is on your chart."

She attempted a smile. "Not fair," she said.

After a moment, she continued, "I look fifty."

"No you don't," Paul lied.

"I have a granddaughter," Cynthia said.

That caught Paul's attention. He did the calculation mentally. It was biologically possible. Barely.

"How old is she?"

"She is ... nine months."

"A fun age."

"I have never ... seen her."

"Why?"

"You really want ... to know, boy?"

Paul nodded.

"I had a daughter ... when I was fifteen. I was ... in bad company."

Cynthia was pacing herself in the conversation. She lifted the mask occasionally. She was quite coherent. When she got out of breath, she quickly put it back on.

"Bad company," she repeated.

"We all do things that we are not proud of," Paul agreed.

"Not proud of," she echoed. "I got into ... drugs. Heavy drugs. I did ... bad things."

Paul waited.

"I was ... a crack whore. Do you know ... what that is?"

Paul nodded his head. He could have guessed.

"Sometimes I did it ... for five dollars. Sometimes three. Even two. All I wanted ... was to ... get my drugs. Day and night."

Paul felt her venting. He wanted to see with her. He was in no position to judge.   "Where?" he asked gently.

"Balti ... more."

Paul waited.

"More crack than DC."

"Where do you live now?" Paul nudged gently.

"With my sister. In DC." She took a deep breath of oxygen. "Not far from here. Off Florida ... Avenue."

"I see."

Paul wasn't sure what to say. She was not done. He looked into her eyes. She wasn't frightened. She knew she was going to die.

"I did bad things," she repeated.

She paused.

"Where is your daughter?" Paul asked.

"She is on … the streets. How can I … tell her not to?"

Cynthia rested. Then restarted. "I have a son. Six years old."

Paul was a bit surprised. "Where is he?"

"He lives … with my sister. My grandbaby with … my mother. My son … with my sister," Cynthia clarified.

"Is your sister well?"

"She uses. Heroin."

Paul again waited.

"Heroin … and needles. Her own … needles."

Her sentences were becoming shorter. Paul took a chance. "Is she well?"

"She looks so. She doesn't do sex. Heroin only."

She caught her breath, then restarted on her own.

"More than … ten years. Heroin. Heroin people … don't do sex."

That was news to Paul. He had read it somewhere but doubted its authenticity. "Was she ever tested for HIV?"

"I don't … think so." Cynthia was getting very tired. "She looks good."

Paul knew he has to steer the conversation to an end. But he couldn't rush a dying woman.

"Cynthia, does she visit you?"

"Yes." Cynthia smiled warmly.

"That's good," Paul said firmly.

"Yes. I want to ask … you something."

"Yes, Cynthia?"

"Don't let them … put me … on that machine?"

Paul looked at the floor.

"You hear me?" she persisted.

Paul nodded.

"I did … bad things. I know … I will … die soon. Let me die … here."

Paul nodded his consent silently.

Her eyes continue to plead with him.

Paul got up. He squeezed her hand.

He looked directly into her eyes. "I will do my best, Cynthia. I promise."

4

PAUL GOT UP EARLY ON SUNDAYS. TODAY WAS NO DIFFER-
ent. He thumbed through the bulky edition of the *Washington Post*. An
early start meant he could have coffee with Karissa before heading out to
do hospital rounds.

Karissa sat next him at the kitchen table. She flipped through the
ads section of the *Post*. The morning sun streamed into the kitchen. Paul
browsed over page 3 of the paper.

"You heard about the shootings over the weekend?"

"There are always shootings in DC," Karissa replied.

"This weekend was really bad," Paul said.

Karissa didn't respond immediately. After a moment, she said, "I just
don't look at the news anymore."

Paul wanted to talk. However, he hesitated at every opening. He didn't
want to get specific. "Eleven people shot dead over the weekend. Seven
separate shootings."

No answer from Karissa.

Paul continued. "And that might not be all of it. The paper goes to
printing just after midnight. That number is just for Friday night and early
Saturday night."

"I know, Paul. It is pretty bad," Karissa agreed.

"Bad is an understatement," Paul said firmly. "It didn't even make the
front page of the newspaper."

"People are just used to it," Karissa said, still not looking at him.

If she was concerned, she didn't show it.

"That's only part of it," Paul stated.

"Part of what?" Karissa finally looked up.

"Look, if eleven people were shot in Georgetown, it would have been on the front page. It would have made CNN and the national news. But look at where they occurred."

Karissa waited.

"Martin Luther King Avenue, South Capitol Street, Mississippi Avenue. All in Southeast DC. Places I have worked. All close to Greater Southeast Hospital."

Karissa still did not answer. She knew he was venting. She wasn't sure if he was scared.

"In fact, nineteen people were shot. Eleven died. All young men."

"Probably gang related," Karissa offered.

"Gang and drug related."

Karissa heard that word again. *Drugs.*

"Life is too cheap, Karissa."

Karissa nodded.

"Too cheap," Paul repeated, shaking his head.

"I agree, Paul," she replied.

A week later, Cynthia died.

She died in the same room on the fourth floor where Paul first met her. He had returned three times to see her even though she wasn't under his direct care. The last time, she was barely able to talk. She had signaled with her eyes. They both knew the end was near.

Paul managed to get Cynthia what she wanted. It wasn't easy. The medical resident who oversaw her care didn't share Cynthia's view of death and dying. Paul had to overreach. Paul had a long discussion with her attending physician. He documented in detail all of Cynthia's wishes. He itemized the care she didn't want.

In the end, they didn't transfer her to the ICU. They didn't put her on the ventilator. They gave her generous doses of morphine. It decreased her sensation that she was suffocating. Her rapid breathing was trying to pull more oxygen into her lungs. Morphine greatly aided her comfort.

Cynthia died peacefully in her sleep. The nurses told Paul they checked on her at the shift changeover. She had passed on.

Paul had made another promise to Cynthia. He had promised to get her sister tested for HIV. If she was positive, he would treat her. According to Cynthia, her sister had not seen a doctor in years. Cynthia thought she had the virus.

Paul explained to Cynthia that there were newer drugs in the pipeline. It was too late for Cynthia. It might not be for her sister. Cynthia wanted her sister to live. Cynthia wanted a mother for her son.

Several times, she brought up the subject. Paul couldn't deny a dying woman. He committed. She gave him an address and a phone number. He promised he would find her soon.

Cynthia believed him. She wanted to. It allowed her to let go.

Paul entered his apartment with his briefcase in one hand. In the other hand, he had a dozen shirts on small wire hangers. He had to squeeze the briefcase between his knees to free a hand to open his door.

Karissa was already home. They now had a second car so she didn't have to wait for him. She looked up from the couch. She got up to meet him as he struggled with the laundry and his work bag.

She pecked him on the lips. "I'm glad you're home early."

"I could have been here even earlier."

"How so?"

"They postponed the evening case presentations. So I decided to stop by the cleaners."

She smiled. "You got tired of doing your own laundry."

"Yes." He averted his eyes.

"Recently, you were doing laundry two, three times a week," Karissa chided.

"I tried."

"I was getting worried," Karissa joked.

"Doing laundry is not fun," Paul agreed.

"I knew it wouldn't last."

"Shirts are just ninety-nine cents each. No point in doing them myself," Paul lied.

Karissa didn't respond. She had found the new obsession with his clothes quite unlike Paul.

"I could take yours. There is a place in the strip mall just out front," he continued.

"No thanks," Karissa said. "You know I prefer to do my own."

Paul wanted to press the subject, but he didn't know how. He wanted to tell her to avoid the laundry room. Avoid it as much as she could. But that would require an explanation. He left it alone.

She was correct. Over the last few weeks, he had made numerous trips to the laundry room. It was in the basement, connected to the storage area. He couldn't help himself. Doing laundry was a legitimate cover.

The suitcases Felipe left there were undisturbed for a week. Then they disappeared. After another week, Paul was beginning to relax. Then suddenly six new cases appeared. No one spoke to him about it. They just appeared.

Once when Paul was waiting for his clothes to dry, curiosity got the better of him. He opened the storage locker. He lifted up one of the cases, then a second and a third one. They were heavier than he expected.

Paul saw the small lock on it. He could force it open if he wanted to. Instead, he pulled the zipper and managed to get nearly an inch of separation. He went upstairs and got a small flashlight. One that he normally used to look into the throat of patients. With the light, he could clearly see the contents of the suitcases. Tight stacks of one-hundred-dollar bills.

He dropped the case and quickly pushed it back among the other storage items. He had no idea why he was prying. He tried to estimate the amount of cash those cases would hold. He knew it would be hundreds of thousands of dollars.

Afterward, Paul stood there in silence. He finally made up his mind. He would not return to the laundry room. He would get his clothes done at the cleaners.

Every time he had looked at the suitcases, he remembered Cynthia. She was one of the thousands who had lost their lives to drugs. Some quickly. Some, not so quickly. His conflict felt heavy in his throat.

As he climbed the stairs to his third-floor apartment, he reflected on his situation. How did he end up in this position? All he ever did was choose the wrong seat on a plane, he reminded himself.

He reassured himself that would never touch the money. He would never touch the cocaine. He would continue with his life as planned. Yet he saw no end in sight.

5

IT WAS WEEKS AFTER CYNTHIA'S DEATH BEFORE PAUL MUS-
tered the courage to look for her sister. He got the next of kin information
from the medical chart. Her name was Brenda Jones. He tried the phone
number listed. It was a not a working number.

The address listed was close to the hospital. He had promised Cynthia
that he would get her tested for HIV. He would go find her if necessary.

Before he met her, he outlined the plans he had for Brenda in his
mind. If she was HIV positive, as they suspected, she could get treatment.
Preferably with one of the newer medications that was becoming available.

Paul hoped he could enroll her in a clinical trial for newest HIV
medications. He also thought the chance of her having the virus was very
high. Ten years of injection heroin use was a steep cumulative risk.

Brenda's listed address was a fourth-floor apartment between Second
and Third Streets. Not many people walked the area. Drug dealers inhab-
ited every corner. It was considered highly unsafe, even in the middle of
the day. An occasional police car passing through did little to change it.

Paul rarely went on foot in the local neighborhood. He didn't have
good memories of it. Twice his car had been broken into. Both times,
the windscreen was smashed. Once parked on Fifth Street when he had
left his coat in the back seat. Another incident was on the campus of the
hospital itself. He had left two six-packs of Coca Cola on the passenger
seat. He never left anything visible in his car since.

Paul did his homework. In casual conversation, he had found a cafeteria worker who lived a few blocks away. One late night on call, Paul sat
with him in the empty cafeteria.

Paul garnered that the price of crack was cheaper there than on
Florida Avenue. The more travelled artery was just three blocks away. He

also found out that some of the cops were considered insiders. They often sold drugs that were seized in raids to the local dealers. The locals knew which ones were considered safe.

His new friend told him that only the hardened buyer ventured into the local neighborhoods. If Paul was trying to get some stuff, he would bring it to him right there in the hospital. No need for him to go on the streets. He advised Paul never to go alone in those streets. He would stick out like a Christmas tree in the middle of a football field.

Paul made up his mind. He would sneak away in daylight. During clinic hours and return before evening rounds. He packed a small kit. It contained needles, syringes, and alcohol pads. Blood tubes, a rubber tourniquet, and a few gauze pads completed his supplies.

His plan was simple. He expected Brenda to refuse to come to the hospital. He would draw her blood and bring it to the hospital. He was friendly with the nighttime lab technician. They could run her blood under Jane Doe. He was hoping against hope that she would be HIV negative. That would be the end of his commitment to Cynthia.

The sun was bright. It lifted the temperature as Paul headed out on foot. He found the apartment building easily. He felt eyes looking at him. From the street to the building. No one spoke to him.

He tried the elevator. The button lit up, but no lift came. He looked around and saw the stairs. He took them and headed up to the fourth floor. The stairwell was cold. Many of the windows that lined it had broken glass. He had noticed that most buildings in the block had broken glass.

He reached the fourth floor slightly out of breath. He pulled out the piece of paper from his pocket. The apartment was number 434. He headed down the wrong side of the hallway. He quickly turned around and followed the sequence of numbers. He stopped at the faded lettering on the door: *434*.

Paul took a deep breath and knocked.

No answer.

He knocked firmly again. Still no answer.

He waited. He looked at his watch. It was 2:58 p.m.

Another minute passed. It felt like ten. Paul knocked again. Still no response.

Just as he was about to leave, the door opened. A woman, with her coat on, opened the door.

"Who are you?" she demanded.

"I am Dr. Karan."

She looked at him blankly.

"A friend of Cynthia's," Paul added hurriedly.

"What do you want?" she asked, still speaking through the half-opened door.

"Are you Brenda?" Paul asked.

She looked at him from head to toe before answering.

"Yes," she said finally.

"I am a friend of your late sister. She asked me to come."

She looked at him suspiciously. "What do you want?"

"I want five minutes of your time."

"I don't have any. I am going out now."

"Just five minutes, Ms. Jones," Paul pleaded.

"What for?"

"Cynthia asked me to do your blood tests."

"For drugs?"

"No, no," Paul said quickly, realizing his ambiguity.

"For what? For AIDS?

"Yes. For HIV," Paul confessed.

"Look, I don't want any of your tests," Brenda said firmly.

"Ms. Jones, if we know, we can treat you."

"Treat me?" Brenda asked incredulously. "For what?"

"For HIV. That is, if your test is positive."

"Look, those drugs kill you faster than HIV."

"Ms. Jones, the newer medications are much better."

"You saw what happened to Cynthia!" she said flatly.

"Cynthia's condition was end-stage. Sorry."

"You expect me to believe you?" Brenda asked incredulously.

"I can explain the options," Paul pleaded.

"I don't have time right now. I have to go."

"Please. It will take just five minutes."

"School already finished. I'm late."

She read the question in Paul's eyes.

"I have to get Cynthia's son."

She slipped out of the door. Before Paul could respond, she closed the door behind her. She headed down the narrow hallway.

"I can wait," Paul said desperately.

She didn't turn around. He was sure she heard him.

Paul just stood there. His head dropped. He had failed again. He gathered his thoughts. As he was trying to decide what to do next, Brenda's apartment door opened again.

A large black man stood there. He was about six five. Paul looked up at him. He wore ill-fitting jeans and a faded Houston Rockets T-shirt. Paul stared.

He returned Paul's stare with kind eyes. He spoke first.

"I heard everything," he said.

Paul nodded without thinking.

"You must go now."

"I can wait."

"No need to."

"How long before she returns?" Paul asked.

"Maybe, forty minutes. She has to walk to the boy's school. It's about a mile away."

"I can wait," Paul insisted.

"She won't change her mind."

"Are you sure?" Paul asked.

"I axed her many times before. To get tested, that is."

Paul was silent.

"Please leave," the man said.

"Why?" Paul asked

"You won't last twenty minutes here.

"What do mean?" Paul asked.

"You're not safe here," he repeated.

"I'm a doctor."

"Nobody knows that. They know you're a stranger."

Paul looked at him questioningly.

"They will think you're an agent or something. Or an outside dealer."

Comprehension was hitting Paul.

"Either way, you're in big danger. You shouldn't come here by yourself."

Paul's heart was racing. It had finally sunk it.

"Look, I will walk you to the corner street. It's safer than this building."

"Thanks," Paul said.

"You can leave that bag with me."

"Why?"

"I'm sure you have clean needles in it."

Without any protest, Paul gave up the bag. He was stunned and confused. One thing was certain—he was out of his element here. His logic and reasoning didn't apply to this world.

He tossed the bag into the apartment and closed the door. He headed down the hallway toward the stairs. Paul quietly followed him.

6

Not a day passed without Paul thinking about drugs.

The drugs in his basement. The drugs on the street. The drug-related killings in the news. The drug shows on TV. Now, the daily deaths from AIDS in his patients.

He saw it in the day. He saw it in the night. He saw it in his sleep. He saw it in his nightmares.

For most Americans, the drug news faded into the background. They went about their daily lives as if it didn't exist. The war on drugs on TV was less important than a fender bender on a busy street. People just flipped past the channel. Paul couldn't understand it.

The "Say No to Drugs" campaign and "This Is Your Brain on Drugs" commercials garnered interest for how funny the commercials were. Not on the actual importance of the message. Everything screamed for the public's limited attention span. In an attempt to up the ante, hockey games reverted to ambulance sirens for celebrating. The perversion caught on and became the norm. It made even less sense to Paul.

Several drug-addicted patients told Paul that he could make a lot money on the streets. This offer usually came when he skillfully threaded IVs through their badly sclerosed veins. One patient offered half of his drugs if Paul could give him a regular hit through his nonexistent veins.

At today's Morbidity and Mortality Conference, Paul noted that all four of the cases presented died of AIDS complications. The medical residents were fascinated by the adrenal complications of AIDS. They never gave thought to how long the twenty-two-year-old had the infection. The cases were quickly forgotten as they ate free pizza, brought in by the drug company.

With a two-hundred-pound weight pressing on his shoulders,

Paul drove home that evening. He couldn't forget the case of the twenty-two-year-old. He couldn't shed the weight.

He stopped at the mailbox as per his routine. As he sifted through the mail, he noticed an unusual stamp on an envelope. It stood out from the mostly junk mail. He opened it as he walked up the stairs.

It was a letter from Andreina. It was short and to the point.

Dear Paul,

I know you are in Washington. I got your address from Javier. He would not give me your phone number. I know they have been in contact with you. I do not want to imagine what they have asked of you.

I hope you are doing well in your medical specialty training. Not much has changed here. I am still locked up in this prison. I do get to visit my family frequently. But I am often followed there. Ramon is in Colombia more often now.

I believe that they know I helped you escape. No one has said anything to me, but Javier has hinted of it. A few weeks after you left, my cousin, Sebastian, was killed. My sister told me. He was run over by a truck in broad daylight. They made it look like an accident.

Please do not try to contact me. It is for your own safety. I will try to write again when I can.

Love,
Andreina

Paul reread the letter twice. He gripped it so tightly that his knuckles turned white. It played over and over in his head. Caracas was now as close as Baltimore in his mind.

He already knew what would happen tonight. He would wake up screaming. He would be back in the prison cell in Ramon's mansion.

Thank God, Karissa would be next to him when he awoke. He consoled himself that he was in Washington, DC, not Caracas.

7

NOBODY WAS TALKING ABOUT DRUGS, AND THEN SUDDENLY everybody was. All because of one night in January, 1990. January 18, 1990, to be exact.

The mayor of Washington, DC, Marion Barry, was arrested in a downtown hotel for possession of cocaine. It was an undercover operation. There was video. The video was released by the FBI to justify their prized catch. For several days, CNN played it every few minutes. The local TV stations each played it at least a hundred times.

Still the debate was not on drugs itself. The debate was whether Barry was framed. His supporters were convinced he was set up. It polarized the population of the DC Metro area. Not surprisingly, the camps aligned themselves along racial lines. Paul thought that it was a sad outcome. A real opportunity was missed to delve into the devastating effects of drugs.

For months, Paul kept abreast of the drug trafficking news. It was overwhelming. There were weekly drug seizures at the airports in New York, Miami, and Toronto. It made about a paragraph in the newspapers.

Paul doubted that he heard of many of the West Coast busts. There was one he couldn't escape. A mega bust in Sylmar, California, late in 1989. Twenty-one tons of cocaine with a street value of more than $7 billion was seized. It made the news for a day or two. Then for most, it receded into history.

Paul went to the Greenbelt library every day for two weeks to read the *LA Times*. After digesting every detail, his conclusions were the same. The news reiterated what he already knew. The reaches of drug trafficking were expansive. It was but a churning, tumultuous, and treacherous ocean.

Dr. Paul Karan was but one little, dispensable fish. In an instant, he could be gobbled up by sharks. And the sharks were many.

✝

Paul did his best work when it was quiet. Around 8:00 p.m., he decided to do some reading. He wanted to prepare for his upcoming lectures. He flipped the pages to the chapter on tropical infectious diseases. He quickly became absorbed in it. It had been weeks since he had some real free time in the evening.

Paul was well into the tapeworm infestation of pigs when he heard a knock. He wasn't expecting anyone. He didn't get up immediately. A second, more urgent knock followed. He made his way hastily to the door.

He opened it. It was Felipe.

"Come with me," Felipe instructed.

"What are you doing here?" Paul hissed.

"*Come with me,*" Felipe insisted.

"For what?"

"Boss wants to see you."

"I don't want to see Ramon."

"You don't understand. Come now."

"Go to hell."

"It is not Ramon. It is the big boss!"

"Which big boss?"

"Senor Luis. Luis Alvarez."

"Why do I want to see him?"

"He is waiting for you."

"Where?"

"Get ready. I will take you."

"And what if I don't go?"

"Nobody says no to Luis."

"Maybe this could be a first!"

"Don't do that, Paul. Not even Ramon, his own brother, would refuse to see him," Felipe warned.

Paul groaned. He couldn't envision how this nightmare would end. Their timing was not random. They must have known that Karissa was working this evening. They knew more about her whereabouts than he did.

He got into Felipe's car. They drove quickly to DC. Paul knew the roads well. They headed down New York Avenue and into downtown DC. Felipe pulled up in front of the Sixteenth Street Hilton. Uniformed attendants took the car.

Felipe escorted Paul to a luxurious penthouse suite. He opened the door with an electronic keycard. Felipe ushered Paul inside. He did not follow him.

Paul stepped into the suite. He had never seen anything as grand before. It was humongous. The furnishings spoke of excesses. He wondered whether the painting of the walls were originals. He had little time to ponder. To his right, he saw four men sitting at table. It was a grand, darkly polished, oval table. They were deep in conversation. They looked up when he entered.

He immediately recognized one of them. Javier. He didn't know the other three, although one of them looked familiar.

Javier got up and approached him. Javier gripped his hand and shook it heartily. "Paul, it has been a long time."

"It has been a while," Paul replied quietly, showing little emotion.

Javier had changed little. Still holding Paul by the arm, he continued jovially, "I am glad you came."

Paul didn't answer. Javier seemed to be playing for his audience. "Come on, let me introduce you."

One of the men at the table stood up. The other two remained seated. Javier started with the men seated. "This is Mr. Joel Chadee, head of our operations in Trinidad."

Joel Chadee nodded.

"And this is Mark Munoz, adviser and chief financial officer for Mr. Alvarez."

Paul acknowledged the greeting.

Then turning to the man who had stood up to greet him. "This is Mr. Luis Alvarez. He is the head of our family."

Luis reached across the table. Paul took his extended hand. His handshake was warm.

"Pleased to meet you, Paul," Luis said.

"Pleased to meet you too," Paul replied.

"Have a seat," Luis continued on politely.

"Would you like to have a drink?" Javier asked.

Paul politely declined.

"Well, gentlemen, let's get down to business. Dr. Karan's time is limited," Luis said.

They all looked at Luis. He began as if he were speaking about the Washington weather.

"Paul, we would like to make a deal with you. The exact terms will be worked out by my team. I will outline it in principle."

No one said anything. Paul waited.

"Our family would like to have a greater presence in the Washington area. We need your help with that. We do have a presence here, but we plan to expand it. We are seeking multiple avenues for that growth. For years, the Medellin cartel has stolen our lunch in this area. In the past, we chose to ignore it. We can no longer afford to."

He took a breath and continued.

"We are now well set in Miami, New York, Toronto, and Philadelphia. We can compete with them there but not here. We do not have any consistently reliable structure in place. In fact, the fastest-growing market is nearby Baltimore. We have virtually no presence there."

Paul finally spoke up. Completely bewildered, he said, "I know nothing of these things."

"Not to worry. We will give you the particulars in good time."

"I still don't understand how I can help," Paul said.

"Paul, we are asking you to be a full member of our team," Luis stated matter-of-factly.

Paul still had a look of incomprehension.

"You will be well compensated," Luis added.

"What is well compensated?" Paul stuttered.

"Two million dollars per year with a 50 percent increase each year."

"Two million dollars?" Paul asked incredulously.

"Correct."

"So you expect me to quit my medical career?"

"Not at all, Paul. Actually, it is the reasons we chose you. As a physician here, you are under the radar. One of the conditions of our deal is that you remain a doctor."

"What exactly do I do?"

"Very little, Paul. My men will work out the details. You will be under the management of Javier and Mr. Chadee. We will take care of the rest."

"Ramon?"

"I understand that you are not fond of my little brother," Luis replied.

Gathering a bit of courage, Paul persisted, "Can you give me an idea of my role?"

"All I would say, Paul, is America is a great country. You need a search warrant to go on private premises."

Luis didn't have to spell it out. Paul already had a clue. His place was going to be their safe house. They had already piloted him. His mind immediately went to the safety of Karissa. No, he would not get involved any deeper. No amount of money would make him do that. They must have noticed the expression on his face.

For the first time, Mark Munoz, Luis's advisor, spoke up. "So, Paul, do we have a deal?"

Paul shook his head in refusal.

"No," he said, getting up.

Munoz raised his eyebrows.

"No," Paul repeated firmly, as if to reaffirm his refusal.

He started for the door.

Luis's voice was as calm and conversational as when he started. "Paul, I would like you to take a few days and consider my offer. My men will be in contact."

Paul didn't answer. He opened the door and headed down the hallway. He was looking for a nonexistent elevator when Felipe suddenly appeared.

"I will take you home," Felipe said.

†

In the days that followed, Paul could not clear his mind. He had met with the drug cartel's top leaders. He had seen them. He could identify them. It was with him in every waking moment. In the shower. While he drove to work. While listening to his lecturer droning on. Before he went to sleep.

He couldn't shed it. He knew sooner or later they would be in contact. He was on constant edge. He knew they wouldn't just let him go.

Karissa sensed something was wrong. She probed gently. He did not tell her. She knew he was jumpy. She came home one evening, and he had forgotten to walk the dog. The one thing he promised to do on the days she worked in the evenings.

Paul apologized profusely. He decided to join them for a walk late that night. The white German Shepherd jumped around in joy. She had been locked up in the apartment for twenty-four hours. It was an American White with a thick, furry coat. Karissa had named her Lily.

Lily was Karissa's pride and joy. Some time ago, she had expressed interest in a companion dog. He bought it as a wedding present for her. Actually two months before they got married. Lily grew quickly. At seven months, she was sixty pounds and a handful to manage. Paul knew they would soon need more yard space for her.

A week passed, and no one bothered Paul Karan. He made some plans. He had heard about the witness protection plan. He researched it. Now that he and Karissa were married, she would be offered protection too. He hoped his story was important enough that they would help him. He had read that his testimony would have to lead to some high-level conviction. That would qualify him for the program. How they would convict a Colombian and a Venezuelan drug lord, he had no idea. He had to try.

Paul waited. He knew why he waited. He would have to give up his career if he chose that path. It was a difficult decision. Shouldn't he discuss it with Karissa? He thought that was fair. He didn't know where to start. He convinced himself he would wait a few more days. Then he would go to the authorities.

Paul knew he needed to talk to someone. Logically, it should be Karissa. Yet, in an effort to protect her, he had isolated himself even more. He knew he would explode if he kept everything to himself.

He made a conscious decision. There was a young Trinidadian doctor whom he had developed a friendship with. Dr. Roger Ramsammy was one year his junior. He would speak to Roger in general terms. His head had now become a pressure cooker. He hoped that, by releasing some steam, he might be able to keep his sanity for a bit longer.

✝

Paul pulled off Kenilworth Avenue and onto Greenbelt Road. He was almost home. He decided to avoid the BW Parkway today, as two accidents had been reported. He made good time.

Ten days had passed since his meeting with Luis Alvarez. Not a word from the cartel. He was starting to hope that they might leave him alone.

He opened the door to his apartment. Karissa sat there, tears streaming down her face.

"What wrong, honey?"

She didn't answer.

"What happened?"

She still did not answer. Paul was churning inside. He didn't know what to think. He knew it had something to do with Ramon's men.

Karissa got up and grabbed him by the arm. She was leading him somewhere. He followed as she bolted down the stairs. Along the path and around the building.

"Come see this!" she hissed.

She skirted around the man-made lake at the edge of the woods. They passed the tennis courts. The route was familiar. It was where Karissa walked Lily almost every day.

She passed the No Outlet sign. She headed to the end of the community. She tugged his arm and walked furiously. Then she stopped and pointed, "There!"

Paul looked at the ground where she pointed.

He wasn't sure how to react.

Lily was lying on her side. Lifeless, in a pool of blood. A single red spot was on her head. Paul didn't have to ask any questions.

Karissa knelt beside Lily's body. She sobbed openly. The words came out gushed. "I was walking her. Just before you came ... home."

"I heard ... I heard a loud sound. Like a firecracker. I saw Lily fall to the ground. Somebody shot her! Somebody shot her, Paul!"

"I am sorry, dear. I am really sorry." That was all Paul could muster.

"Who would do such a thing, Paul? Who?"

Paul had no answer.

"What do we do now?" Karissa wailed. He continued to sooth Lily's fur.

"She's gone, Karissa." Paul tried to calm her.

"What do we do with her, Paul?" Karissa insisted.

"We don't have a yard."

Karissa looked at him uncomprehendingly.

"I'm not even sure about the county laws," Paul stated.

"What?"

"We cannot bury her, Karissa."

She finally understood. "What do we do?"

"Let's go home. I can call the City Sanitation Department. They'll pick her up."

Paul had hoped to say these words gently. They still came out cold.

"What?" Karissa said, her tone rising.

Her mood had changed to anger. Paul was the only one around.

"I'll call them," he said calmly.

"You go!" Karissa shrieked. "I'm not leaving her."

"I'm not leaving you here," Paul said firmly.

"Why not?" Karissa yelled.

"It's not safe," Paul said.

"Safe from what?" Karissa shouted.

Paul couldn't answer that question honestly.

"Okay. I'll stay with you."

Karissa didn't answer. She tried to gather herself. After a couple of minutes, she appeared to accept his support.

"I have my on-call cell phone. I should be able to get them."

"Thanks," Karissa muttered.

"It could take hours for them to come," Paul said.

"I will stay here. I will stay until they come!"

8

PAUL KARAN HAD HEARD THE PHRASE "CAUGHT BETWEEN A rock and a hard place." He had never given it much thought until recently. It appeared gentle given his present situation.

He saw a sheer, thousand-foot, perpendicular cliff as the rock. He was standing at the foot of it. The hard place was a massive, metal wall being pushed by gigantic, invisible bulldozers. He was trapped in between. The cliff and the wall were so high that he barely saw a small sliver of the sky. His rock and a hard place were no longer a metaphor.

Immediately after Lily's death, Paul expected to hear from them. Maybe a note under his door. Or in his mailbox. Maybe another anonymous phone call.

Nothing that day.

Nothing the following day.

They were giving him time to think, he surmised.

Two days later, he opened the door of his car. It was sitting there. On the driver's seat. Paul didn't even concern himself about how they got into his car. They seemed to have access to everything.

He ripped open the white envelope as he sat behind the wheel. He didn't start the car. The note was longer than previous ones. Typed in simple uppercase letters. One could infer that the writer's English was not good. Either that or it was simply a case of stating it bluntly.

YOUR WIFE'S HEAD IS LARGER THAN HER DOG'S.
WE KNOW WHERE YOUR FAMILY LIVE IN TRINIDAD.
FELIPE WILL PICK YOU UP AT EIGHT O'CLOCK TONIGHT.

A stamped picture of the dagger tattoo served as a signature.

The message was clear. They were giving him one last chance. They owned him. He had to do what they wanted.

The witness protection plan would not help him now. It was too late. The metal wall moved closer to the cliff. Paul had no energy to push back.

He didn't feel like going to work. A deep medical sense of duty pushed him on. He drove to the hospital in a daze. He didn't register the traffic around him. He didn't see anyone or anything.

†

At 8:00 p.m. sharp, Felipe knocked on his door. Paul was waiting. His heart pounded without his permission. He complied and followed Felipe. No point in objecting now.

Felipe must have been waiting in the parking lot. He was impeccably dressed. It was hard to imagine that this groomed Felipe was the same one he knew in Caracas.

They headed to DC entering via Connecticut Avenue. The destination was another plush hotel. Just off M Street in Georgetown. Javier and Mark Munoz were waiting for him.

Another charade and offer of a drink by Javier. He looked surprised when Paul accepted. It was clear that Javier wanted to advance in the organization. He was trying to impress Munoz.

"Mr. Munoz was kind enough to remain in town while you were considering our offer," Javier said.

Paul nodded. The cynic in him smiled at the choice of words.

"Let's go over it again, Paul. I have prepared a document that requires your signature. We will keep the copies for security reasons. They will be available for future negotiations between you and our group."

Again Paul nodded.

Mark Munoz chimed in. "If changes are to be made, please let us know now, Dr. Karan."

"Okay" was all Paul could mutter. These guys actually believed they played by the rules, he thought.

"The offer is $2 million per year with a 50 percent increase every year," Javier said.

Paul nodded.

"In return, you will abide by the goals of the group. You will deny knowledge of our existence or any association with it. Understood?"

Paul nodded again.

"Do you have any questions?" Javier asked.

"Yes."

"Go ahead," Javier urged.

"The IRS is not stupid. How do I explain suddenly getting $2 million?"

Mark Munoz smiled. He was waiting for his opportunity to be useful. Javier nodded in his direction.

"Paul, that's why we have financial specialists. Like Javier and me."

Paul waited.

"Paul, you will be a part owner of a business registered in the Cayman Islands. I should tell you that we own several business entities registered in the Cayman Islands and the Bahamas. They have all been scrutinized over the years and have been found to be legitimate. You do not have to concern yourself with these matters."

Paul took a moment to digest this. Like the rookie he was, he asked, "How do I actually get my money?"

"Simple, Paul." Munoz was only too happy to explain. "We will do it the old-fashioned way. I have in my possession a set of addressed, postage-paid envelopes. Enclosed in each is a transaction number. It links our business account in the Cayman Islands to your personal account here. All you have to do is put a figure in the space provided and place it in any mailbox. In less than a week, the amount will be paid into your account. It will show as income from our business of which you are a legitimate part owner. I should add that the transaction number is specific and is only valid for those accounts."

Nice, Paul thought. They had it all worked out. He had no reason to doubt them. He realized that they must have done this many times.

"What is the maximum amount that I can transfer?" Paul asked.

"Of course, you cannot exceed two million in the next year. All single transactions over $500,000 are reviewed by me. That is my directive to the bank. I recommend that you keep it around fifty to a hundred thousand per month. That will keep you under the radar. We also note that your financial needs at this time are not high."

"Anything else, Paul?" Javier asked.

"Yes."

They waited.

"I would like a 100 percent increase each year."

Javier looked over at Mark Munoz. Was he testing them? Mark was quick on the draw. "That would be untenable if we have a long-term relationship, Paul. I am sure you know that math gets complicated with percentages increase. I am generally not in favor of them."

Paul was pushing to see how far he could go. "So let's keep it simple then. Two million in the first year, four in the second. Six in the third, and then we renegotiate."

Javier looked over at Munoz. They concurred with facial expressions. To Paul's surprise, Mark Munoz said, "Done. I will adjust the contract to reflect that."

"Anything else?" Javier asked.

"What do I do now?"

The men exchanged looks.

Mark Munoz was correct. He and Javier were more of the boardroom type. They were patient with Paul Karan. They had taken his opinions into consideration. Paul knew Javier had been a bank manager. His guess was Munoz had a similar background.

"Paul, we took care of all the arrangements. Felipe will be posted to Washington. You seem to get along okay with him. He knows the area well," Javier said.

Paul waited.

"Felipe will explain all of this to you. I will outline it."

"What specifically do I do?" Paul insisted.

"Nothing, Paul. You do nothing unless Felipe contacts you directly."

Paul looked blankly at him. They were not paying him $2 million per year to do nothing.

"I have in my possession a set of keys," Javier began. "Also the title of a house. You own this house, Paul. You will move in this weekend."

Paul blinked. He never had any choice. They were way ahead of him. They had made plans for him, weeks before. Maybe even months.

"The address is here. Felipe took me to the premises yesterday. He says it is just off New Hampshire Avenue. About one mile north of Randolph Road," Javier continued.

Paul waited for him to go on.

"The house is a bit old. We recently renovated it. It has a very large yard. No neighbors within a hundred meters. The garage is not attached to the house. There is a large tool shed behind the garage. The entire house is yours. However, you do not have access to the garage and the tool shed."

Javier paused for a moment, then resumed. "The driveway has been widened. You will always park your cars to one side of it, never blocking access to the garage. The gate is remotely locked. Only Felipe, you, and one of his men has access."

"Karissa?"

"Paul, to be honest, our lives are less complicated without wives."

"She is not going anywhere!" Paul insisted.

"For now, she can live with you. Everything should be as normal as possible."

"What do I tell her?"

"You are smart enough, Paul. Come up with something. Just minimize visitors. If she wants to have a party, have it at a hall or somewhere. You can afford it."

"How often will Felipe come by?"

"That I do not know, Paul. You will have visitors. Maybe a few times a month. Maybe a couple times a week. They will come through the gate and park in the garage. They will leave without ever bothering you. Felipe will try to contact you ahead of time, when possible."

"I cannot move this weekend," Paul protested.

"Why?"

"I have a lease with the apartment building." Paul knew his protest was feeble.

The beginnings of a smile formed at Javier lips. "The lease has already been taken care of. It has been paid off in full."

Paul was now immune to surprises. They were miles ahead of him.

"Sign here." Mark Munoz's voice interrupted his thoughts.

Paul signed without reading the contract.

"Good luck, Paul," Javier said.

Paul barely heard Javier's voice. His life was being charted. He had no say whatsoever in it. He was plunging headlong into another dark alley. And he wasn't even equipped with a functioning flashlight.

9

THE NAMED GREGORY LONDON WILL BE ETCHED IN PAUL'S brain forever. It was one patient Paul Karan would never forget. Paul could still hear his voice, "How are you, Dr. Karan?"

Gregory was the born the same year as Paul, one month apart. He was from The Islands. He left his fiancée and young daughter to seek his fortune in America. He hoped to return for them in a year, when he got settled in Washington, DC.

For months, he did odd jobs to make ends meet. One weekend, he accepted a coworker's invitation to go to a late-night party. He didn't want to say no to the guy who helped him load trucks daily. More as an act of team spirit than one of celebrating.

At the party, there was crack cocaine. And a lot of willing women, many of whom were stoned. For the first time in a long time, Gregory let his guard down. Next day, he closed the entire episode out of his mind. He didn't even speak to his coworker about it. He continued to load trucks in the cold morning and in the hot sun. He worked twelve hours per day, seven day a week.

Months later, he noticed he was getting tired easily. He lost weight. He attributed it to working too much and not eating well. One day he fell ill at work. He began to vomit relentlessly. He was taken to a nearby hospital.

He was admitted with a high fever, vomiting, and a pounding headache. He felt as if his head would explode. He was diagnosed with Cryptococcal meningitis. Something he had never heard of before. The doctors told him it was a rare fungal infection. It occurred primarily in people with AIDS.

Gregory denied being gay. No, he didn't use needles. They tested him for the AIDS virus. His test came back positive. They treated him with an intravenous antifungal. It made him nauseated, and his body shook. It affected his kidneys. Gregory fought through the side effects and won.

They discharged him as soon as they could. He had no health insurance. They gave him a prescription for an antifungal pill called Diflucan. They sent him on his way with a week's worth. Gregory counted the seven pills. He took them as directed. When they were gone, he tried to fill the prescription. The pills cost more than ten dollars each. With the cash he had, he could afford only eighteen pills.

Gregory was too weak to return to work. He quickly used up his supply of medications. But he refused to give up.

It was at this intersection Paul Karan met Gregory London. He showed up at the free AIDS clinic in DC. He had already been out of his medications for several weeks. Gregory was happy to meet someone from The Islands. He put his trust in Dr. Paul Karan.

Paul gave him a few of the Diflucan pills. He kept some medications in his desk drawer. He had obtained them from another AIDS patient who had died. Gregory was able to restart the Diflucan immediately.

Paul filled out dozens of forms for Gregory to get free medications. There was an AIDS drug-assistance program available. Only problem was it took them months to respond. Too often, it was not a stitch in time.

Gregory grew on everyone at the clinic. Paul saw him almost weekly. The nurses, the clerks, and the health techs all loved him. He resumed his twelve-hour days. He made plans as if he had never fallen ill.

The medications eventually came. As the months passed, Gregory's headaches returned. His vision was now affected. His fungus had become resistant to the Diflucan. He needed intravenous medications.

"Don't worry, Dr. Karan, I will be fine," Gregory often reassured Paul.

Several times, Paul referred Gregory to the hospital. On each occasion, they evaluated him in the ER. Then they sent him home. Paul knew the real reason. He tried multiple hospitals. Same result. No insurance, no admission. Hospitals were losing money. They didn't want patients like Gregory.

Gregory developed lesions on his face and his nose. The Cryptococcus grew on his skin. It literally grew out of his brain. Gregory's sight deteriorated rapidly. His body began to waste. He moved around wearing a big coat. His effort to conceal his skin and weight loss was marginally successful.

Gregory finally told his mother in Trinidad. She promised to come to see him as soon as she could. She negotiated the visa quagmire and made it to Washington, DC.

Gregory brought his mother to meet Paul. He drove her to the clinic. Paul had repeatedly warned him not to drive. His vision was poor and deteriorating rapidly.

"Dr. Karan, this is my mom," Gregory said proudly.

She had the same smile as her son. Paul was happy to meet Gregory's mother. But Paul also faced a dilemma. Gregory had endangered his mother and the public by driving nearly blind. Paul knew that Gregory should not drive. He should report Gregory to the DMV. Gregory begged Paul to let him keep his license. Gregory explained that there was no one to take his mother around. In the end, indecision froze Paul. He did nothing.

Gregory lost more weight. He became skin and bones. He was forced to give up working. The social worker eventually got him to agree to enter a hospice for AIDS patients. He never told Paul the reason he agreed. He had been evicted from the room he was renting. He had no money. It was the hospice or the streets.

Every day when Paul looked at his garage, he thought of Gregory. He thought of Cynthia and the many others who had stumbled upon crack cocaine. And the thousands who would begin to use crack. Crack cocaine that was stored at his house. Crack cocaine that he was peddling. Directly or indirectly. He had to face that hard, cold fact.

Paul mustered his courage. He would visit Gregory next week. He would go to the hospice early one morning. He would do it before work. It was the least he could do.

He would like to hear, one more time, the melodious voice of Gregory London. "How are you, Dr. Karan?"

✝

Paul got up early that Wednesday morning. He was going to see Gregory London. He was excited and scared at the same time. Inwardly, he knew the reason.

Gregory was him. It could have easily been him. Their ages, roots, and demeanor were almost identical. They wanted the best for their family and those close to them. Only difference was Paul had some luck in his career path.

As Paul was getting dressed, he vividly recalled another Gregory story. It happened two weeks before Gregory entered the hospice.

Paul was at his desk one Monday afternoon when his phone rang. The caller ID listed the number as unavailable. Paul answered. It was the Newark police. Paul was normally downstairs in the clinic at this time. He was reviewing some labs results, as his new patient was late.

The police verified that he was Dr. Karan. Then they asked if he knew someone by the name of Gregory London. Sure, Paul said. Gregory was his patient. What was he doing in Newark? Paul had asked.

The police informed him that Mr. London was in their custody. They had found him in the predawn hours that morning. He was semiconscious and naked. He was left in a side alley. He was bleeding from his mouth and nose. The only thing he could remember was Dr. Karan. He said, "Call Dr. Karan." Miraculously, he remembered Dr. Karan's phone number.

When Paul saw Gregory later that week, he pieced together the full story. Gregory had somewhat recovered by then. The previous Saturday morning, some friends had asked him to go New York with them. Gregory agreed, as he had a couple of high school friends there. They took Amtrak, and everything went according to plan.

On Sunday afternoon when they were scheduled to return to DC, his friends changed their minds. They decided to stay an extra day. Gregory, not being of full mental capacity, couldn't deal with the change. He decided to return alone. On the way back to DC, the conductor asked him for his ticket. He had no ticket or money. He was tossed out in Newark. During his wandering there, he was mugged.

Paul was still meandering in this memory when he heard sirens coming up New Hampshire Avenue. His heart skipped several beats. Every time he heard sirens in his neighborhood, he feared the worst. The police were coming to raid his house, he thought. It was well known that the Montgomery County Police were no-nonsense guys.

Karissa was still home. Paul decided to wait. He didn't want to leave her alone. He froze as the cars turned onto his street. Now he was sure that the police were coming for him. Another two police cars joined the convoy. Paul quickly closed his front door and went inside. Through the open bedroom door, he saw Karissa getting dressed for work. Unperturbed.

Paul peeked through the drapes. The first car was getting close to his driveway. The moment he had feared for months was here. It was only a matter of time, he had reasoned. Someone would eventually spill the beans.

To his amazement, the first car passed his driveway. It continued on down the road. So did the second. Followed by two others. He exhaled slowly. Soon an ambulance followed.

Paul later learned that there was a big accident on Chaney Street. They had used his side street as a shortcut. The traffic began to pile up. He would be late for work. He would have to postpone his visit to Gregory until tomorrow.

Later that evening, he got a call from his head nurse at the clinic. She was calling to inform him that Gregory London died that afternoon.

10

THE LEAVES CHANGED COLORS. THE WEEKS MOVED INTO months. Paul continued his work in DC's poorest areas. His AIDS clinic was visible to all. The rest to himself. Some of it to Felipe and Javier. As well as his bosses in Cucuta and Caracas. Paul never felt so alone.

This afternoon, he was hosting his colleague and friend. They would be visiting his house in Silver Spring. Dr. Roger Ramsammy and his fiancée, Jennifer. Paul was happy and apprehensive at the same time. He was glad to have company. Jennifer and Karissa got along particularly well. It was Karissa's idea to have them over.

Anytime someone came to the house, Paul got anxious. Suppose Felipe and his men made a sudden appearance? He hadn't seen or heard much recently. But he knew that they came and went. Usually in the wee hours of the morning. Felipe had all but forgotten to inform him about their comings and goings.

Roger Ramsammy was an interesting guy. He was from Couva, Trinidad. His grandfather was a cane cutter. His father, a small-time building contractor. His older brother was an engineer, and his older sister, an obstetrician. Roger had come to the DC area to go to college. He took a fast track into medical school and was just about completing his residency in surgery. He was ambitious and talented. He already had an offer to specialize in transplant surgery.

He and Paul had a lot in common. He met Roger one late night in the hospital cafeteria. They were both on call and were grabbing a midnight snack. They had traded stories. They got closer in the months that followed. Paul recognized a quiet, deep determination in Roger that he had seen in few. Added to his prodigious talent, he knew Roger was going places. Paul wished that he didn't have a leash around his neck. Then he could dream about the future like Roger did.

They opted to sit outside that afternoon. Sipping a cold beer with the sound of a lawnmower in the distance, they chatted idly. Karissa and Jennifer were inside catching up with girl talk. Paul decided that today would be the day. He would tiptoe in when he got a chance.

"Did you see the Raiders game last weekend?" Roger asked.

"I caught a few minutes."

"Only?"

"I flipped the channel during halftime of our game."

"They smoked the Chiefs."

"Yep. That was a big win," Paul answered, unenthused.

Paul didn't understand how Roger lived in DC for years and supported a team in California. He still had a lot to learn about American culture, he thought.

Paul had only one subject in his mind. He knew had to tell someone, otherwise his head would burst. He imagined the vessels in his head as over-pressurized pipes waiting to explode. He trusted Roger fully. Yet he didn't know how to approach the subject.

"Want to take a trip to Annapolis this weekend?"

"What for?" Roger asked.

"They have a boat show up there."

"Didn't know you like boats."

"I like the water," Paul replied.

"Sorry. On call this weekend."

Roger noticed the disappointed look in Paul's face.

"Perhaps next weekend?" Roger offered.

"I'm on call next weekend," Paul said.

Roger didn't respond. He knew Paul wanted to talk. He waited.

Paul finally made a feeble attempt.

"Roger, did you ever have something to tell someone and you didn't know how to?"

Roger looked at him for a few moments. Then he answered, "Not really. Nothing major."

"Suppose you did. How would you go about it?"

"I guess it depends on what it is," Roger replied.

"Something private. Something personal."

"You mean like an old girlfriend?"

"Kind of."

Another silence from Roger. He toyed with the cap from the bottle of the Amstel Light before asking, "Are you and Karissa having problems?"

"No, no," Paul said quickly.

"Well … in this hypothetical situation of yours, my advice is to be direct. I would tell her exactly what's bothering you and hope that she understands."

"What if it's something that could ruin our lives?"

"Then I would carefully weigh the risks and the benefits."

"And?"

"If there is no upside, I might consider keeping the past in the past."

"And what would be the downside?"

"The downside would be carrying the weight and the burden alone."

"I see," Paul said

"That is not something to be underestimated," Roger said.

Paul nodded. He was living proof of that. He didn't know how to take the conversation any further. Not without making Roger an accomplice.

†

Paul turned off the *Arsenio Hall Show* and got ready for bed. Karissa had already gone upstairs. She began her day earlier than he did.

Paul passed by the window close to the garage. He heard voices. Intense voices. They were clearly having a disagreement. The garage door had been left open.

There was a vehicle in the driveway. A Toyota 4Runner. He recognized it as belonging to Felipe. They had never left the garage door open before. There was another vehicle parked inside. Paul saw the glow of the rear lights.

Paul waited. The voices got louder. He wasn't sure if Karissa had gone to bed yet. Annoyed and angry, he opened the kitchen door.

They stopped arguing when they saw him. Felipe was facing two other men. He did not know either of them.

"We were just about leaving," Felipe said, apologetically.

"After waking up half the neighborhood?" Paul's tone was acid.

"Sorry," Felipe said.

Paul was quiet for a moment.

"Since I'm already here, you might as well introduce me to the people who visit my house without my knowledge."

"Your garage, Paul. Not your house," Felipe corrected.

"Don't be a smartass, Felipe. You said only one person beside yourself would have access. There are two here."

"Paul, you know things happen. We have to have backup," Felipe explained.

"For what?"

"The boss says so."

Paul didn't answer.

"This is Tomas, and that is Manuel," Felipe continued, pointing at the men.

Paul acknowledged their presence without shaking hands.

"I am Paul Karan."

"We know who you are," Tomas responded.

Paul looked at him then at Manuel. Without another word, he turned and headed back to the house.

Felipe got into his vehicle. As Paul closed his door, he heard a vehicle going down the driveway. One vehicle only.

Paul shook his head. Even though he had agreed to this, there was something unsettling about the encounter. He was left to guess that the other men left with Felipe.

11

PAUL TOOK THE ELEVATOR TO THE SIXTH FLOOR OF THE University Hospital. The medical unit was always filled. He walked slowly down the hallway.

He started his rounds. He saw only two patients before his mood sank.

Paul gently bit his lower lip. He was still amazed at how strong the human heart was. The younger the heart, the longer it could go, he reasoned.

His work cell phone rang. He answered, already getting a pen out to jot down the name and room number of the patient. It was going to be another infectious disease consult for an AIDS patient. It would have to wait until after clinic. He would give the resident a curbside for now. He had late clinic that evening.

Except it wasn't. It was Felipe.

"I told you not to ever call me on this phone!" Paul hissed.

"I know," Felipe said. "But it is urgent."

"You know your number will be listed on the department's bill.

"I am on a payphone. Let them look up that."

"What do you want?"

"Javier is here to see you."

"When?"

"Tonight."

"I can't see him tonight. I have late clinic."

"Get out of it somehow. Javier is in a rush to get back home."

"I have a lot of sick patients, Felipe," Paul protested.

"Let one of the other doctors see them."

"Felipe, I can't. I have been treating some of these patients for months. Only I know them well."

Felipe was silent.

"I will see Javier tomorrow night," Paul added.

"He won't be happy."

"That I know. But he doesn't own me."

"He pays you," Felipe said.

"He can take his money and leave me alone."

"Okay, I will tell him tomorrow night."

"Good. Let him wait."

"Don't ever say that to Senor Luis. Just my friendly advice, Paul."

"Anything else?"

"I will pick you up at eight."

The phone went dead.

Paul slipped out of the cubicle that he had stepped into to take the call. He had to pass the room of one of his patients he had just seen. His thoughts went right back to her. He couldn't shed it. Perhaps he didn't want to, he thought.

Her name was Lakisha Barclay. She was twenty-one years old. Paul first saw her four months ago. She had end-stage AIDS. How long she was infected with the virus was anyone's guess. She had become sexually active as a teenager. She presented to Paul's clinic with advanced AIDS.

Lakisha was young and pretty. She had a two-year-old daughter. By the time she sought medical attention, she was emaciated and withered. She couldn't take care of her daughter anymore. Her mother took on the responsibility.

For months, Lakisha had chronic diarrhea and no appetite. She had thrush growing out of her mouth. More specifically, she was diagnosed with disseminated Mycobacterium Avium infection. She did not respond to any of the dozen medications tried.

Her HIV virus continued to overwhelm her body. The opportunistic infection ran rampant. The relative of the tuberculosis bacteria took one hit after another but didn't budge. Her condition continued to worsen. She frequently lapsed into a semicomatose state.

Lakisha had good family support. No one wanted to see her suffer. Her family and Paul's medical team came to a decision. They would stop all further treatment. Lakisha's condition was terminal. She would be given pain medications and fluids only. It was expected that she would last a few days. She would become acidotic and breathe deeply. Her breathing would eventually stop. Morphine would prevent her from the feeling of gasping for air.

Every day since, Paul's first stop had been at her room. And every day, she was still breathing deeply, eyes shut. Her treatment was stopped three weeks ago. Lakisha's heart was still pounding away. A twenty-one-year-old heart could beat in saline, he concluded.

Paul tried to push the emotion away. He knew the pain of waiting for someone to die was not limited to family members. It took its toll on everyone involved in her care. Right down to the lady who cleaned her hospital room daily. Every day, she too turned up, not knowing whether the room would be empty.

As Paul reached the far end of the hospital corridor, he pushed Lakisha to the back of his mind. Little did he know then that Lakisha's slow death would haunt him for decades.

12

FELIPE WAS AT THE HOUSE PROMPTLY AT EIGHT. ACTUALLY, he was there five minutes early. From the bedroom window, Paul saw his car coming up the driveway.

Paul made him wait. Paul stepped out of the house five minutes after eight. Felipe didn't comment. The rush-hour traffic had subsided, and the trip to Javier's DC hotel took only thirty-five minutes.

Paul asked Felipe for the Javier's room number. He expected Felipe to park under the hotel. Felipe ignored the question. Instead, he used valet parking and had Paul follow him to Javier's room.

Javier greeted him like a long-lost friend. Paul wasn't quite as enthused.

"I wish you came yesterday," Javier said.

"Why?"

"Mark was here."

Paul didn't answer.

"Mark Munoz. Remember him?"

Paul nodded.

"He had to go back to Colombia."

Paul remembered only too well. Similar situation, different hotel. Just as luxurious. The bigwigs saw Paul only when they wanted something. It usually came with a lot of money and very little choice.

"Why all the interest?"

Paul tried to act as casually as possible. His tone must have portrayed his anxiety. Javier picked up on it easily.

"Sit down, Paul."

Paul dropped down in a plush leather sofa.

"A drink?"

Why not, Paul thought. Felipe would drive him home. And he wasn't on call. He nodded. "Scotch and ginger."

Javier poured a generous drink. He handed the glass to Paul.

Paul took two sips and waited. He stared closely at the ice cubes. Nothing from Javier. Felipe was within earshot in the far corner of the large suite.

Paul stirred the ice with his index finger. He found it hard to remain silent. He planned to outwait Javier.

Javier finally spoke. Not a subject that Paul was expecting.

"I have a letter for you," Javier said.

Paul looked up.

"From Andreina."

Paul couldn't hide his surprise. He saw out of the corner of his eye Felipe turned to face them.

"What did you say?"

"A letter from Andreina."

Paul took the envelope. He examined it. White but opaque. His full name was written on the front. He turned it around. No sender's name. He carefully placed it in his coat pocket.

"How is she?" Paul finally asked.

"I am sure she will tell you in the letter."

Paul's heart skipped a beat or two.

Javier must have noticed the apprehension. He quickly added, "She was okay when I last saw her. She knew I was coming to DC. She asked me to hand-deliver a letter."

"Thanks," Paul replied, looking in the direction of Felipe.

Javier understood his unasked question.

"Don't worry, Paul. I think everyone in Ramon's family knows Andreina was fond of you. Even Ramon."

Paul was stoic again.

"Ramon had asked me about that. For her safety, I denied it."

"Thanks," Paul said again, not knowing why he was thanking Javier.

Another silence.

Paul's thoughts had shifted to Andreina.

Javier finally spoke up. "Paul, since you've been in this area, we have done well."

Paul half-nodded.

"In fact, very well."

Paul waited. This was leading up to something, he guessed.

"We have more than quadrupled our business in DC and Baltimore. We continue to expand. We now have multiple distributers in Richmond and Harrisburg."

Paul couldn't bring himself to say thanks this time. He just nodded. Felipe was delighted.

"Luis and Mark are happy with your performance. Even Ramon is."

Still no answer from Paul.

Javier waited.

Paul finally obliged. His cynicism got the better of him. "What do you have in mind?"

"I am glad you asked," Javier continued, cheerful and unruffled.

"Couldn't wait."

"Well, wait no longer. We want to appoint you head of our operations in Trinidad."

"Trinidad?"

"Yes."

"Why Trinidad?"

"It's our largest transshipment port to North America."

"Really?"

"You heard correctly. Not Colombia. Not Central America. *Trinidad.*"

"Why would I want to go there?"

"We will pay you $20 million a year."

Paul appeared unimpressed. Javier thought more money might make a bigger impact.

"That is *US* dollars, Paul! More money than I am making."

"Not interested."

"Mark is not here. He told me his best offer. Twenty-five million!"

Paul didn't answer.

"Paul, think about it! You will be the head of *all* Caribbean operations. *And* you get to return home!"

Paul remained silent. After a while, he spoke calmly. "Javier, I want to continue my medical career here. I am in the middle of some very important work."

"Paul, we have looked into that. You got a year off for excellent performances in residency. That is what you came here for, isn't it?"

Paul nodded.

"What you are doing now is additional. Correct?"

"Yes."

"This infectious diseases and AIDS business. You can stop at any point. You don't need the money."

Paul repeated firmly, "I want to complete my specialty training and fulfill my obligations. Then I will consider it."

Javier wasn't sure if Paul was trying to push him. Paul sounded serious. "Are you sure?"

"Positive."

"That is a lot of money, Paul. You can live like a king in Trinidad."

"I already have more money than I can spend. And I am not proud of it."

"You want to think about it and get back to me?"

"No."

Javier sighed. "I told them you wouldn't go for it."

"How did you know?"

"Life is complicated there. The place is too small."

"You were right," Paul replied, the firmness in his voice returning. Here he could hide. There was no way he could remain anonymous in Trinidad. Not drowning in money like that. He would attract friends like honey drawing flies.

"I do have a question."

"Go ahead."

"Wasn't there a local boss in Trinidad?

Javier nodded.

"What happened to him?"

Paul was still sharp. Javier chose his words carefully. "His position was eliminated."

"Was he eliminated along with his position?" Paul persisted.

Javier nodded.

"Ramon got him?"

"Paul, you know I can't answer that."

"You don't have to. I can fill in the blanks."

"I can tell you he hoarded some of our merchandise. Worse yet, he sold it to our rivals."

"I see," Paul said.

✝

On the way back, Paul was quiet. In the faint light, he tried to skim the letter from Andreina. He gleaned that there wasn't much in terms of specific news. She said she was doing okay. She still lived at Ramon's mansion. She hoped he was doing well.

Paul sensed an undertone of worry. He wondered if she omitted events because she thought her letter would be opened. Maybe it was and had been resealed. He couldn't be sure. Regardless, he was glad to hear from her. He would read it more carefully later.

Felipe, on the other hand, was humming. He was noticeably happy. He must have received a raise too. They were pleased with his work in Caracas and Cucuta. Now he was excelling in DC. He was a big part of the expansion.

Felipe did seem to enjoy American life. Paul wasn't sure how often he made the trip back to South America. He left Paul to his own thoughts. As they were nearing the house in Silver Spring, Felipe decided to test the waters.

"Paul, I heard you put Javier's offer on hold."

"Correct."

"Can we talk a bit more?"

Paul hesitated. Felipe had been good to him. He had kept his side of the deal. He rarely involved himself in Paul's affairs.

"Sure."

Felipe pulled off Georgia Avenue. He took a side road to a small playground. He parked next to a basketball rim. It was late. No one was around. The swings and plastic slides reflected the dim light. Felipe turned off the engine.

After a few moments, he spoke. "Paul, I want you to be in charge of the DC region."

Paul was surprised by the topic. He scratched his chin before he replied. In a measured voice, he said, "I am not interested."

"Why?"

"I want to be left alone."

"You cannot get out, Paul."

"Then I want to be as uninvolved as possible."

"Not possible. Once you are in, you are in," Felipe stated flatly.

"Maybe there is a way out."

"Trust me, there is no way out. I know."

"Well then, let's leave it as it is."

"You don't have to do much, Paul. Attend a few meetings now and then." Felipe tried one last time.

"What stake do you have in this, Felipe?"

"If you move up, they will make me your deputy," Felipe stated bluntly.

"Don't you have a regional boss already?"

"*We* do. But we don't like him."

"That's not my problem."

"That's because you don't have to deal with him."

"He won't just vacate the position, would he?" Paul asked.

"He can be taken care of."

Paul didn't respond.

"I lost a couple of good friends because of him, Paul. I think he is playing both sides."

Paul didn't want to know more. He sidestepped.

"Why don't they make you the regional boss, Felipe?"

Felipe didn't answer.

"You've been very loyal to the organization. According to Javier, we've done very well in the last couple of years."

Felipe laughed. Paul waited.

"Paul, you still surprise me."

Paul looked at him questioningly.

"For a position like that, they need a person without a record. Someone with a background that can be verified. Someone who lives above ground. Someone who could be detained and answer police questions. Without giving anything away. That is you, Paul. Not me."

"I see."

"Those people are hard to find, Paul. You can name your price."

Paul didn't respond.

"Just let me know when you are ready. We can create the opening for you."

Paul felt a tingle going down his spine. He could read between the lines. *Uneasy lies the head that wears the crown, indeed,* he thought.

13

It was almost midnight when Paul opened his front door. Karissa was still up. She was working in the morning, so Paul was expecting her to be asleep by now.

"What are doing up so late?" Paul asked.

"Watching TV," she answered in a not-convincing voice.

"Movie?"

"No."

Silence.

Paul sensed that something was wrong. He had no idea of the problem. He waited. Sure enough, it came. The tone was much stronger than the words.

"Where were you, Paul?" Karissa asked.

"I had to attend a meeting."

"What kind of meeting?"

"A business meeting," Paul replied offhandedly.

"Are you sure?"

"Yes, I am," Paul said firmly.

"I do not believe it."

"What do you not believe?"

"That you went to a meeting."

Paul took off his coat. He draped it over the back of a chair.

"Where do you think I went?

"Paul, these meetings are getting too frequent."

"I agree," Paul replied, trying to relax.

"Weren't we supposed to go out for dinner tonight?"

"I don't recall."

"You never recall the important things."

"I'm sorry. I will make it up to you this weekend."

"That is what you always say, Paul. This weekend or that weekend. You are never here. You are either on call or at some stupid meeting." By now, Karissa's voice was emotional.

"Listen, honey, didn't you hear the car drop me off? It was one of *those* meetings."

"How convenient!"

"What is convenient?"

Silence.

Then it came out.

"Paul, I think you are seeing someone."

"Karissa, I am not."

"You have been very distracted recently."

"Does that mean I am seeing someone?"

"That is how it feels."

Paul was beginning to get testy. He had had a very long day. "How do you know how *it* feels?"

"So you are going to dissect what I just said? You are going to change topics? Like you always do?"

Karissa was really hot now. Paul knew this wasn't going well. He took a deep breath. He lowered his eyes.

In a resigned tone, he said, "A lot has been going on, honey. A lot at work. A lot with other things too."

"Tell me about it."

"I know I haven't been home as often as I should. I promise to spend more time with you."

"I have heard *that* before."

"I mean it."

"Right!"

"I'm serious."

Paul waited for her to deescalate. She appeared to be calming down. He switched his attention to the TV screen.

"What is this, Paul?"

Paul froze. She had just reached into his coat pocket. She raised the envelope in the air.

"It is a letter," he stuttered.

The guilt must have been obvious on his face. She picked up on it.

"From whom?"

"An old friend," he managed.

She removed the letter from the envelope. She looked at the bottom of it.

"Andreina?"

He nodded.

"She lives here now?" Karissa stated more than asked.

Paul was too stunned to respond. He tried to gather his thoughts. The night had been a roller coaster. Before he could answer, she stormed out of the room.

She ran up the stairs. She slammed the bedroom door. She had found the answer she was looking for. In Paul's coat pocket.

✝

Karissa didn't speak to him for two full days. The first night, Paul slept on the couch. The second night, thankfully he was on call. He got a couple hours of sleep in a hospital bed.

Karissa remained cool after that incident. They didn't speak about the letter. Paul saw no trace of it. He was glad he had skimmed it before she laid hands on it. It was probably in pieces in the trash somewhere. He thought of looking for it. He doubted that she would put it anywhere he could find it.

Paul buried himself in his work. He felt safe there. He was sure of himself in his chosen specialty. Outside that, he was frequently in turmoil.

Two weeks passed before any semblance of normality returned. Fortunately, Felipe did not bother him in that time. Paul doubted his explanation of a sudden business meeting would be well received by Karissa. She would think Felipe was playing along with him. And the meetings were just another ruse.

Paul was now rich. He had more money that he could use. Yet he longed for the simple life. How he wished he could roll back time and return to San Fernando General Hospital. An altruistic, innocent young doctor seemed like a distant dream. Water under the bridge, he told himself. He could not undo what had happened. And a lot had happened.

He and Karissa got closer again. He could have never imagined what would bring them back together. It unfolded in front of her very eyes. After that night, he didn't think she would doubt him again.

Paul had a late patient that evening. By the time he turned off New Hampshire Avenue into his side street, it was dusk. He saw the vehicle behind him also made the turn. He glanced in his rearview mirror and recognized it. It was the Toyota 4Runner that Felipe often drove.

Paul tapped the remote. The gate to his driveway opened. He pulled up close to his house. The Toyota followed him into the yard. It stayed at the end of the driveway. They didn't lock the gate behind them.

Paul went into the house without paying the vehicle any mind. He saw Karissa peering through the drapes. He looked over her shoulder to the driveway. He saw a man standing next to the open door of the 4Runner. It was not Felipe.

In the fading light, Paul recognized the man as Tomas. One of the guys Felipe had brought to his house. He was obviously waiting for someone. Perhaps Felipe, Paul thought. He nudged Karissa away from the window. He knew they could be seen easily from the outside. The lights were on behind them.

"Who is he, Paul?" Karissa asked.

"I don't know," Paul lied.

"Shouldn't we call the police?"

"No, no," Paul said quickly. "It's probably one of Felipe's men."

She looked at him, not fully believing what he said.

"Should we get dinner?" Paul asked, trying to change the focus.

"I have some leftovers from yesterday," Karissa said apologetically.

"That's fine," Paul said.

"I had a long day today," Karissa added.

"I'll change and help you."

Karissa headed into the kitchen in the rear of the house. Paul went up to their bedroom. He quickly changed into slacks and a T-shirt. On his way down, he took a quick peek outside.

He noticed another car had joined Felipe's vehicle. He could hear animated voices. They had to be quite loud, he thought. The windows and doors were all closed. He was glad that the neighbors were a fair distance away. He knew that was by design.

Karissa set out plates and forks as she waited on the microwave. Paul joined her and tugged the placemats into position. He tried to push the image of the strangers in his driveway out of his mind.

Suddenly, they heard two short, sharp explosions. It sounded like gunshots to Paul. He wasn't quite sure. He opened the front door and heard the roar of engines. One of the vehicles disappeared down the narrow street. It was Felipe's 4Runner.

The other remained in the driveway. Paul heard a croaking cry. *"Help!"*

The voice choked off. It was coming from the car in the driveway.

Without thinking, Paul rushed to the vehicle. The doctor instinct in him took over. He got to the car in less than ten seconds. Slumped backward in the driver's seat was a man in distress. Paul had never seen him before.

His eyes were wide open. His eyelids flickered. He stared at Paul. His shirt was soaked with blood. Paul knew he was still alive. Barely.

Paul looked at the man. He looked back at his house.

"Help," the man's eyes pleaded at him.

Paul knew he had to do something. Even at that time, he knew this could be the end of his facade. He would never be able to explain a man gunned down in his yard.

He reached over the man and felt for a pulse. Faint. He looked up in front him. He saw the gates were still open. His mind was racing.

The keys to the Honda Prelude were still in the ignition. Paul yanked the gear shifter into neutral. He gave the car a quick push. It rolled down the inclined driveway. Thirty feet later, it went through the wide-open gate. It picked up speed before settling into the shallow ditch on the other side of his street.

Paul was right behind it. He reached for the occupant again. No pulse. He looked up. He saw Karissa staring at him. Her eyes widely dilated.

"Call 911!" Paul hissed.

She looked at him in confusion.

"I will start CPR."

She understood and nodded.

Paul began chest compressions.

Karissa turned to go to the house. Paul pulled out his cell phone and tossed it to her. His hands were bloody. He had no gloves. There was blood everywhere.

Paul barely heard her speaking into the phone. He was trying hard to push a few breaths into the stranger's lungs. He returned to chest compressions. Deep in his mind, he knew his efforts were futile.

He soldiered on.

Paul saw the entry wound. He knew his patient's heart and aorta was shattered. His lungs were full of blood. Each compression caused blood to ooze from his mouth. Paul kept going. The EMTs would be here soon, he hoped.

They would take over. He could use any help.

14

THE CHIEF OF POLICE RARELY LEFT HIS BED IN THE WEE hours of the morning. Tonight was the exception. He needed to speak with Dr. Paul Karan. In person.

For the third time, he asked the same question. Different words. Just more direct and blunt this time. As if Chief Slater was in Paul's corner.

"Are you certain that you don't want an attorney?"

"I am sure, Chief."

"So everything you told us is correct?"

"It is."

"We will require that you sign the statement that you gave to us. Once it is signed, it is an official legal document. I suggest you take a few minutes and read through it. Just to verify its accuracy."

"Okay," Paul said.

Paul was very tired. It was 3:00 a.m. He had not slept since the previous night. He just wanted to go home. *Karissa must be very worried*, he thought. He hadn't had time to call her since getting here.

The ambulance had arrived in seven minutes after Karissa called. It was Montgomery County. They were quick. The EMTs took over. They sped off to nearby Holy Cross Trauma Center, sirens blaring.

Paul knew the man was dead. More than half his blood was in the car and around it. Paul was later informed that the man was pronounced dead at Holy Cross ER. No surprise to him.

The police came immediately after the EMTs. As soon as the EMTs left, the police took over the scene. Less than an hour later, they asked Paul to come down to the station to give a statement. That was several hours ago. He told them what had happened. All of it. Almost.

He was taking an evening walk when he had heard what sounded like gunshots. He had run to the scene and offered his medical help. The shooting took place on the street, just outside his driveway. The driver lost control and ended up in a shallow ditch. Paul's wife was also roused by the noise. She came out and called 911. He was just being a Good Samaritan. That was all there was to it.

Paul was taken to the main police station. Not the one in nearby Colesville where he lived. The one in downtown Silver Spring. He wasn't sure why. He thought they didn't have enough staff at the local one. Paul had given his version of the events. It was received, recorded, and transcribed.

The sergeant, the lieutenant, and the poor clerk were the only people present. When Chief Slater came in, they had all left the room.

"Before you sign the statement, Dr. Karan, you *can* make corrections," Chief Slater said.

Paul looked up questioningly.

"Sometimes, things get transcribed incorrectly."

"Thank you, Chief."

Paul continued reading.

The police chief interrupted again. "You said you were taking the dog for a walk?"

"That's correct."

"Dr. Karan, can I call you Paul?"

"Certainly. I would prefer that."

"You may call me John, if you wish."

"Chief Slater is good for me."

"Paul, our records show that you don't own a dog."

Their eyes locked. Slater was reading him.

"No dog is registered at your address," Slater repeated.

A long pause. Paul lowered his eyes.

Slater spoke first. "Perhaps you misspoke. A lot was happening at the time."

"That's correct, Chief. We *had* a dog."

"So you went for a walk?"

"Yes. I went for a walk by myself."

147

"That is what your wife, Karissa, said. That you went for a walk by yourself."

"Karissa?" Paul asked, clearly surprised.

"We got a statement from her as well," Chief Slater said.

"When?" Paul stuttered.

Slater did not answer. Paul waited. He was trying to decide how much to trust Slater. He appeared to be a nice man, but he was the police chief. He might just be playing him for more information.

"Well, we need to correct the statement."

Paul nodded.

"Paul, you are not being recorded. This conversation is just between us."

Again Paul nodded.

"Your story checks out. There are some minor inconsistencies. We can sort those out right here. I can have it corrected before you sign it. With your medical standing and the good work you've done, I doubt we'll ever have to speak you again."

"What inconsistencies?" Paul obligingly asked.

"First let me say the man who was shot was a known criminal. He was wanted for drug trafficking in DC and murder in Baltimore. The police found two guns in his car. One in the glove compartment and one under the mat of the passenger seat. I would like nothing more than to put this case to rest."

Long pause. Paul waited.

"I have to ask you again, Paul. Did you know this man?"

"I never saw him before last night, Chief. I give you my word," Paul replied truthfully.

"Good."

Slater's eyes penetrated to the back of Paul's brain. Paul didn't respond. He scratched the side of his neck. Slater decided to resume talking.

"We also spoke to one of your neighbors. He said *he* was walking his dog at the time. He also heard gunshots. He saw a vehicle speeding away. He said it looked like a 4Runner, but he wasn't sure. He said he was too afraid to go to the scene. Did you see a getaway vehicle, Paul?"

"Come to think of it, I heard a speeding vehicle. I didn't actually see it. I was busy helping the victim."

"That's more like it, Paul."

Paul nodded.

"I will have this updated before you sign it."

"Thanks, Chief."

"No problem, Paul. It is good to help good people."

"You are too kind, Chief."

"Karissa Karan is also on the record with the same version of events."

Paul exhaled slowly.

"Chief, I will need a ride home."

"Karissa can take you."

"She is here?"

"She drove in at our request."

✝

Paul badly wanted to call Felipe when he left the police station. He resisted.

Two reasons. Firstly, Karissa was with him. Second, there was chance that the police were listening to him. He would wait. He would try tomorrow from a work phone at the hospital. Felipe probable knew everything already.

Paul was dog-tired. He reminded himself to be patient. He kept his thoughts to himself.

Karissa didn't pry. She understood so much more now. She rested her hand on his lap. It was calming. That was enough for him. They drove home in silence.

✝

Chief Slater joined Sergeant Wilson in his office. It was almost four in the morning. Wilson was on duty. Slater was not.

"Wilson, what do you think?

"Not sure, Chief."

"Not sure about what?"

149

"He hesitated a lot."

"Do you think he's lying?"

"I don't think so. But I think he's holding back something."

"What?" Slater asked.

"Something doesn't add up. He wasn't afraid. He wasn't shaken. It was as if he had expected all of this," Wilson replied.

"He's a doctor. They tend to be pretty calm," Slater said.

"I suppose," Wilson agreed.

"His background checks out. This is not the kind of guy who would be involved in murder."

"I agree."

"You still seem to have doubts," Slater said.

"The boys on the scene said there were no tire marks alongside the ditch. They said the tracks were at right angles to the road. Just outside Dr. Karan's property."

"Perhaps the victim lost control after he was shot?"

"They didn't report any significant skid marks," Wilson objected.

"Maybe the car had stopped. Remember that there was no shattered glass. The shots were fired at point-blank range."

"More than likely the gunman knew the victim. They were probably talking with windows down," Wilson opined.

"I agree."

"But if they were not moving, there would be no tracks," Wilson objected.

"Correct. Maybe the Prelude was just idling. The rendezvous took a turn for the worst. After the shooting, the victim lost control, and the vehicle slipped into the ditch."

"That sounds more like it, Chief."

Wilson was glad to have contributed. Not every day the police chief came down to the station on the graveyard shift.

"Anyway, I'm glad that scumbag is off the streets. I didn't want it to happen in our county, though. Makes our numbers look bad," Chief Slated added.

Wilson wasn't expected to comment. He knew how much pride the chief took in the low murder rate in his county. Especially, when it was compared to the neighboring counties and DC.

"What do we do now, Chief?"

"Find the 4Runner."

"The boys are already working on it."

After two hours of what could barely be called sleep, Paul heard his alarm. He dragged himself out of bed and made coffee. He pretended he was on call the previous night. He doubled the strength of his coffee.

He showered slowly, wiping sleep out of his puffy eyes. He jolted his brain with cold water on his head. His body ached. It was taking a beating.

It crossed his mind to stay home. He quickly put the thought away. It wasn't a realistic option. He had too many sick patients. The nurses would bug him all day on the phone. He still wouldn't get any sleep.

He would survive, he told himself. Just another day in the life of a doctor. Paul called his medical resident on his drive in. They would start rounds a half hour late today. He reminded the resident physician to check all the new lab results.

Paul rested his cell phone in one of the cup holders in his car. He noticed a brownish stain on it. It was blood from last night. He recoiled as he thought of the messy CPR. No gloves, no mask. Splashing blood and an infectious disease doctor was a no-no. He reminded himself to get HIV and Hepatitis testing in a couple of weeks.

As soon as he had started rounds, he happily forgot the events of last night. Even the blood-borne exposure and risks. He got in a couple of hours of steady work.

He took a break between inpatient rounds and new consults. He decided to call Felipe. It quickly came flooding back. He couldn't avoid it. It played over and over in his mind. Felipe was surprised to hear from him.

"What do you want?" Felipe hissed.

"Last night, a man was shot in my driveway."

"I know."

"That's it?"

"He was an enemy of ours," Felipe replied.

"Did *you* arrange it?'

"No. There was a dispute. Tomas got him."

So it was Tomas, Paul thought.

"I tried to save him."

"I know."

"You know everything?"

"I have my sources."

"I called to tell you to get rid of the 4Runner. A neighbor saw it speeding away."

"Already taken care of, boss."

"Don't call me that," Paul hissed.

"Good work in getting the car out of the driveway."

"Never do that again!"

"I promise, Doc. No more meetings at your place."

"Good."

"Paul?"

"What?"

"Don't call me for a couple of weeks. Let things settle," Felipe said.

"How about never again?" Paul asked, cynicism gushing forth.

Felipe did not respond.

Paul hung up the pay phone. He looked around. The visitors' lounge was empty. He hoped no one had heard him.

The following day, Paul left work late. His flipped the dial away from the sports-talk radio. It settled on WTOP, the news station. As he crossed into Maryland from DC, a news item caught his attention.

A vehicle had just been pulled from the Potomac River, just south of Alexandria. Two bodies were removed from it. According to the Virginia police, they had several bullet wounds. The vehicle was a Toyota 4Runner.

CARTELS

1

It took Paul seventy-two hours to get the information. In the end, he got a name. The name was Steve Johnson. He was a county executive in neighboring Prince George's county. He was also the boss of the Medellin cartel for the Washington and Baltimore area.

Paul knew that Felipe would have known. He didn't want to ask him. He had treaded into dangerous territory. The less Felipe knew, the better. Paul's life was under threat from too many people. He didn't want to add Felipe to the list.

Paul used the yellow pages to find a private investigator. No meeting. An anonymous phone call from a pay phone. A very generous money order, courier delivered. He would call again in forty-eight hours. He just wanted a name.

The intelligence must have been difficult to obtain. When Paul called, he was informed that the data was still pending corroboration. They needed another twenty-four hours.

A day later, he checked back. They delivered a name and a description. Steve Johnson. Holds public office in Prince George's County.

Now that Paul had a name of a public official, the rest was easy. Soon after, he found an office address, a home address, and several telephone numbers.

He considered that the PI could have given him false information. He reasoned that any real PI who didn't deliver wouldn't last very long. Referrals were usually word by mouth in that world.

Paul couldn't decide what to do with his newfound knowledge. It took him forty-eight hours to make a decision. It was risky. He carefully weighed his options before accepting the risk.

He decided to pay Mr. Johnson a visit. He doubted that anything short of a personal visit would be useful. He preferred to do it during the day. He planned to do it as soon as he could take off from work.

✝

A week passed, and Paul still wasn't able to escape from work. Several times, he doubted the logic of his decision. He was preparing to play ball with the big boys. And he was in this boat alone.

Today, his last two patients were no-shows. He rushed out the hospital and got into his car. He had parked in the outdoor lot to save time. Rush-hour traffic was not yet in full flow. He managed to get to the Beltway in twenty minutes. Paul exited 495 and headed for Upper Marlboro.

He had no trouble finding Steve Johnson's office. There was a big sign in the parking lot with his name on it. Paul took the stairs to the second-floor office. He was greeted indifferently by a secretary.

"I' am here to see Mr. Johnson," Paul said.

"Do you have an appointment?"

"Sorry."

"Mr. Johnson is in a meeting."

"It's important. I can wait," Paul added quickly.

She didn't respond.

The waiting area was well decorated. The carpet was new and thick. Paul thumbed through a couple of magazines. He looked up from time to time at the secretary. She pretended to be busy on the phone with an air of feigned importance. After a long twenty minutes, Paul got up and approached her. She raised her chin in a questioning manner.

"Is Mr. Johnson in the building?"

She fiddled with her nails and nodded.

"When do you expect him to be free?"

"Don't know," she replied in a disinterested manner.

Paul returned to his seat. A few minutes later, a man in an expensive-looking white suit exited the inner office. He left with barely a glance in Paul's direction. Paul guessed it was either Steve Johnson or the person he had been meeting with. He waited. The secretary said nothing.

Paul approached her again. "Does Mr. Johnson know that I'm here?"

"I buzzed him when you first came," she replied.

"Is his meeting over?"

"His client just left," she answered, gesturing toward the door.

"When will he see me?"

"He didn't say."

Paul was getting desperate. He had rushed out of the hospital and driven all the way out to meet Steve Johnson. He had agonized over the decision. He didn't want to let the opportunity pass. He might not have the courage to do it again.

"What time does Mr. Johnson leave?" Paul asked.

"His driver will be here anytime."

Paul looked at his watch. It was after four thirty. He put on his best imploring smile. "Can you kindly remind him that I would like two minutes of his time?"

"What should I tell him this is concerning?"

"Business."

"Look, Mr. Taylor. That is what you said your name was, correct?"

Paul nodded.

"If you don't have an appointment and you can't tell me what this is about, Mr. Johnson will not see you."

Paul smiled charmingly. "Tell him it's an old friend from South America."

Reluctantly, she got up. She went into the inner office. A minute later, she returned and motioned for Paul to enter. She closed the door and left.

A fortyish-looking, well-dressed man got up from behind a table. He extended his hand.

"Steve Johnson," he said, introducing himself.

"David Taylor," Paul replied.

Johnson motioned to a chair. Paul sat.

"Have we met before?"

"I don't think so," Paul answered directly.

"My secretary told me that you claimed to be an old friend …" He trailed off with a clear question at the end.

Paul wanted to make the most of his time. "We have many friends in common."

Johnson waited for him to elaborate.

Paul tiptoed in. "We have many common friends in South America."

Paul thought he noticed a flicker in Johnson's eyes. Still no verbal response as Johnson waited.

"Yes, Mr. Johnson. Most of them are in Colombia."

Paul had his attention now.

"What do you want, Mr. Taylor?"

"I have information that may be useful to both of us."

"What kind of information?" Johnson pressed.

"Information about your business rivals in this area."

Johnson stared at Paul for a full fifteen seconds. He twitched his nose. He appeared to be convinced.

"I don't discuss such business here," Johnson murmured.

"Give me a time and place. We can talk privately then."

Johnson passed his hands though his hair. He appeared to be thinking.

"I have an event at the Inner Harbor in Baltimore this weekend. I' am staying at the Renaissance Hotel. We can meet there."

Paul nodded.

"I will inform the front desk. They will be expecting you," Johnson said.

"Let's meet at the hotel's restaurant," Paul countered.

Again Johnson sized him up. This one was sharp, he thought. *He doesn't want to take too many risks.*

"No," Johnson said firmly.

Paul looked at him questioningly.

"Across the street from the hotel, there is a row of shops. Right on the waterfront. At one end, there is an Irish pub. I will be having a drink with my driver."

"What time?"

"Six."

Paul nodded.

A light knock at the door followed. Paul was beginning to get up. He expected the secretary. In came a muscular and well-groomed man.

"Your ride is ready, boss," he stated.

His tone really asked, *Everything okay, boss?*

Johnson nodded.

"I was just about to leave," Paul stated.

Paul felt the driver's eyes examining him as he walked out of the office. His heart was pounding. There was no turning back now. The die had been cast.

Paul knew that was no driver. He noticed the bulge under the man's well-fitted jacket. He shouldn't have been surprised that Johnson had an armed bodyguard.

2

THE NEXT DAY, FELIPE SHOWED UP IN PAUL'S DRIVEWAY.
Paul was almost relieved to see him. It somehow suggested that things
were normal. Paul's chest tightened when he thought of the upcoming
meeting. Felipe would be firmly casted on the other side.

Karissa had gone to her favorite activity of late. Shopping. Paul didn't
mind. Money was a nonissue. His guilt of having her in this mess took
many forms. His encouragement of her indulgence was one. Piles of shopping bags cluttered the house. Paul hardly noticed them.

On a whim, he opened the front door. Felipe saw him. Paul motioned
him over. Felipe obliged. He stopped at the bottom of the steps.

"Come in," Paul said.

"Karissa not home?"

"She's gone shopping."

Felipe entered the house. He sat down at the kitchen table. It was a
first. Paul got a couple of Red Stripe beers from the fridge. He knew Felipe
liked the tropical lager. He had seen him drinking it.

Felipe took a swig. He wiped his mouth with the back of his hand.

"What's the occasion?"

"Nothing."

"Boss?"

"I told you not to call me that."

Felipe didn't say anything.

"Is Felipe your real name?" Paul asked after a while.

Paul's tone was more of a conversation starter than an information
seeker. He wasn't sure if his subconscious played a part. He had used a
fake name to meet Steve Johnson the day before.

Felipe took no offense. "It is now."

"What was it before?"

Felipe took another sip of his beer. He took his time to reply. "Not Felipe."

Paul didn't press.

Felipe played with the beer bottle.

"Do you have a family, Felipe?"

"I have two kids."

"In Caracas?"

"Yes."

Again silence.

"Do you seem them often?" Paul asked.

"No."

"Time?"

"No."

"Why?"

"Their mother told them that their father is dead."

"Why?"

"It's better that way."

The men said nothing for a few moments.

Then Felipe continued without prompting. "I am hardly in Venezuela now, boss. I mean Paul."

Paul nodded.

"She has someone else in her life. The kids' mother, I mean."

Another pause.

"He treats them well. So I let it be."

"I see," Paul murmured.

"Ramon asked me if I wanted to get rid of him."

Paul raised his eyebrows.

"I said no."

Yet another pause.

"I want them to grow up with some stability. I don't want them to be like me."

Felipe's voice changed. Paul knew what he was hearing what few had heard. Felipe didn't talk about his personal affairs. Paul now had some history with him, and this was still a first. Paul found it hard to believe that the man sitting across the table had helped to torture him.

Felipe had changed a lot since. His English was excellent. He had a good grasp of the larger world. Paul connected with the genuineness of his feelings.

"That must be tough," Paul said.

"It is."

Paul waited.

"The last time I was in Caracas, I asked to see them. She said she couldn't explain me to them."

Felipe took another sip of his beer and continued. "I told her to tell them her cousin was visiting or something."

Felipe paused.

"She still said no."

Paul again waited for him to continue.

"She has no problems taking my money. I send money for them every month. Her boyfriend doesn't even work. But I want the kids to have a good life."

"I'm sorry to hear that, Felipe. I didn't mean to pry."

"It's okay."

"You know what the worse feeling is, Paul?"

Paul didn't answer.

"The last time I went there, I parked in the street. Just outside the house. I waited to see the children. I waited for hours. When the ice-cream truck passed, they came out."

Felipe caught his breath.

"My daughter is four. She is very pretty. My boy is two. I couldn't go and touch them. Not even buy ice cream for them. Their mother was right there with her man. When I left, I was crying. A grown man like me. Crying."

Felipe's voice choked off with emotion.

"Sorry," he said after a while.

Paul didn't know what to say. With all his training and empathy with patients, this was different.

"Can I get you another beer?" Paul mustered.

Felipe nodded.

Paul felt for Felipe from inside. He knew Felipe was vulnerable. He didn't want to seem predatory. It came out anyway. It was something he had always wanted to know, but the time was never right.

"Felipe, we have been through a lot."

"We have, boss."

Paul ignored the "boss" this time.

"You're a nice guy."

Felipe waited.

"How did you get involved with Ramon?"

"That is a long story, Paul."

"We have time."

"The less you know, the better for you, boss."

"No, I really would like to hear."

Felipe appeared to be thinking.

Finally he said, "Okay, this is for you only."

Paul nodded.

"It was many years ago. I was eighteen or nineteen."

Paul waited.

"I was in prison. The big one, outside Caracas. They gave me ten years."

"For what?" Paul couldn't help himself.

"For stealing cars. I stole cars and got caught."

"I mean, why did you steal cars?"

"Look, Paul, I know you are from Trinidad. You have poor people there. But nobody *starves*! Many people in Caracas starve."

Paul waited. He realized his interruption was insensitive.

"I was the oldest of nine children. My father left when I was twelve. We lived in a shack on the hillside. In the slums. A few galvanized zinc sheets and some blankets. That was it. When it rained, we got wet."

Paul waited.

"When he left, we were going to starve. Either that or prostitute for tourists."

"My mother, she got real depressed. She lost her mind. I knew I had to feed the children. That is how I started stealing cars."

"I see," Paul said.

"I managed to feed them somehow. I didn't even make much money. But it was enough to buy food."

Paul gave him an understanding look.

"I had a good run, Paul. I stole the cars. I drove them to a shop. They chopped them up and sold the parts. They gave me two hundred pesos for every car. That was it. But that was a lot of money then."

"Then?"

"Then I got lazy. It was getting too easy."

Again Paul waited for Felipe to continue.

"I went back in the same street a second time. In the same week. It was a fancy sports car. I liked it. The police were waiting. They got me."

He paused and then continued. "They promised me a light sentence if I told them everything. I was stupid. I told them everything. The judge gave me fifteen years. He said I could be out after ten if I behaved well."

Another pause.

Felipe didn't continue this time.

"Do you see your family when you go home?" Paul asked gently.

It was at that point Felipe's tone turned acid. A voice Paul had never heard before.

"See them, Paul? Do you think we had a *lease* in the slums?"

Paul was taken aback by the sheer intensity of his voice. He didn't answer. Felipe swallowed. He tried to deescalate.

"They are all gone, Paul. *All gone.* My mother spent months in a hospital ward. Then she killed herself."

Paul did not interrupt.

"Remember, nine of us, Paul. The two boys after me joined gangs. They got killed. I was still in jail then."

Felipe paused again and then resumed on his own.

"My two youngest brothers are in jail. Still alive, but in jail. My oldest sister became a prostitute. They said she died of a drug overdose. Two younger ones got married. Both of their husbands are wife beaters. The last one met a man from Guyana. I am told she moved to Essequibo with him."

It was quite an earful for Paul. Finally, he said again, "I'm sorry, Felipe."

Felipe looked at him and nodded. He knew Paul meant it. He had vented. He said more than he ever thought he would to anyone.

"You see, Paul, I fed them. But I couldn't save them."

"You did the best you could, Felipe."

"Yes, but I didn't save them. I just showed them how to steal."

Paul had no answer to that.

"I have to go, Paul. We will talk about Ramon another time."

3

PAUL GOT TO THE INNER HARBOR IN BALTIMORE EARLY. HE wanted to take a look around. He didn't park under the hotel. He parked across the street in an uncovered lot. He sat for a moment in his car and collected his thoughts.

He was jumpy. Nervously, he got out of his car. He crossed over Pratt Street. It felt better to have his legs under him. With half an hour to go before his meeting, he had some time to kill. He uneasily strolled down the Inner Harbor at the water's edge. He made it to the aquarium and then retraced his steps. At five minutes to six, he entered the pub.

He gave his name to the host. They told him his table was ready. His party was waiting for him.

The host took him to a secluded area at the back. Sure enough, with a big smile, Steve Johnson was waiting. He was seated, facing them. He got up and offered his hand.

"Good to see you, Mr. Taylor."

"Good to see you too, Mr. Johnson."

"Call me Steve," Johnson insisted.

The host left quickly. Paul took his seat, and Johnson resettled.

Paul didn't reply.

"Do you mind if I call you David?" Johnson asked.

The flicker of hesitation must have been enough for Johnson.

"I know it's not your real name. It would do for this meeting," Johnson stated.

Paul nodded sheepishly.

He was already on the defensive. He reminded himself again he was dealing with pros. He had been extremely lucky so far. Just to be alive. A lot of that had to do with Felipe and his men. Paul was alone here.

"I took the liberty of ordering a beer for you. The house beer is very good," Johnson said.

"Thanks."

"I am on my second," Johnson said.

"Good stuff," Paul concurred, after taking a few sips.

"I have to make a trip to the men's room. You?"

It sounded like an invitation to share a private word. Paul hesitated at first. Then he quickly followed Johnson. The pub was almost full. He caught up with Johnson at the rear of pub. The restroom was down a narrow hallway. Johnson held the door for him. Paul stepped through. Johnson didn't follow.

A split second later, a muscular arm grabbed Paul from behind. He felt the butt of a gun on his spine. Paul turned his head to the side. He stared directly into the eyes Johnson's bodyguard. He had made no attempt to conceal his face.

"Show me the dagger!" he hissed.

Paul didn't understand.

Johnson's man moved the gun up to Paul's head. A silencer stuck out of the muzzle.

"Show me the dagger and you live!" he demanded.

A light-bulb flashed in Paul's head. Of course he meant the tattoo. The dagger tattooed on his lower back. The genuine identification of his cartel allegiance.

Relieved, Paul lifted up his shirt. He pulled the back of his pants down slightly. His assailant looked. He quickly put his gun away.

"You may rejoin Mr. Johnson," he said.

Paul headed sheepishly back to the table. Johnson had the same big smile.

"Sit down, Mr. Taylor."

Paul took his seat again.

"Looks like we do have business to discuss," Johnson continued.

Paul followed Johnson's eyes, looking past him. With jacket donned, standing innocently behind him, he saw Johnson's bodyguard. The man who had just mugged him in the men's room.

"Do you mind if Omar joins us?"

"Not at all," Paul replied.

Omar was already taking his seat at Johnson's side.

✝

Paul heard the doorbell.

He wasn't expecting anyone. Karissa was at work. He hadn't told anyone that he had taken the afternoon off. It was one of those rare days when the clinic schedule was light. The nurses urged him to take a break. There was another staff doctor and two volunteer doctors in the clinic. They assured him that they could manage without him.

Paul gently pulled the drapes and peeped out. It was Felipe. His heart skipped a beat. Several beats. He feared the worse. Somehow, Felipe had found out about his Baltimore activities over the weekend. Paul tried to appear calm. He couldn't think clearly. If Felipe knew he was home this afternoon, Felipe knew everything. So it seemed, anyway.

The doorbell rang again.

Paul collected himself and opened the door.

"Wasn't expecting you," Paul said.

"I was in the area and just wanted to stop by," Felipe said hesitantly.

Paul refrained from asking why. He felt a bond with Felipe a few nights ago. He knew this visit wasn't random.

"Can I come in?" Felipe asked.

"Sure," Paul replied.

Without asking, Paul walked to the refrigerator and got two Red Stripe beers. The men didn't say anything for a bit. After a couple of sips, Felipe played with the short bottle.

Then he spoke. "I am going to Venezuela tomorrow."

"Business, I guess?" Paul asked.

"Yes."

Another pause.

"I was wondering if you wanted to send anything for Andreina. I can personally deliver it."

"I hadn't thought of it."

"Well, if you decide, leave it in the mailbox next door. That house is empty for now."

"Thanks, Felipe."

Felipe waited.

"Actually, I think I will. It has been a long time," Paul said.

Felipe nodded. More silence.

Finally, Felipe cleared his throat. "The other night, you asked me how I met Ramon."

"I did."

"I told you I met him in jail," Felipe said.

"That's about all you said," Paul replied.

"Well, it's a longer story than that."

Paul waited. He knew Felipe wanted to talk. It was the real reason for his visit. Not that his offer to courier a letter to Andreina wasn't genuine. He meant that too. A few nights ago, Felipe had unlocked doors to his past. There was more.

"Go on," Paul nudged.

"I told you I was in for fifteen years. Ten if I behaved well."

Paul nodded.

"Well, it was really fifteen. You can't survive in jail and behave well at the same time."

"I see," Paul said.

"Good guys don't last long in the big prison," Felipe reiterated.

Felipe paused, then resumed.

"When you are eighteen, fifteen years is a life sentence. No hope. No future."

Paul nodded again.

"I was in jail for a couple of years when they brought in Ramon. I remember it well. It was late one night."

Felipe had a habit of speaking and pausing. He wasn't expecting a response. It was as if he was waiting for Paul to digest the information. He was very deliberate with his words. It was his way of planning what to say next, Paul thought.

"They brought him to a cell opposite mine. I saw everything. I knew right away he wasn't your ordinary crook. The prison officials treat him differently."

Paul had no doubt Felipe was telling the truth. He had no formal education, but he was brighter than most. Felipe was astute and learned quickly.

"The key to survive in jail is the first few months. If you make it, you learn the rules of jail. Then you have a chance. To live a life in jail, that is."

Paul nodded.

"Anyway, Ramon would have been killed quickly. He was arrogant, and he had money."

"How did you know?"

"Everyone saw the arrogant part. He was unfriendly. He refused to talk to the other prisoners. He refused to join any gangs. He was a loner. The money part I picked up on. The second night he was there, he had a visit from a high-up official."

Again Paul waited.

"Life in a big prison is rough, Paul. Assault and rape is a daily thing. If the weak don't get friends, they perish quickly."

Another silence.

"I saved Ramon, Paul. That's the bottom line. The details don't really matter. I knew the ropes. I protected him from the other inmates. In return, he promised to get me out."

Paul nodded again.

"I didn't know all of it at the time, but later I joined the pieces. Ramon was sentenced to twenty years for trafficking. The regular judge was in his pocket. That judge was transferred two weeks before Ramon's trial. The new judge refused all Ramon's money. They tried to make an example of him. This judge wanted to repay his political bosses. They had promised to fight a war on drugs," Felipe continued.

"Ramon knew he would get out sooner or later. He would beat the system. Money in Venezuela does a lot of things, Paul."

"But Ramon would have been dead long before they could get him out. His brother took out a hit on the new judge. He paid off a lot of people. He forced a fake appeal case. Ramon walked free in six months."

Felipe paused again.

"But it still took *six months*."

"I see," Paul murmured. He had witnessed firsthand the corruption in the Venezuelan prison.

"For protecting him in prison, he promised to get me out. I had acted as a go-between for him. I picked up his money from the outside and paid the prison officials. That kept him safe."

"Ramon kept his promise. Four months after Ramon left jail, I became a free man. He managed to get his own judge to review my case. That my crimes were committed as a juvenile helped. Lots of money changed hands. The end result was I got out jail."

"I am glad you got out, Felipe."

"At the time, I was too."

Paul looked directly at him.

"Now, I am not so sure," Felipe added.

Paul waited.

"After I got out, Ramon offered me a job."

Another pause.

"I had no choice. I took it. After all, I owed him my freedom. I became his bodyguard once again."

Paul nodded once more.

"Since that time, I have worked for him."

Yet another pause.

"I have done bad things for him, Paul. Worse things than I did before I went to prison. Like when you first met me."

Paul flinched inwardly. The memory of when he first met Felipe and Alonzo still jolted him. He quickly pushed it out of his mind. This was a different Felipe. He should judge him now, not back then.

"Who else knows this?" Paul asked.

"Ramon and now you. That's it."

Paul nodded. He guessed as much. It was quite a load.

"Javier, maybe a little. Bit and pieces, Alonzo. We spent lots of time together back then," Felipe added.

Felipe got up to go.

"I will leave a letter in the mailbox tonight," Paul said.

Felipe nodded.

"Your story is safe with me," Paul assured him.

"You are a good man, Paul."

Paul watched as Felipe headed for the door.

4

ANDREINA STARED OUT OF THE BEDROOM OF HER MAGNIFI-
cent prison. Her view was spectacular. She didn't see any of it today. The
green rolling hillsides appeared invisible to her. A thin film of tears coated
her eyes. They gradually got filled. A single drop landed on her bare toe.
It startled her. It brought her back to the present.

Ramon had gone to Colombia the day before. Andreina pooled her
courage. She finally went to see the doctor. But she couldn't do it. In the
end, all she told him was she was there for a health checkup. He had
obliged. He had done the routine things. Still, she kept silent. Hoping
against hope, that all was well.

Her thoughts became muddled in this grandiose of bedrooms. She
couldn't escape Ramon. He was everywhere. Even though he wasn't present. She walked down the stairs and entered the small room that Paul had
occupied. She sat on the bed and put her hands to her face. She sobbed
silently. She didn't know how long. Andreina finally lifted her head and
stared through the window. The view was not as good as from upstairs.
But it looked better. She saw the green of the hillside.

Andreina walked to the window and stood there. She pressed her
forehead against the glass. It was cool and soothing. She tried to return
to the present. It wasn't pretty. Ramon would return next week. She will
have to cope or face the consequences. She knew Ramon didn't make idle
threats.

It was a week to the day that she buried her sister. Her mother and
her alone with their grief.

An empty church. A pastor and a couple of Ramon's thugs. They were
the only ones present.

The suddenness. The indignity. She would never forget. The thought that her mother would lay one of them to rest had never occurred to her. Without any family or friends was unthinkable.

Andreina thought her sister was unwell. She had lost weight. Andreina had seen her about three weeks earlier. She didn't pry. The next thing Andreina heard was she had been taken to hospital. They said it was for rapid breathing.

She died forty-eight hours later. The doctors said it was rare form of pneumonia. One that only people with AIDS got. There it was, written all over the death certificate. Cause of death: AIDS. Even the few friends of her mother shunned the funeral. Rumors had already spread. Fear and stigma prevented friends and family from attending the funeral.

Andreina went to the doctor earlier in the day to get tested for HIV. She knew that Ramon had sexual relations with her sister, as he did with many other women. There was a good chance that he infected her sister, Andreina reasoned. So she knew she herself was at high risk. Yet she couldn't bring herself to do it. She made it to the doctor's office. But she didn't have the courage to ask for the HIV test.

She wasn't sure why she changed her mind at the last minute. It was the sole purpose of her visit. In the end, all she got were routine blood tests. Maybe one day she would return, she kidded herself. Deep down, she knew the real reason. She was afraid of knowing. This way, she could hold out hope that all was well.

There was a light knock on the door. She thought it was Javier. She opened the door. She stared in surprise. It was Felipe. He didn't know what to say.

Finally, he mumbled, "I have a letter for you."

Her heart skipped a few beats.

"From Paul," he confirmed.

She broke down in tears again.

✝

Just before midnight, Paul pulled up to the old farmhouse. He was late. He had gotten lost. He didn't expect the place to be so close to I-270.

He had driven way past into the countryside. The farmhouse was at the junction at Key West Avenue and Darnstown Road. It belonged to Steve Johnson.

Paul followed the instructions for his 11:30 p.m. meeting. The farmhouse appeared abandoned and deserted. The garage door opened as his car neared it. It started to close even before he came to a stop. It was huge. An old tractor sat on one side. Farm equipment was scattered at the far end. He doubted that they had been used in years.

A door from the adjoining farmhouse opened. Omar stuck his head out. He beckoned him to follow. Paul entered the house from the side. Omar led him to a room at the rear. It served as conference room. Plush leather chairs surrounded a huge, oval mahogany table.

Two of the chairs were occupied. Omar motioned him in. Omar closed the door behind Paul without entering the room. Steve Johnson got up to greet him. The other man stayed seated.

"Mr. Taylor, good to see you again." Johnson greeted him like an old friend.

"Sorry about being late."

"Don't worry about it. It's easy to miss this place," Johnson replied, with feigned understanding.

Paul nodded acknowledgment.

"Meet my boss, Mr. Martinez."

The man who stayed seated swiveled his chair to face Paul. He locked eyes with Paul. He didn't get up. Instead, he stuck his hand out. "You may call me Jimmy. My friends do."

"David Taylor," Paul replied, taking his hand.

Jimmy Martinez examined him from top to bottom. He didn't let go of Paul's hand as he scrutinized Paul's face. Paul's discomfort grew. Finally, Martinez let go of his hand.

"Good to meet you, Dr. Karan," Martinez said.

Paul pretended to be surprised. Martinez spoke before he could respond.

"If we are going to do business, we have to be transparent, Dr. Karan."

175

Paul nodded.

"We have to trust each other."

Even at the time, Paul thought his statement was ironic.

"We did our research, Dr. Karan. You would not be meeting with Mr. Martinez if you didn't check out," Johnson said.

"Okay. Then you can call me Paul."

"Well, Paul, let's get down to business."

Paul looked across the table. He held their gaze. He appeared calm but could feel his heart palpitating all the way to his temples.

"Sure," he replied.

Martinez took the lead. "Steve told me about the Baltimore meeting."

Paul nodded and waited.

"You do have some interesting information."

Again, Paul nodded.

The rest of the meeting proceeded like a routine business meeting. It could have easily been about selling cars. Instead, it was about selling cocaine.

Paul was impressed with the acuity and knowledge of both Martinez and Johnson. Their attention to detail was remarkable. Their background information about their business matched that of any CEO's of a big company. Paul drifted off as they explained the business aspect of the cartels.

"It is true that your organization is still a tenth of ours. But we have lost significant market share recently," Johnson droned on. "Twenty percent in the Washington area and 50 percent in Harrisburg and Richmond. The biggest concern to us is your rapid growth. As such, it does pose a significant threat."

"We can eliminate your regional bosses. That doesn't really solve the problem," Martinez said. "From our experience, it creates disorder. Then someone will step up to fill the spot. So we have deferred that option. We prefer to deal with this problem at the root."

"That's sound reasoning," Paul managed.

"We will need in-depth information. We will need details at multiple levels, Paul," Johnson said.

"I will do what I can," Paul stated.

"Perhaps you can enlist Felipe," Johnson prodded.

This surprised Paul. He told himself he shouldn't have been. If they knew his personal details, they would know his associates. Yet Johnson was a full step ahead of him. The thought that Felipe had access to the details they needed had entered Paul's head moments earlier. Johnson spelled it out for him.

Once again, Paul reminded himself that he was dealing with seasoned pros. They lived in a dangerous world. They had no room for error. They had tools that he didn't have.

"We will pay him well," Johnson added.

"I will see what I can do," Paul replied, trying to remain levelheaded.

"Finally, Paul," Martinez said.

Paul waited.

"Steve told me that you didn't want any money?" Martinez asked.

"Correct."

"Are you sure?"

"I have enough money, Mr. Martinez. I just need my freedom. I need to keep my name and identity clean. That is the only way I can keep a medical license."

"Understood."

"Thanks."

"If your information is adequate, I promise you that. We will keep your identity to Steve and myself. If for some reason I am eliminated, I cannot guarantee it. That is the best I can do."

"Thank you, Mr. Martinez," Paul replied.

†

Andreina read the letter for the hundredth time. She soothed the paper at the edges. She caressed the words. She heard his voice saying them. It made her feel close to him. She folded it neatly and put it back in her pocket. When she was done, Paul was still three thousand miles away.

Truth be told, there weren't many specifics in the letter. But she treasured it. Every time Ramon went on a business trip, she went to Paul's old room and read the letter. She journeyed through the memories. It still remained the best times for her in this prison mansion.

Andreina got more information from Felipe than the letter. He came to the house a few times during his trip. On one occasion, she had managed to corner him and ask about Paul. Felipe filled her in as best as he could, leaving out the criminal details. She didn't pry.

Andreina knew he had married Karissa. Oddly enough, she wasn't envious. She hoped he was happy. She knew life had dealt them some strange cards. She could never hope to have him for herself. But she wanted him to be happy. Karissa was a lucky woman, she thought. She had Paul in her life every day. Andreina would give the world to have him for *one* day.

Andreina drifted to their intimate times together. Recently, it had become clouded. Clouded with the possibility that she could have been infected at the time. The thought lingered on. She doubted it would have happened that early. But how could she be sure? She had read that HIV could be dormant in a person for years. That it didn't usually cause symptoms early on. She was more worried about his health than her own.

Andreina learnt from Felipe that Paul's specialty was infectious diseases and HIV/AIDS. *What irony*, she thought. Perhaps if he knew about her, he could do something, she reasoned. Once again, she promised herself to go back and get tested. Even it was for Paul's sake, she rationalized.

She also gleaned that Luis and Ramon had Paul in their grasp. She knew they would find him. They had spared him because they had found him useful. They had forced him to cooperate. Just like her. He was trapped. So was she.

For the first time in a while, Andreina didn't cry in Paul's old room. Once again, she made plans. This time, she would act on them, she reassured herself. She would get out of this prison. She would put all her energies into it. Even at the cost of her life.

5

PAUL SAT ON HIS DECK ON A COMFORTABLE SATURDAY AF-
ternoon. He heard the sound of a lawn being mowed in the distance. He
flipped through the Outlook section of the *Washington Post*. He browsed
without reading anything in depth. He was alone and moved at his own
pace.

Today was the day. He was nervous despite his mundane surround-
ings. He had asked Felipe to meet him at the house that afternoon. Today
was the beginning of the end, he told himself. One way or another, he was
going to escape their grasp. He knew he could pay with his life as well as
the lives of those close to him.

Karissa had gone to Trinidad to see her family. He had encouraged
it. He didn't know if she would see them again. If things went according
to plan, he hoped she might. He told her that she should stay for a few
weeks. Instead, she decided to visit for a week. She claimed that she didn't
want to leave him alone for too long. And that she wanted to get back to
work, as her time off was limited.

Paul was flattered she wanted to be with him despite the incessant
danger. He didn't fight it. He knew she would be safe in Trinidad. As long
as Paul complied with the cartel, she was safe. If not, all bets were off.

He remained guilty about dragging Karissa into this mess. She didn't
deserve it. He led a complicated life. She preferred a simple one. He
wanted a simple one too. All he had ever done wrong was to sit next to
a bad guy on an airplane, he reminded himself. Since, his life had been
charted for him.

Before Karissa left, they spent some quality time together. He had
finally gone into the details about the tattoo on his back. She had asked
him about it numerous times over the years. His response, until now, was

always the same. "I didn't want it. They did it to me." And that was how he had always left it. Locked away in a crevice of his memory.

This time, he provided her with all the details that he could remember. The table. The lack of sterile technique. The blood. The pain. He saw the hurt in her eyes. She felt his pain. At the end of it, she kissed it. She vouched that it would never be an intrusion into their lovemaking again as it had been in the past.

Paul wasn't sure why he was sharing with her the details years after the trauma. Maybe he inwardly thought that the end was near. That if she survived him, she would understand why he lived the way he lived. Why he made the choices he did.

When he had returned to Trinidad after his capture in Venezuela, he told her about his ordeal. But he told her in a summary way. Not the details. Just the overview of what happened. She never really pried, until recently. Somehow she sensed something was different. The questions popped up in indirect ways. This time, he didn't push them away.

He must have been engrossed in his thoughts. He heard the doorbell ring. He hadn't heard any vehicle coming up the driveway. Felipe was early.

†

Felipe pulled up a chair next to Paul. The sun was still up but sinking quickly. Paul tried to make small talk. Felipe noticed he was edgy.

On his second beer, Felipe took the direct route. He looked directly at Paul.

"Why did you do it, Doc?"

Paul almost dropped his beer.

"Do what?" Paul fumbled.

"Don't play innocent with me, Doc. You know what you did."

Silence.

Felipe had taken to call him "Doc" in the last few months. He knew Paul disliked being called *boss*.

"If I had told anyone, you would have been dead already. But I wanted to hear from you," Felipe continued.

Still no answer from Paul.

"I regard you as a friend, Paul."

So Felipe already knew, Paul reasoned. He shouldn't have been surprised. He had already met with Steve Johnson *three* times. If these guys knew when he left the clinic early and when Karissa went shopping, they knew everything. His zest to get out of this mess had left him tunneled vision.

"Let's talk, Paul."

"About what?"

"You called me here, didn't you?"

"Okay, Felipe. Tell me what you know."

Felipe stroked his chin.

"If it is correct, I won't deny it," Paul said, reversing the topic on him.

"I know you met with the Medellin bosses," Felipe stated matter-of-factly.

"Who?"

"Steve Johnson and Jimmy Martinez."

Paul lifted his eyebrows. Felipe really did know everything.

"How do you know?"

"I followed you to the farmhouse. We know Steve Johnson owns it."

"That is true," Paul admitted.

"I also know that you met with Johnson before."

"How do you know that?"

"Look, Paul. I've been around. Martinez does not meet with anybody at a first visit. He has underlings to do that."

"Do you know where I met Johnson?"

"No, Paul. I might have been in South America at the time. Where is not important."

Felipe stopped in mid-thought, as he often did.

Paul waited.

"*Why* you met him is the important thing."

181

"How long did you know?"

"Honestly, Doc, only since you went to the farmhouse."

Paul nodded.

"I didn't feel the need to stay too close to you. I trusted you."

"What are you going to do?"

"Paul, you will get us killed. People have been killed for less."

"I know it's dangerous."

Felipe waited awhile. Then he spoke slowly. "*Dangerous*, Paul? Do you know what is dangerous? Do you know *how* dangerous?" he asked incredulously.

Paul didn't answer.

"Paul, these men are ruthless. They only have to snap to their fingers, and you are done. You are not equipped to deal with them. *I* am afraid of them."

"I was desperate."

"Desperate, Paul? You have it easy. You are never where the blood is. You are a respected doctor, for God's sake!" Felipe shrilled.

Paul stared at him coldly.

"Felipe, I know that you have protected my life many times. I thank you for that. But *this* is not the life I dream of!"

"Do you think this is the life I wanted?" Felipe asked hotly.

Paul didn't answer.

"Do you know how many friends I lost, Paul?"

Paul wasn't expected to answer.

"More than you can count!"

Felipe paused and then resumed more calmly.

"If I know someone for a few months, the only thing I can count on is … is them being dead. Sooner or later."

"I am sorry, Felipe."

"I have been lucky, Paul. Nobody at my level lasts this long. Not in this business!"

"I think I know that," Paul replied softly.

"Now that you have become a friend, you decided to give them your head on a platter!"

Paul was pensive. He knew the reason Felipe was so upset. Felipe was worried for *him*. Felipe had protected him for a long time. And now Paul had suddenly decided to offer himself up to the enemy.

"Let's go inside, Felipe."

⸸

Paul sat at the kitchen table. He still had a hard time discussing business in his living room. The small kitchen table somehow made it seem transient. He hoped that a third beer would make it easier to enlist Felipe.

"Well?" Felipe asked.

"I thought you wanted to know why I met with Johnson and Martinez."

"You said you were desperate. I know they will pay a lot for info."

"It is not about the money, Felipe."

Felipe stared directly into his eyes. He appeared to believe him.

"Well, what is it about then?"

"I want to be free, Felipe. I want to remain as Dr. Paul Karan and practice medicine. I do not want to be a drug dealer. I just want to take care of my patients and live a normal life."

"How do you propose to do this?"

"I cannot be free unless Ramon and Luis and this entire operation is eliminated."

Felipe looked at him for a long time.

"Are you crazy, Paul?"

Paul did not answer.

"Do you realize that you can never escape a cartel?"

"I can try."

"And retain your identity?" Felipe asked, dumfounded.

"Why not?"

"They will kill you."

"I can move to Utah or somewhere far. Some rural area where I can practice medicine."

"Do you think they wouldn't find you?"

"Not if they are all gone."

"Paul, there will always be people left. If not ours, the other cartel. They will find and kill you. Or worse."

No one spoke for a while. Paul didn't give up.

"Felipe, you have to help me."

"Why?"

"Because I have already made commitments to Johnson and Martinez. If I back out, I am dead anyway."

"How much are they paying you?"

"No money."

"What!" Felipe exclaimed.

"Just my freedom."

"Doc, I am going to ask you this again."

Paul didn't respond.

"Are you really crazy?"

Paul suddenly felt sheepish.

"Listen, Doc, I know you have a good heart and all. But this is insane. The only thing these people understand is money."

"Are you saying that I should ask for money?"

"A lot of money."

"How much?"

"Tell me what exactly they want, and I will give you a figure."

"It is quite a bit."

"Go on."

"Well they want the name of all the regional bosses. The location of the warehouses in the big US markets. They also want to know the details of operations in Cucuta and Caracas as well as the storage facilities in our top five transshipment ports. I think those are Trinidad, Aruba, Jamaica, Guyana, and Panama."

Felipe took a long, hard look at Paul. The silence became uncomfortable. Finally he spoke. "Paul, when you dumped that body from the driveway for us, I told myself not to underestimate you. Looks like I have done so again."

Paul looked at him questioningly with raised eyebrows.

"All along, you had me in," Felipe said.

Paul nodded.

"You made the commitments without having most of the information. You knew that they would kill you if you didn't deliver," Felipe said slowly.

Paul nodded again.

Another long pause.

"Meet with them and ask for $100 million," Felipe said.

"What?" Paul asked.

"It is worth at least that to them."

"I already told them I don't want any money."

"They don't expect you to stick to that. And *I* want escape money."

"That much?"

"Yes."

"They will refuse."

"No, they won't. They are asking for the regional bosses. That is the head of operations in New York, Miami, DC, Atlanta, Philadelphia, and Toronto. We have warehouses in more than a dozen cities, including Chicago, Detroit, and Cleveland. They want information on our South America operations. Do you think that is worth something?"

Paul nodded feeble.

"Okay, suit yourself. Ask for a hundred and agree and settle for fifty minimum. They will negotiate. Trust me, they will be happy to settle for fifty."

"Okay."

Paul felt his heart pounding. He was still sitting still, but he felt as if he was galloping. His thoughts were.

"Thirty for you and twenty for me," Felipe said.

"Okay."

"Ask them for time. I will need to go to Colombia and Venezuela. I need to update details of our operations."

"How much time?"

"A couple of months."

"So long?"

"They will wait. They want to burn this thing to the ground."

"I see."

"I don't want to be here when the bloodbath starts," Felipe said quietly.

6

ANDREINA STARED IN THE BATHROOM MIRROR. SHE BARELY saw her reflection. The mirror was foggy from the water condensing. The toothbrush hung limply in her hand. She knew. She was numb. No tears came this time.

Her appetite over the last couple of months had been poor. Now she was losing weight. She had kept her promise to herself. She had gone back to her doctor for the HIV test. She asked specifically for the test. He didn't ask why.

Andreina had asked him not to call with her results. She said she would return to his office. She would get them in person. He assured her that the final result would be ready in three days. That was almost two weeks ago.

She wiped the condensation from the mirror. She tried again. She tried to scrub the white patches that were stuck on her tongue. They wouldn't come off. She managed to get rid of those on the inside of her cheek. But she knew it would reappear by tomorrow. In desperation, she dug into her tongue with the toothbrush. It started to bleed. The white spots remained.

Andreina was a trained nurse. She knew the cause. It was thrush. And she knew what it meant. She would return to the doctor for confirmation.

She had to take action soon. There was wasn't anyone in the house she could talk to. Not even Javier. They would evict her out of fear. It was only a matter of time before they noticed her weight loss. Then they would put the pieces together.

✝

Paul called Steve Johnson's office. He didn't expect to get him. He told the secretary he would call again in twenty minutes. He asked that

Johnson leave him a number. He told the secretary that it was urgent. This time, she took him seriously.

When he called back twenty minutes later, sure enough he was given a phone number to reach Johnson. A cell phone number. Paul was certain Johnson used multiple cell phones that he discarded frequently. Steve Johnson answered on the first ring.

"This is David Taylor," Paul stated.

"Why are calling me in the middle of the day?" Johnson demanded.

"We need to talk."

"I cannot talk from here. I *am* at the office."

"Let's set up a meeting. We need to clarify our agreement."

A long silence.

Finally Johnson said, "Tonight at nine?"

"Where?" Paul asked.

"Do you know Laurel?"

"I can find my way around."

"On Route 1, just south of 198, there is a seafood place. Chesapeake Seafood. Meet me at the booth in the rear. The owner knows me."

"See you at nine."

The phone went dead. Paul knew he wouldn't be the first to meet Johnson there.

✝

Paul pulled into the restaurant's parking lot at fifteen minutes to nine. He looked around cautiously. A minute later, he stepped out of his car and headed for the entrance. The bulk of Omar suddenly appeared, confirming that he was in the correct place. Omar followed him but stayed a respectful few steps behind. Paul wondered if Johnson went anywhere without Omar. Probably not, he guessed.

Paul walked into the small lobby. Not unexpectedly, the owner of the restaurant welcomed him. He was taken directly to a booth in the back. It was a weeknight, and only a few patrons remained. Paul knew they didn't have to worry about closing time.

Johnson stood up and greeted him with a big smile. The owner and Omar quickly disappeared.

"Please sit." Johnson motioned.

Paul took a seat directly opposite Steve Johnson.

"I took the liberty of ordering crab cakes and shrimp for us," Johnson said casually."

"Thanks," Paul said.

"Drink?"

"A beer would do."

"That's what I thought," Johnson replied.

"You know everything about me?" Paul asked, with an attempt at humor.

"Just about," Johnson replied.

Paul's attempted humor fell flat.

The food arrived with Omar in close tow. There was an exchange of looks between Omar and his boss. He closed the door to the small room and left. Paul knew Omar remained close by.

After a few bites, Johnson went directly to the point. "Why do you need to see me?"

"It is about our agreement."

"What about it?"

"It will take time to get all the information you need."

"How long?"

"A couple of months."

"Is Felipe on board?"

"Yes."

"Good."

"He has to go to South America to get updated info. As you know, stuff changes," Paul stated.

"I figured as much."

Johnson was silent for a while. Paul cleared his throat. Johnson waited.

"Is there something else, Paul?"

"Yes."

"Tell me."

"I … was hoping Mr. Martinez would be here."

"He couldn't be. He has important business in New York this week."

Paul looked at him questioningly.

"I assure you, I speak for him."

Paul was still hesitant.

"How much, Paul?"

"What?"

"How much do you want?"

"Well, when I spoke to you last—"

Johnson cut him off. "We knew Felipe wouldn't do this for free. He refused our generous offer in the past."

"You met with Felipe?" Paul asked, genuinely surprised.

"Not me. My people."

Paul looked puzzled.

"Very few people in the organization have met me in person, Paul," Johnson continued.

Paul nodded understandingly. He reasoned the same was true for him.

"Consider yourself special. You found me. How is not important right now."

"And Felipe?"

"One of my trusted men met with him a year ago. He refused to join us then. We lost that guy soon after."

Paul was still digesting this when Johnson spoke again. "Do you know why he refused, Paul?"

Paul rarely lost his composure. This time he did.

"Not really," Paul said.

"I am told he didn't want to sell you out."

The look of relief in Paul's eyes must have been obvious. It appeared that everybody knew each other in this world. Except him.

"Anyway, what's your price?"

Paul mustered his courage and spoke. "One hundred million."

Johnson just stared at him.

"For the both of us," Paul added quickly.

"That is *a lot* of money."

"Felipe said you will make that back in a month if our organization is disabled."

"Felipe may be correct. But you are not the only one who needs to get paid."

"Seventy-five million?" Paul asked timidly.

He wasn't good at this kind of thing, and Johnson knew it.

"We have to split it," Paul added nervously.

"How you split it is your problem."

"Seventy?"

"No."

"What do you have in mind?" Paul asked.

"Martinez has authorized fifty million max for this entire operation. This is information only. You do not have expenses."

Paul was hesitant.

"Fifty tops," Johnson stated.

Felipe's estimate and Martinez's were identical. Felipe had a much better idea of the markets than Paul did.

"We will take it."

"Good."

"Anything else?" Paul asked.

"We need *everything* before the last day of February."

Paul nodded. That was enough time for them to be thorough.

"The day before you deliver, send me the numbered accounts. With the splits for you and Felipe. We will deposit it within minutes of getting the info."

Again Paul nodded agreement.

"If you don't deliver by the agreed date, the deal is off."

Paul nodded.

"I am sure you know we take our business deals very seriously."

Johnson stared directly into Paul's eyes. His expression spoke for him.

Paul nodded.

Johnson stood up. Paul followed his lead.

John reached out his hand. "Good luck."

Paul shook hands silently. As he walked out of the room, he felt his heart thundering all the way up to his neck.

†

Andreina walked out of her doctor's office, confirming what she already knew. She was HIV positive. Now she had an official piece of paper to prove it. It was in black and white. The word *positive* was stamped in uppercase.

Her doctor appeared more nervous than she did when he gave her results. He tried to explain the preliminary and the confirmatory tests. Oddly enough, she didn't say much. She listened. She asked no questions.

Andreina remained stoic. That made her poor doctor even more confused. He was apologetic. He kept repeating that he wanted to call her earlier. But she had left instructions not to call her home. He told her that he could try to treat her, but the choice of medications was limited in Venezuela.

He advised her that she would best be served going to the General Hospital in Caracas. There was a clinic for AIDS patients only, he explained. They were very experienced with such cases. Andreina knew the reputation of that clinic. One visit there, and everyone would know.

Andreina thanked him for his efforts. He tried one last time to give her hope. He said he knew of some newer drugs called protease inhibitors. They were being studied. They were not yet approved but should be in a year or two. Andreina deduced that it would an additional couple of years before they reached Caracas. That would be far too late for her, she thought. Maybe in time for other people, but not her.

She mulled over this strange conversation with her doctor as she drove down the street. She stopped at a hardware store a few miles from the doctor's office. She sat in her car in the parking lot for a sometime. She didn't move. Tears finally welled up in her eyes. Even though she had known all along, there was a certain finality having the official lab results. It wasn't 95 percent anymore.

Andreina wiped her eyes. She stepped out of the car and put on a pair of sunglasses. No one could see her puffy eyes now. She walked to the trash can at the end of the parking lot. She carefully tore her test results into small pieces. She tossed it in the trash can.

An illegible bit with a few words missed the bin. It settled on the ground about ten feet away. She walked over and picked it up. She tore it into even smaller pieces. She put it in the bin again. There was a transient riddance from shredding the results. Discarding it in a parking lot bin helped her to renounce it. A peculiar form of catharsis, she thought.

Andreina entered the store and walked slowly up the aisle. She found what she thought would work. She bought six packets of rat poison.

That should be more than enough, she reasoned. She swore to herself she would use it. She would wait. Until the right time.

7

IT WAS AFTER DARK THAT SATURDAY EVENING WHEN FELIPE showed up at Paul's house in Silver Spring. He had called earlier in the day to tell Paul he was coming over. He didn't give Paul a time. Felipe had told him Javier was in town. Javier wanted to meet with Paul.

Felipe didn't conceal himself the way he used to. He parked in the middle of the driveway. He walked up to the front door and rang the bell. Karissa answered it. She led him into Paul's study and then excused herself. She went upstairs and pretended to be busy.

Karissa had returned from Trinidad and tried to return to her regular life. Life was anything but normal. Since Paul had given her details about the tattoo, he noticed a subtle shift in her behavior. When he mentioned business dealings, it became very obvious.

It appeared to Paul that she somehow hoped everything would magically disappear. No such luck. Her consent was always silent. She never verbally objected to what he did. But her expressions bore her unspoken thoughts. Paul had taken years to give her details.

Paul still wasn't sure if he did the right thing in sharing everything. Now that she knew, she understood his life better. But the burden he had gotten used to carrying was weighing heavily on her. His thoughts returned to the present.

"Why didn't you come earlier?" Paul asked.

"Javier didn't give a time. He said later is better," Felipe replied.

"Do you know what it is about?" Paul persisted.

"No."

"Any thoughts?"

The men were now pretty open with each other. Felipe stroked his chin and then replied slowly, "It didn't seem to be about business as usual."

"How do you know?"

"Just a feeling."

"You don't usually go for 'just a feeling,' Felipe."

"Okay, two things are unusual."

"What?" Paul couldn't help himself.

"First, he came up here alone. Second, he didn't give me a specific time. From that, I know he isn't planning to have other people at the meeting. Javier is usually a stickler for time."

"Do you think he suspects anything?"

"Come on, Paul. Only you and I know about this."

"You're wrong, Felipe."

Felipe looked at him quizzically.

"Johnson and Martinez knows too," Paul stated.

Felipe was silent for a moment. Then he said, "You continue to surprise me, Doc. You are right." Full comprehension had entered his voice.

"Maybe you've been asking many questions recently?"

"Not really, Paul."

After a moment, Felipe added, "I've been very careful with whom I speak and what I ask."

Another silence.

Felipe finally broke it. "Something on your mind, Doc?"

"Not really."

"Come on, Doc. I know you."

"Why do you ask?"

"You are jittery today."

"Well to tell the truth, I been thinking about Andreina."

"What about her?"

"Well ..." Paul stopped.

"You can talk to me."

"I was thinking that when we gave them all this info, they would act on it. Right?"

"Why else do you think they are paying us fifty mil?"

"They will wipe out the people in Caracas, right?"

"Yes, in San Tome compound."

"Is there some way to warn Andreina?"

"I see," Felipe said.

"What?"

"You are worried that Andreina will be killed with Ramon and the rest."

Paul nodded. He had finally gotten around to it.

"Doc, you are brilliant and still simple at the same time."

"What?"

"Look, Paul, you agreed to this deal. Didn't you think people would be killed?"

"Yes."

"Friend and foe."

Paul didn't answer.

"Paul, there are many people I work with that I don't like. The world would be better off without them. They deserve what they get."

Still no response from Paul.

"But there are some whom I have known for a long time. A few, I might even consider friends. At the end of this thing, most of them will be dead. That is just a cold, hard fact."

Felipe stared at him. Paul held his gaze and then turned away. Finally in a meek voice, Paul asked, "Could we still warn Andreina?"

"We could have if we knew when, Doc," Felipe said.

Paul nodded silently.

Felipe looked at him with soft eyes. Here was a man who was not thinking with his head. He was a good man. It was the main reason Felipe hadn't sold him out. But his lack of real exposure to Felipe's world still made him naïve. He would never be fully one of them.

"We don't know *when* they will strike," Felipe repeated gently.

Paul leaned back in his chair and closed his eyes.

Felipe left him alone for a full ten minutes. Then he nudged him gently. "Let's go, Paul. It's getting late."

Paul groaned. He dragged himself out of the chair. The one weekend he wasn't on call, he had to spend with Javier.

"Is he staying at the same place?"

"Yep," Felipe replied. "You know Javier. He lives it up when he comes to DC."

†

Javier usually stayed at the Hilltop Hotel at the edge of DuPont Circle. A penthouse suite was a given. No luxury was spared. He looked upon it as an opportunity to use some cash that he had stockpiled. From the hotel's point of view, he was an excellent customer.

The traffic was light at this time of the night. Felipe made good time until they got inside the DC line. The restaurants along Connecticut Avenue were still doing good business at this hour. Between a turning lane and cars parked in the right lane, they slowed considerably. They passed the National Zoo and over Rock Creek into the city proper.

Felipe opted not to use valet parking. He politely declined the attendant's offer. He pulled under the building himself. The first couple of levels were filled. He found a spot on the P 3 level. They took the elevator from the parking garage and headed to the penthouse. They switched lifts on the ground floor. Felipe knew his way to Javier's suite.

He knocked gently on the door.

No answer.

He knocked again. Firmer this time.

Still no answer.

Felipe tried the door. It was open.

He headed into the vast suite with Paul close behind.

"Oh shit!" Felipe hissed.

Paul gasped. His own eyes took in the scene before him.

Sprawled backward in the large sofa was Javier. His head was tilted at an odd angle sideways and backward. Like a drunken man in a stupor. His hands hung limply to his side. His eyes were wide open. A half-finished bottle of Scotch was on the table next to him.

197

The white shirt he was wearing had three bright red stains. All on the left side of his chest. Barely larger than the size of a quarter.

"Let's get out of here," Felipe said sharply.

Paul couldn't help himself. He reached for Javier's neck to feel for a pulse. Felipe grabbed his hand before he could touch the body.

"Come on, Doc. He is dead," Felipe hissed again.

Paul looked around quickly. There were two drinks on the table. The blocks of ice had not melted yet. Whatever had happened was just *minutes* earlier.

Felipe was correct. Javier was dead as a doornail. It looked like a professional job.

Paul tried one last time. "Shouldn't we call the police?"

Felipe's voice got cold.

"Paul, follow me! Now!" he ordered.

Paul didn't object this time.

"Damn good thing I kept my keys," Felipe muttered.

8

PAUL AWOKE EARLY THE NEXT MORNING. TAKING CARE NOT to rouse Karissa, he quietly headed down to the kitchen. He made coffee. The smell of brewed coffee temporarily lifted his spirits.

It was Sunday. He wanted to sit on the deck and stare into the openness. Look quietly at the trees in the distance. No such luck today. It had gotten cold over the last few days. He sat by the kitchen table instead and tried to clear his mind. Try as he might, he couldn't shed the events of the night before.

He had hardly slept. The image of Javier kept playing over and over in his mind. In the short time he slept, he dreamt Javier was talking to him. Calling out to Paul to help him. Pleading for Paul to take him to the hospital. As a doctor, Paul had seen a lot of death in his career. Usually not like this.

Felipe had dropped him back home around midnight. Fifteen minutes after they escaped from the hotel, Felipe was back to his usual demeanor. Paul's heart was still pounding. The difference between Felipe's world and Paul's. Every traffic cop and every flashing light Paul saw, he was certain they were going to be stopped. Yet the drive back was completely uneventful.

As Paul continued to ruminate, he heard footsteps. Karissa came down and joined him. She pulled up a chair and sat next to him.

"What's wrong, honey?" she asked.

"Nothing," he deflected.

"You're sure?"

"Why?"

"You were tossing and turning all night," Karissa stated.

"Really?"

"Yes."

"Didn't know that," Paul mumbled.

"One time, I heard you cry out."

"I must have been having a nightmare or something," Paul said, trying to sound nonchalant.

"You can talk to me, you know."

"Karissa, the less you know, the better for you."

"How so?"

Paul didn't have an answer.

"We are in this together, Paul. I know you went out with Felipe last night."

"Okay, then," Paul conceded.

She waited.

"You remember Javier?"

"The guy from Caracas?" she asked.

"Yep. He was Ramon's business manager."

"You told me he treated you okay."

"Well, he was in DC this week …"

Paul related the events of the night before. Karissa was a good listener. Paul noticed she became tense. She clenched and unclenched her fists. She bit her lower lip. But she didn't interrupt him. When he was done, she looked at him as if she was seeing him for the first time.

"I am sorry," Paul said.

"Sorry for what?" Karissa asked in a gentle voice.

"Sorry I had to drag you through all of this."

She took his hands and held them tightly.

"I am sorry too, Paul."

He raised his eyebrows.

"I am sorry you have to go through this."

He was quiet for a while.

"This is not fair. You didn't ask for any of it," Karissa added.

"I know. But there is no going back now."

"That I understand only too well," she said.

"Karissa, you don't have to be part of this."

"Paul, they already know me. Whatever happens, I am going to be with you."

"These guys are not playing games, Karissa."

"I am not going anywhere, Paul."

"It is the one thing I am thankful for."

"Paul?" Karissa nudged.

"Yes?"

"I have something to tell you."

"What?"

"Something recent. Something happened when I was in Trinidad."

†

Paul walked over to the microwave. He reheated his coffee and sat down close to Karissa. He took her hand.

She was a deliberate, cautious speaker. He waited patiently. Finally she looked at him. She looked directly in his eyes. Then she looked at the floor.

"I've been meaning to tell you."

"Go on," Paul nudged.

"Since I got back, I was planning to tell you."

Paul waited.

"Some people tried to *kill* me in Trinidad."

"What?" Paul couldn't help the alarm in his voice.

He felt her startle. He gently rubbed her left knee, encouraging her to go on.

"Not only me, Paul. My brother and his wife and kids."

Paul didn't say anything. He waited for her to continue.

"We were going to the beach in Maracas. My brother, Amal, was driving. We were close to the top of the mountain. You know the cliff there. Just before you go downhill."

She paused, then resumed.

"A pickup truck tried to run Amal off the road. It came up suddenly. From above. It cut him off. Amal had nowhere to go."

Karissa was out of breath by the time she got this out. She continued on her own.

"We thought the driver was drunk. Amal hit the guardrail. It buckled. But it held. The car didn't fall off."

"I was in the back seat with the kids. Amal's wife was in front. The kids started to scream. The pickup trunk then raced down the mountain. We never saw the driver."

"So you didn't think it was an accident?" Paul asked gently.

"I wasn't sure at first."

"Are you now?"

"Well, that is one part of the story. We thought it was an accident. Some crazy drunk person. So we talked. We decided that going back home would just spoil everything. So we still went to the beach. On the way back is when I knew it wasn't an accident."

This time Paul waited.

"Again, it was when we got to the top of the mountain. We heard gunshots. The driver in the car in front us must have been hit. His car went out of control. It went clean off the cliff. Our car was hit in the side."

She caught her breath.

"Something made me look up. In a small side road, I saw it. The same pickup truck that tried to ram us off the mountain. I know it was the same one. I still remember the reddish-brown color. It had dirt stains all over."

"Why didn't you tell me this before?"

Paul stopped dead in his tracks as he realized his insensitivity.

Karissa was trembling.

"It brought back all those memories, Paul."

"I see."

"The accident and everything. I just wanted to shut it out."

"I understand."

"I am not sure if Amal remembers *that accident*. But every time I think of what just happened, I remember."

Paul wrapped his arms around her. She buried her head in his chest. He had seen her cry. Karissa began to sob. He tried to say soothing words. She took her small fists and pounded his leg. He stopped speaking but held on to her. After a few minutes, her sobbing subsided. She wiped her eyes and looked up. Her pupils were still wide.

"I am scared, Paul."

"Me too," Paul confessed.

9

IT HAPPENED TWENTY-FOUR YEARS AGO. KARISSA HAD ONLY told him the story once. It was very early in their relationship. Paul often forgot because each day he saw her, he saw a smiling face and cheerful outlook.

It was that night that had shaped Karissa's life forever. She had buried it deep in her brain. The recent attempt on her life had brought everything to the fore again. He was finally sharing in the repercussions.

He knew some of it from her. The rest of it he had filled in with what her family provided. It was too painful to pry. So he had contented himself with what he knew.

It was around midnight, in Trinidad. Karissa's parents were returning from a visit to her maternal aunt. Karissa was four, and Amal had just turned two. They were both sleeping in the back seat of the car. As they neared their home in Trincity, her dad got the green light from the side road.

He started going across the Roosevelt Highway. Out of nowhere came a truck. It went through the red light at full speed. He didn't have time to react. The small car had no chance. The full weight of the truck crashed into the side of it, contorting the metal.

Karissa's father was killed instantly. Her mother died a few days later, never recovering from internal injuries. But miraculously, Karissa and her brother survived. A broken arm and leg was what she sustained. Physically. Amal was in a car seat and escaped serious injury.

The part Karissa never dwelled on was what Paul knew affected her most. He had pieced it together over time. They had taken almost an hour to cut her out of the twisted metal. She had lived several lifetimes in that time. Touching her the entire time was the dead body of her father. Beside her was an unconscious mother, whom she thought was dead. A screaming baby was strapped in a car seat next to her.

It was something Karissa and her brother never spoke about. She remembered it but refused to take her mind back. It was too painful. She hoped Amal was too young to remember. But she knew he had heard the story told several times. Told by relatives with many versions. She, herself, had heard several versions in her childhood. She never corrected them.

The aftermath of the accident was messy. The driver was found drunk and jailed for two years. The insurance company settled for a significant sum of money. The ensuing battle to keep Karissa and her brother was unpleasant.

Eventually Karissa's aunt, the one whom they had visited on the fateful night, adopted her and her brother. She already had six children of her own, all older. That was how Karissa became part of a large family. She and Amal were treated well for the most part. But it was her older siblings who provided their care. Not her adopted mother and father.

Karissa was an obedient child. She kept her feelings inside. She didn't compete with the older children. She always looked out for Amal, and she remained very close to him.

The first opportunity that she got to escape from the overcrowded household, she took. It came when she was accepted at the University of the West Indies. A year later, she met Paul.

Karissa's past became alive on that cliff to Maracas Bay. He knew she was deathly scared. The evidence was in front of him. Paul was nowhere around to comfort her.

He tried his best now. It was never going to be enough. Even if he personally hunted down the driver of the pickup truck, he knew the damage was done. They had shattered the protective wall she had built around her childhood trauma. A fragile Karissa stared at him.

10

FELIPE KNEW HIS SURVIVAL WAS NOT RANDOM. HIS LONGEVity in this job was the exception. The most important reason he believed was his meticulous nature. He always planned well. He paid attention to details.

Ever since he was caught stealing as a teenager, he had vowed not to get careless. He knew he was sloppy when he went back to the same street in the same week. He never wanted to see the inside of a jail again. He knew he could be killed any day. That didn't bother him.

He also knew he could be captured. *That* bothered him. He had a plan for that. A little vial he kept with him at all times. He was not going to jail again. They could take his body if they wanted to. But after his experiences in the Caracas jail never again.

Paul had once jokingly asked him how many passports he had.

His response was, "Take a guess."

"Five?" Paul asked.

"More," he said.

"How many?"

He didn't answer.

Paul didn't know which ones he used to travel to Cucuta and Caracas. His guess was that Felipe was a native everywhere. Less scrutiny.

Felipe made yet another trip to South America. He was carefully gathering information. Updating details. Martinez was paying $50 million for it. Felipe was surprised about how much they knew already.

Earlier in their operations, Felipe had hoped that the Medellin boys would mistake them for the Cali cartel. He thought that because the Cali cartel was growing so rapidly, Luis could fly under the radar. No such luck. Martinez and Johnson knew that there was a significant third player. Three was a crowd. The weakest would be gobbled up first.

Felipe was smart. In another life, he could have been a lawyer or a doctor. His circumstances had barely allowed him a couple of years of school. He knew that his time and Paul's time was limited.

They had probably not yet made a move on Paul because no one benefitted from a gang war. However, things were happening quickly now. No one was safe any longer.

Felipe had hoped Paul would ask Karissa to stay in Trinidad. The Medellin men often get messy. Under pressure, family was not out of bounds for them. She would be safer there. There was no reason to go after her unless they wanted to get to Paul.

It was Felipe's last day in Caracas when it happened. He got most of it from Alonzo's firsthand description. He was glad he wasn't there.

†

The small airstrip was a half-hour's drive from Ramon's mansion in San Tome. An hour outside Caracas. Deep in a wooded area, it was well concealed. Ramon's small plane was chockfull with tightly packed cargo. There was barely room left for the four occupants. Ramon, Alonzo, the pilot, and another bodyguard.

It was the return leg from Cucuta. It was a routine trip for them. The cargo was several hundreds of kilos of cocaine. They were all thinking of home as the pilot started his descent. It was about this time that Ramon felt a salty taste in his mouth.

Ramon had planned to be away for a week. That was what he told Andreina. He was returning in five days. They needed to get this shipment off quickly. Deep-pocket customers were waiting at transshipment ports.

Since Ramon was on board, they didn't wait for a night landing. All the permits were legit. Every major lawman around this area was in his pocket. The territory was friendly. No need for the additional secrecy.

As the pilot dropped altitude, Ramon rubbed his lips. The small plane circled the airstrip. Ramon stood up. He cleared his throat a couple of times.

"Everything okay, boss?" Alonzo asked.

Ramon responded with a choked-off unintelligible answer. It made Alonzo look up. He saw Ramon's face in the light. It started to turn blue.

Ramon continued to make gurgling sounds. He tried to but couldn't speak. His eyes began to protrude from their sockets. He reached up to his neck as if trying to remove an invisible hand. One that was strangling him.

Alonzo and the other guard stared at him. They didn't know what to do. The pilot was too busy with the landing to look back.

Alonzo noticed the vessels in Ramon eyeballs bulging. He saw one burst and squirted blood. Ramon blinked his eyes reflexively.

Ramon coughed as his head leaned forward. A half pint of blood gushed out of his mouth. He started to fall forward. Alonzo and the other bodyguard tried to hold him up.

Ramon coughed again. Blood started to ooze from his nostrils. His face was still blue. He was drowning in his own blood. He coughed one more time. A deluge of blood came from his lungs through his mouth. It landed on Alonzo.

Alonzo temporarily released his grip on Ramon. Ramon fell forward. He landed on his face in the small plane. His body squirmed, and then it became still. Blood continued to pour from his mouth even though he was dead.

As the plane landed, the blood flowed forward and then leveled off. The pilot looked over his shoulder. Ramon had made his last trip with them.

Five days earlier, Andreina had cooked Ramon's favorite meal. He had cleaned his plate and asked for seconds. He felt great when he left for Cucuta. After five days, Ramon's blood was at its thinnest. The Warfarin from the rat poison was at the height of its action. The unpressured aircraft magnified the hemorrhage in his lungs.

That same night, Felipe was scheduled to leave Caracas. He had personally witnessed Alonzo storming into the mansion. Bloodied shirt and all. He came to get Lorenzo, Ramon's nephew. He took him to scene to show him Ramon's body. Lorenzo was next in line.

Alonzo recounted the scene to Felipe later that evening. They did go way back with their old boss. It marked the end of an era. Alonzo was already getting ready to serve his new boss.

When Felipe returned to DC, he shared the news with Paul. He reiterated that little would change. Lorenzo was now Ramon. Business would go on as usual.

DEATH

1

THE BALL DROPPED AT TIMES SQUARE. THE EXUBERANT cheers were contagious even through the TV. Confetti flew everywhere. Paul and Karissa watched from their warm living room. They had decided to stay in because Paul was on call for the New Year's Day weekend.

At exactly 12:04 a.m., the phone rang. The TV channel had not yet gone on commercial break following the countdown. Dick Clark was still on his adrenaline high. Paul muted the TV and answered. It was the hospital operator.

"Is this Dr. Karan?"

"Yes, it is."

"A Joseph Summers wants to speak to you. He said he is one of your patients."

"He is."

Paul knew Joseph Summers quite well. He first met him and his partner in the hospital when Joseph was being treated for pneumocystis pneumonia. After a tenuous period in which his life was in the balance, he recovered.

Three weeks of IV antibiotics and ten days on the ventilator, he was eventually weaned off. Oxygen by mask and more antibiotics, his infection acquiesced. The oxygen continued at home.

Joseph lost a lot of weight. He had little muscle mass left. But he left the hospital in better shape than he came in. He had bought a temporary lease on life.

Charles, his partner, was with him every hour of every day. Charles comforted Joseph. He held his hand. He spoke to him even when he knew that Joseph couldn't hear a word. Sedation didn't deter Charles. He was as committed as any black-necked swan. Paul had rarely seen such love in a relationship.

"Connect me, please," Paul responded to the operator.

At the other end of the line, Joseph was holding. So too was Charles.

"It is time," Joseph said softly.

Paul wanted to be sure, so he asked again.

"The time has come," Charles said.

"We want to do it, Dr. Karan," Joseph said, as firmly as he could.

"We planned to wait until the new year," Charles said, supporting Joseph.

Paul knew the end of the unsaid statement. *And we have reached that goal.*

Paul was not the admitting physician when Joseph first came to the hospital. As such, he was not the physician of record. Dr. Reddy was. Paul had taken care of Joseph several times in clinic. He filled in for Dr. Reddy when she was on hospital duties. He was quite familiar with Joseph's case. Charles was always present with him.

Charles was externally well. He never revealed whether he was HIV positive. Paul didn't pry. Joseph had AIDS, and that was the reason for the visit. Charles was not their patient.

After Joseph's bout with pneumonia, he did fairly well for a few months. Then his gradual decline resumed. He had a very low CD4 count. The different infections kept coming. Each ensuing one became harder to treat.

Dr. Reddy's philosophy was well known to all the other doctors in the group. In cases like Joseph's, if the patient desired, she would provide comfort measures only. Joseph and Charles had discussed this with Dr. Reddy months earlier. They had agreed on it in principle. They would notify her when they made that decision.

Joseph and Charles made the call at 12:04 a.m. on January 1. They had decided on Paul's watch. Paul knew the timing was not random.

"Joseph, I will confirm with Dr. Reddy."

"Sure, Dr. Karan."

"Then I will call the pharmacist."

"Thanks," Joseph whispered.

"We already have a visiting nurse," Charles stated. "And Joseph has IV access."

"Thanks for reminding me, Charles."

Charles waited for him to continue.

"It could take a few hours, Joseph," Paul added.

"We know, Dr. Karan."

"Joseph?"

"Yes?"

"You are a good man."

"Thank you, Dr. Karan," Joseph whispered.

"You too, Charles."

"Thanks, Doc."

Paul hung up.

He called Dr. Reddy's home telephone. He knew her number from memory. Dr. Reddy confirmed that they had all agreed on comfort measures. The exact timing was up to Joseph and Charles. She promised to speak to them later in the day.

Paul asked the hospital operator to page the pharmacist on call. An hour later, the pharmacist returned Paul's called. He apologized for the delay. He and his wife were at a New Year's Eve party. He hadn't checked his pager for a bit. Paul placed the verbal order for the morphine. The pharmacist assured him it would be delivered as soon as possible.

The countdown for Joseph and Charles began.

Three days later, Joseph died.

Dr. Reddy told Paul he died in his sleep.

Peacefully. In his own bed. In his own house.

Charles was by his side.

2

JIMMY MARTINEZ WAS IN RELAXED MOOD AS HE APPROACHED Washington, DC. A couple of Scotch in the back seat of his luxury SUV helped. It made the ride down from New York much easier. They cruised swiftly down I-95 South and were closing in on the DC Beltway. His bodyguards, Mike and Todd, provided occasional conversation. They handled the chauffeuring duties as Jimmy sipped his Scotch.

Martinez allowed his thoughts to drift. After a quick meeting with Steve Johnson, his woman was waiting. The best money could buy. A fancy private apartment and any material comforts she wanted. Just to be available whenever Jimmy was in town. Jimmy always went top shelf. The anticipation and the alcohol put him in a great frame of mind.

Mike roused him from his slumber.

"Boss?"

"What?"

"Somebody is following us."

Martinez was alert instantly. He touched his midsection and felt the comfort of his gun.

"How long?" Martinez asked. His tone was calm, but his body was already alert.

"About five miles," Mike replied.

"Hmmm," Martinez said.

Big Mike had worked for him for years. He knew Mike wouldn't raise a false alarm. Mike was pretty sure about this.

"Todd?"

"Didn't see anything until Mike spoke," Todd answered.

Todd was the quiet type. He was much younger than Mike but just as efficient. He had been with Martinez for about a year. Mike had recommended him after they lost another bodyguard. Many years earlier, Mike had worked with Todd. They worked well together, and that reassured Martinez.

"What vehicle, Mike?" Martinez asked.

"A dark blue Buick. It's hanging about three cars back."

"I see it," Martinez confirmed.

"I don't think they know we spotted them," Mike stated.

Martinez was silent.

"Boss?" Big Mike asked, looking for instructions.

"Pull off at the next exit and see if they follow."

Mike pulled off the interstate without question. He climbed off exit 29 to Route 212 East. Sure enough, the dark blue Buick followed.

"Still behind us, boss."

Martinez knew that Mike was worried. Mike's voice was now slow and measured. No hint of his usual dry humor.

"Try to lose them."

Mike hit the gas, and the SUV lurched forward. The road ahead was empty. The Buick kept pace. In fact, the Buick started to close on them. They had given up on the hide and seek.

"Oh, shit!" Mike exclaimed as he ran the intersection.

Martinez and Todd pulled their guns. Todd started to shoot out of the window. Martinez joined in. The gunshots reverberated in the close quarters. The men in the Buick returned fire.

Mike joined the act. One hand on the wheel, he joined the gunfire. Martinez saw the man in the passenger seat of the Buick slumped forward. He wasn't sure who got him. Didn't matter. One less.

One tire of the SUV took a hit. It exploded. The vehicle skidded uncontrollably. Then it lurched off the road. The Buick continued to stalk. Completely out of control, the SUV veered into the roadside ditch. It came to a stop in the ditch, eventually settling on its side.

Martinez crawled out of a window. He laid on his stomach in the grass. There was blood on his shirt. He decided not to move. In the fading light, he appeared dead. Someone would have to look closely to know if he was alive. He kept his gun under his chest. He listened.

Martinez heard a loud gunshot. A single shot fired at close range. Martinez resisted the urge to look. He figured he couldn't help the dead.

He heard footsteps. Then voices. Todd speaking to someone. The voice that replied wasn't Big Mike's. It was a voice Martinez didn't recognize.

Another loud explosion. Again a single gunshot. He hoped the other guy was dead. Not Todd. He was correct. No more conversation.

Then he heard Todd's clear voice. Very precise and controlled. He was about twenty feet away.

"Hand over the gun, boss."

Martinez turned over and looked up. He took in the scene around him. The surprise must have been evident his face.

Big Mike laid on the ground. Dead. His gun was still in his hand.

The stranger with whom Todd was conversing was also dead. He was lying in a heap on the ground. He was on his back, his mouth open. His arms were contorted at an odd angle. A few feet away, Mike was on his back in the grass. He stared at the sky with wide, unseeing eyes.

The Buick was about a hundred feet away, nestled at the side of the road. The steep embankment made it invisible from the road. Bullets had smashed the windscreen. The SUV was sprawled on its side in the ditch.

Todd stood over him. His gun pointed at Martinez's head.

"Hand over the gun," Todd ordered.

"Let's talk about this, Todd."

"Now!"

Martinez knew that Todd was dead serious. His voice was cold. A tone Martinez hadn't heard before. He tossed the gun at Todd's feet.

"Start walking," Todd commanded.

He waved the gun, pointing toward the Buick.

Martinez got up slowly. He took a few steps forward.

"Todd, let's negotiate."

"About what?"

"How much are they paying you?"

"A lot."

"I am sure I can match it."

"I have my doubts," Todd said.

"Why didn't you shoot me?"

"You are worth twice as much alive," Todd replied.

"Really?"

"If you try to run, I will take the half price."

"Why did you kill Mike?"

"He would get in the way."

"You could have shared the money."

Jimmy Martinez was trying hard to keep the conversation going. He knew Mike wouldn't have sold him out. If he wanted to, he could have done it a long time ago.

"I hate the bastard," Todd hissed.

"Really? I thought you two were buddies."

They were nearing the Buick now. Martinez knew there was at least one dead man in the car. He didn't want to end up in the boot of the car.

"That sonafabitch!"

"Mike?"

"I had to put up with his shit for a year."

"What?"

"He couldn't keep his mouth shut!"

Martinez waited. Todd was getting emotionally involved.

"I couldn't wait to kill him."

"And your buddies over there?"

"Collateral damage."

"I see," Martinez muttered.

"Get into the trunk," Todd ordered.

Martinez pretended not to hear. He knew if he got into the vehicle it was over.

"Come on Todd, give me dollar figure."

"Get in," Todd commanded.

"I am sure I can double it," Martinez said, still trying to stall.

He wasn't sure if Todd heard him. At the edge of embankment, Martinez slipped and fell. Todd moved closer.

The speed at which he tackled Todd surprised even him. Todd fell backward. Martinez reached for the knife that he always kept inside his socks. Todd didn't have time to react.

Martinez drove the blade directly into Todd's chest. A swift single stroke pierced Todd's heart. A shot escaped from Todd's gun. It sailed harmlessly into the air.

Warm blood squirted onto Martinez's shirt. Todd stared at him. Slowly his life slipped away.

Martinez pulled out the knife. He wiped it on his shirt. He calmly replaced it in his sock. He took off his shirt and wiped his chest off. He looked around. Todd's eyes remained open. The surprise was still on his face.

Martinez spat on the ground. He got into the Buick. From the driver's seat, he reached over and opened the passenger door. He kicked the body out. Unhurriedly, he made his way to the main road.

He took a deep breath as he accelerated. He passed some open fields. Jimmy Martinez shook his head. His rough-and-tumble days had not deserted him. These guys had forgotten that he came from the streets of the Bronx. He had started just like them. Twenty years earlier.

3

ANDREINA PACKED HER BAGS ITEM BY ITEM. SHE HAD A couple of weeks to do it, but she kept putting it off. Today, the day of her flight, she no longer could. She knew her choice of destination was not random.

She had considered Miami and New York. She found a reason not to go to either place. She convinced herself that she was heading to the right place. She would get better medical care, she rationalized.

With Ramon dead, Andreina doubt that they wouldn't even bother to look for her. Not unless she went to the police. She planned to drive right up to the airport and park. For weeks, she had been mentally preparing for this trip.

Andreina had lost weight. Her appetite was poor. She knew that soon her illness would become obvious to all. Now that she thought of it, Lorenzo would be glad to be rid of her. If she hadn't been Ramon's woman, she would have already been kicked out.

Business had returned to normal. Alonzo became Lorenzo's bodyguard. Luis was still directing operations from Colombia. The merchandise came and left as it always had. Lorenzo quickly filled Ramon's role.

Both of Andreina's suitcases were full. She picked up a picture from her dresser and examined it. It was of her as a young woman. Smiling and happy, in full bloom. It was taken before she had met Ramon. Life had limitless potential back then. She thought of taking it. After a few moments, she put it back on the dresser. She was hoping to make a fresh start. Some of those new medications they had in America might give her new life. She prayed and hoped.

Andreina couldn't help but feel a smidgen of nostalgia. She had lived in this luxury prison for years. She was now heading into the great unknown. She was certain that she would never see these walls again. She would miss the green grass on the rolling hillside. That was about it.

Her biggest quandary wasn't what possession to take. It was how much money to take. How much money she could conceal without getting into trouble. Ramon had a personal safe in the bedroom. He kept emergency funds there. She knew the combination. There was more than enough money.

She decided on US $50,000. An even number. She had to pay $10,000 to get a US visa. So she opted for $60,000. Even with hundred-dollar bills, it was bulky. The false bottom of her suitcases couldn't fit any more without raising suspicion. That was a lot of money, she thought. She could live on it for years. Living in Caracas was all she knew.

She zipped her suitcases without locking them. One at a time, she took them to her car in the inside garage. The effort taxed her heart and lungs. She rested after each trip. No one appeared to notice her movements.

She returned to her room. She put on some makeup. She looked around one last time. Then she made her final trip to the garage. If all went well, she would be in Washington, DC, before midnight.

✝

The sudden knock on Steve Johnson's front door startled him. He was watching HBO in his living room. His wife was out. He wasn't expecting anyone. He didn't entertain visitors on weeknights. Omar had already left for home.

Johnson put the TV on mute. A second knock broke the silence. More insistent this time. Johnson got up, apprehensive. Stray traffic didn't come into this upscale neighborhood.

He turned on the outside light. He looked out from the side window. Steve Johnson walked to the door and peered through the keyhole. Satisfied, he opened it.

"What are you doing here?" he asked.

The look Martinez gave him required no words.

"Come in," Johnson said.

Martinez entered the house. He plunked down in a sofa. He raised his eyebrows in an unspoken question. He was still his boss.

Johnson answered. "She went out."

"Good," Martinez replied.

"What brought you here?" Johnson asked.

"We will get to that."

"Where are your boys?"

"Dead."

That got Johnson's attention.

"How did you get here?"

"Shut up, Johnson. If you must know, I didn't blow your cover."

"I didn't ..." Johnson started.

"You and your prissy neighborhood. Goddamn."

Johnson was silent.

"I took a cab. I got off five blocks from here."

"Thanks."

Martinez looked around. He took in the luxury of the room. The painting on the walls screamed of money. The furniture did too. So did everything else.

"So this is how you live while we bust our asses. Easy money."

Johnson didn't take the bait.

"Looks like you had a full day," Johnson prompted.

Martinez took off his shirt. Then he removed a small towel he had taped to his chest. A bullet had torn the skin off the left side of his chest. Another two inches, they wouldn't be having a conversation tonight.

"Tell me what happened."

"Looks like the Cali boys are playing hardball."

"What?"

"They tried to kill me."

"Weren't Mike and Todd with you?"

"Both dead."

"You need new men?"

"You know the rule, Johnson."

"I don't like the rule."

"Five of theirs for one of ours."

"That is not a good rule," Johnson protested.

"The rule is the rule. You need to kill ten of theirs."

"What if it doesn't stop there?"

"It will. If we stick by the rule," Martinez said.

"I will give the order tomorrow," Johnson conceded.

Both men were quiet for a while.

Martinez was the first to speak. "Todd double-crossed me."

Silence.

"Didn't expect him to play both sides," Johnson said finally.

"Worse. He killed Mike."

"Sorry."

"Mike is gone," Martinez repeated.

"I know you were close with Mike," Johnson said.

"Yep. They don't make them like Big Mike anymore."

That was the closest Johnson had ever heard Martinez to expressing feelings. For anyone.

"You got Todd?"

"I am here, and he isn't. *Is he?*" Martinez voice was sharp.

Johnson didn't respond. He wasn't expected to. He switched topics.

"You need a doctor?"

"No."

"That thing could get infected."

"A good wash and some antiseptic. I'll be fine."

Another long silence.

"Question for you, Steve?"

Johnson smiled. Martinez was calming down.

"I'm waiting."

"This is out of character for the Cali boys."

"Agree."

"Do you think it could be Luis and the Cucuta gang?"

"Don't think so, but it *is* possible."

Martinez didn't say anything.

"I didn't think they were organized enough to go after us. Not in that kind of way," Johnson continued.

"I told you. You gave them too much time," Martinez said.

"We need to do this thoroughly, Jimmy. You know that. We need to take this thing out from the root. Here and South America."

"Still too much time."

"You know if we make a small hit, they will go underground. In a few months, they will regroup," Johnson said.

"I am not a fool."

"Patience, Jimmy."

"How much longer?"

"They have another three weeks to get everything to us."

"This waiting is killing me."

"A couple weeks after that, Cucuta is done."

"Good."

"Boss?"

"What now?"

"Since Todd was theirs, we only lost Mike right?"

"I guess."

"So five is enough?"

"Fine. They will get the message."

"If they strike back?" Johnson asked.

"They won't. Pacho is no fool."

"He might not know."

"Get one of their local bosses. That will get his attention," Martinez said.

"I am concerned about starting a new war, Jimmy. Remember '94?"

"Don't worry. Things are different now."

"How so?"

"Pacho runs a tight shop. He has New York under control. The last thing he wants is bodies all over the place. It's bad for business."

✝

Paul counted the days. The turmoil inside him was unbearable. He sat in his study alone. He attempted to read a journal. He quickly gave up. He couldn't focus, let alone digest a new study.

He was becoming increasingly anxious as the February deadline zoned in. Everything was now up in the air. So many questions, and he had no answers.

Would he escape with his life? What would become of his patients? Was it fair to drag Karissa into an unknown future? Would he ever see his family again? The more they went around in his head, the more confused he became.

Paul was usually a clear thinker. Normally he was very precise in his planning. Years of training had groomed him for that. But this situation was entirely unpredictable. It had taken control of him. He rarely slept well anymore. He was trapped.

The phone rang. He almost jumped out of his chair.

It was Felipe.

"I am in the area, Doc."

"Aren't you always?"

"Can I stop by?"

"Sure."

"Is Karissa in?"

"Yes, but it shouldn't be a problem."

"Good. I will see you in a few."

Paul walked out of the study. Karissa was in the living room browsing a magazine. A car backfiring in the distance startled him. He stumbled and almost fell over a foot stool. He took a deep breath. Then he sat next to Karissa, resting his hand on her leg.

"Felipe will be here in a couple of minutes," Paul said.

Karissa gently rested the book down. "Do you want me to go upstairs?" she asked.

"No, I want you to stay."

She nodded.

"You have a right to hear everything," Paul continued, almost talking to himself.

"Okay."

Paul heard a car coming up the driveway. He peeked through the curtains. It was Felipe. He opened the front door. Felipe followed him to the living room.

Felipe removed his baseball cap. With a slight bow of the head, he greeted Karissa. "Good to see you, ma'am."

"Likewise," Karissa said, in a pleasant enough tone.

Paul motioned Felipe to sit. He obliged.

Paul quickly got to the point. "What brings you here tonight?"

Felipe looked over at Karissa before he spoke. He was still hesitant.

"Go ahead," prompted Paul.

"I have almost everything they want."

"What else do you need?"

"The exact location of another three warehouses. The name of the new boss in Philly."

"Good news then?"

"No."

"Why so?" Paul asked.

"This is a very dangerous time, Paul."

Paul waited. Felipe wanted to say more. He glanced tentatively at Karissa again.

Paul answered his look. "It's okay, Felipe. She knows everything."

"Look, Doc, I know I don't have your kind of education," Felipe started. "But I've been doing this for many years. I've been blessed with luck. But over time, I have learned a few things."

"I am listening, Felipe."

"Well, for starters, we need to be extra careful. I have the info stored in a secure place. I wouldn't give it to them until we get the money."

"What are you suggesting?" Paul asked.

"You get the account numbers. I will handle the rest."

"Okay?"

"When we give them the info, we shouldn't be here. I will give you specific instructions later."

"Okay. Are you suggesting we move the date up?" Paul asked.

"No. We still have to put some more things in place. We need the time."

"Tell me."

"Paul, you are a smart man. I am sure you have figured out that you cannot live in this area. You and Karissa have to disappear. That is your only chance when hell breaks loose."

Paul nodded silently.

"I will make the arrangements. I know about these things," Felipe said. "That had always been my backup plan."

"Why didn't you do it before?" Paul couldn't help himself.

"Two things. One, I didn't have $20 million."

Felipe stopped.

"The second?"

"You, Doc."

Paul looked closely at him. His eyes seemed to be welling up with tears. Without asking, he continued. "I didn't think they would leave you alone if I was gone."

Paul nodded. He knew he owed his life in DC to Felipe. He wasn't sure what drove Felipe to do what he did. He got a hint of sorts.

"I am sorry about what I did to you, Paul."

"What?" Paul had almost forgotten.

Felipe averted his eyes. "When we first met, Paul."

The apology was unexpected. Paul was moved. So too was Karissa.

Paul got up. He placed his hand on Felipe's shoulder. "You have been a good friend, Felipe. Karissa and I owe our lives to you."

"What is left of it, you mean," Felipe muttered.

Paul didn't want to lose the moment. Yet he could find no words to express his feelings.

"You had another suggestion?" Paul finally asked.

"Yes."

"What?"

"I am getting the dagger removed next Tuesday. You should too."

Paul understood. Felipe was systematically removing all connections from his cartel.

"I know you have friends who can do that kind of thing. Please do everything off the record."

"Makes sense," Paul agreed.

"It will need a couple of weeks to heal."

"Correct."

Felipe got up. "Do everything that you normally do."

"I will."

"I will be staying in touch. No more out-of-town trips."

Felipe got up and headed for the door. He couldn't help but notice the dazed look in Paul's face. "I have two men watching the house 24/7, Doc."

"Thanks."

4

ANDREINA WAS LOST IN THIS STRANGE CITY. SO MANY PEO-ple, no one she knew. A week earlier, she had taken a cab from National Airport. She had checked into a cheap motel in DC. It was in Northeast, just off Bladensburg Road. She was hoping her money would last longer at a low-cost boarding place.

So far, Andreina had no real plans. She had looked up Paul Karan's number in the phone book. No listing. She couldn't find him. She looked up medical clinics. She found quite a few in the DC area.

She mustered her courage and called several. Most of the phones went to a voicemail. She wasn't brave enough to leave a message. Most of the recordings asked to leave a call-back number. She was using a pay phone. She had no call-back number.

The few times she got someone, they asked about her health insurance. She had none. Only one clinic didn't. The earliest appointment for new patients was two months away. She still took it.

With every passing day, Andreina got closer to despairing. Every time she brushed her teeth, she saw the white stuff. It wasn't only her tongue now. It was stuck on the inside of her cheeks. She knew what it was. She tried to scrub it off. It bled before it came off. The next day, it reappeared. It was an exercise in futility. She desperately needed medical help.

Andreina was conscious about her weight. She had lost thirty pounds in the last year. Her clothes had gotten very loose. She had no appetite. She forced herself to eat. Despite this, the weight loss continued.

To add to her troubles, an unexpected problem arose. She became very conscious of her heavily accented English. In Venezuela, she had been complimented on her good English. Now she was ashamed to speak.

She considered returning to Caracas. She forcibly removed the idea. It was too tempting. She thought of ending it all herself. Her personal beliefs wouldn't allow her to use that option. She willed herself to go forward. She reminded herself that she had money. She would walk into a clinic and pay for her care. Next week.

Every morning, around ten, the hotel maid came to clean her room. It was the one thing Andreina looked forward to. Rosa was an older lady. She was from El Salvador and spoke Spanish. Andreina welcomed the opportunity to speak in her own language. They chatted politely about general things. The weather, their countries, and family. Several times, Rosa asked how long she was going to be staying. Andreina didn't give her a definite answer. She didn't know herself.

She was happy it was the same maid every day. It comforted her. She had nearly $50,000 hidden in the false bottom of her suitcases. She tried moving it to the bottom drawer of the dresser under her clothes. It was quite bulky, so she moved it back. Andreina hardly left her room. She was unnerved by the man who came to unclog her sink. When she reported the sink was blocked, he hadn't given her a time. He showed up unexpectedly, late that evening, to fix it.

This morning, Andreina didn't hear Rosa's knock. She was still in bed. She had had a bad night, tossing and turning. She hadn't eaten for more than twenty-four hours. Her sleep was listless. She dreamt about her mother's home in Caracas.

Andreina pulled the covers closer. She felt chilly. Rosa knocked again. Still no answer. Rosa opened the door with her master key. She saw Andreina curled up in bed.

"Ms. Andreina?"

No answer.

"Ms. Andreina?"

A slight murmur.

"Ms. Andreina, you are sick!"

"Is that you, Rosa?" Andreina asked weakly.

"Yes, it is me."

"I am glad you came."

"You are sick, Ms. Andreina. You need a doctor."

"No, Rosa. I am just feeling cold."

"Cold? The sheet is soaking wet!" Rosa said.

"I must have used the blanket last night," Andreina protested.

"You are shivering!"

"I didn't realize it until now."

"Look Ms. Andreina, let me take you to the hospital.

"No."

"Why?"

"I don't have health insurance."

"No matter. You are really sick."

"I will be better by afternoon."

"How?"

"I took some Tylenol. I had a fever last night."

"And that would make you better?"

"I hope so."

"You are really sick, Ms. Andreina!"

"Might just be a cold," Andreina protested feebly.

"Look, Ms. Andreina. This is America. I am going to call 911."

Andreina's protests got weaker.

Fifteen minutes later, the ambulance arrived. The EMTs took her to the nearest emergency room. Washington General Hospital Center.

✝

Paul pulled into his clinic's parking minutes before 8:00 a.m. As per his routine, it was five minutes before his first scheduled patient. He took the spot at the end of the lot, near the dumpster. He left the closer spots for the patients. Too bad some of his coworkers didn't share his conviction.

He grabbed his bag, mind already on the work at hand. He had a full schedule. Three new patients, plus numerous follow-ups. In addition, he had to review the labs of the patients of the volunteer physicians. Then make phone calls to all the patients with critical labs. It was going to be a full Monday.

As he strode across the parking lot, he heard footsteps. He turned and looked. It was Felipe.

"What are you doing here?" Paul demanded.

"Calm down, boss. Just two minutes of your time."

Paul was in his full doctor mode. "I told you not to call me that."

"Sorry, Doc."

Paul softened. "Make it quick. I have patients waiting."

"Paul, can you take leave for the next two weeks?"

"No," Paul stated flatly.

"Why?"

"I have too many people depending on me."

"It is for your own safety."

"How?"

"I could put a few extra men at the house until we wrap up," Felipe explained.

"You want me to lock myself in my house so you could protect me."

A long pause.

"Essentially, yes," Felipe finally said.

"No. I need to be here."

"In another three weeks, someone will have to take over anyway," Felipe pleaded.

Paul studied the expression in Felipe's eyes. He was sincere. He was really concerned. He was right.

"What happened?" Paul asked.

"The Medellin boys are getting messy again. This time, I don't know the reason."

"You mean those five people killed last night?" Paul asked.

"How do you know?"

"I heard it on the news driving in. Five people were shot in a house in Hyattsville."

"Yes, it was them," Felipe said.

"A good guess would be a drug-related crime," Paul replied.

"What you didn't hear was they were executed," Felipe added.

"Same thing."

"Not really. This was a message killing."

"How so?"

"Each person had all ten fingers cut off with a wire cutter. All were shot in the back of the head with a single bullet. They were found blindfolded. They were all from the Cali cartel," Felipe explained.

"How do you know?"

"I have my sources."

Paul stared at Felipe for a long time. He was already late. The first new patient was probably in the exam room by now.

"I will take one week off. Tomorrow, I am going to get this tattoo removed. I will take medical leave for the rest of the week."

"Good. Thanks."

Paul entered the clinic from the side door. His mind completely switched off the conversation he had moments ago. The waiting room was full of patients. His physician assistants had already started.

5

FOR THE FIRST THREE YEARS OF HIS TERM, THE MAYOR OF Cucuta didn't associate himself with Luis Alvarez. In fact, Mayor Esteban avoided him like the plague. Esteban had won on an antidrug and anti-corruption platform. He tried really hard to keep his promise.

That was until recently. Now, Mayor Esteban was facing a tough reelection. His funds were dwindling, and his options were limited. The majority of the populace still supported his policies. But with unemployment rising, his feisty opponent was looking more attractive with each passing day. His critics were beginning to gain traction.

Luis Alvarez was full of cash. He was ready and waiting. He had everything money could buy. Now he wanted status. This afternoon was just one step forward in Luis's grand plan. As Mayor Esteban cut the ribbon for the new soccer field, the photographers were busy. The prize shot for Luis was him shaking hands with the mayor. Luis was sure it would make all the major papers in the morning. It was a priceless picture.

Luis had just rebuilt the entire athletic facilities at one of the best high schools in Cucuta. Simon Bolivar High. He bought the land adjacent to the school and built a new football stadium. All with his own money. To that he added a fat check to the mayor's campaign fund. Luis was pleased with his investment. Mayor Esteban held his breath and shook hands with Luis Alvarez.

Separately, Luis had met with the principal and school board. Following healthy deposits in each of their accounts, the field was named Luis Alvarez Football Stadium. The name was unanimously approved.

Luis toyed with the idea that one day he might run for mayor himself. That would be a great hobby, he thought. Everyone knew Luis was rich. Everyone knew how he made his money. But when money came their way, he was their Robin Hood. Luis planned to repeat the same process with other schools and colleges. Soon his name would be all over the city. He smiled.

Luis had grown up just thirty miles from Cucuta. It was a world away. His parents farmed the hills. They were dirt poor. Luis was the middle of five boys. The oldest one found work with a small smuggling operation. It was Luis's first contact with drugs. His brother was eventually killed taking cocaine into Panama.

Before his death, Luis's brother had made more money than anybody in Luis's entire extended family. The path out of poverty was clear to Luis. The second of Luis's brothers became a drug addict. He quickly moved from snorting to shooting drugs. One day, he went missing. They found him dead in his room. Syringes and needles were scattered all over. On the bed and on the floor. Overdose.

Luis was the smartest of them. He knew he had to manage the operation to be fully in charge. He worked his way up the cartel. He got rid of anyone who was in his path. His most common tactic was to stage gang raids. He killed his immediate bosses in the gunfights. Clearing his way. He didn't stop until he got to the top.

He put his younger brother, Ramon, in charge of operations in Venezuela. His nephew, Lorenzo, was Ramon's understudy. The only person he fully trusted in Cucuta was Benito. His youngest brother.

Luis Alvarez lived in a mansion on the top of a hill. It was few miles off Highway 55. For its seclusion, it might as well have been in another country. Luis knew the area well. The village where he was raised was twenty miles away. Many people had heard about this fortress of a residence. Few had seen it.

Luis owned several miles of real estate around his mansion. The mansion was protected by a twelve-foot stone wall. An electrified fence on top of the wall fortified it. An old-fashioned moat surrounded the mansion, making it completely inaccessible.

The road leading to this fort-mansion was guarded 24/7. Luis resided at the upper level of the mansion. Only Benito was allowed there. And his woman of the week. Not even his top finance man, Mark Munoz, had freedom to roam the entire building. Luis guarded his back pretty well. He never forgot how he himself got to the top.

In the last few years, Luis was clean as a whistle. He had others to do the dirty work. He just gave orders. If it was an inside job, Benito took care of it.

He didn't believe in coincidences. He was still puzzled by Ramon's death. He didn't know where to point the finger. For now, he let it be.

Business was good and getting better each month. The deputy police chief was already in his pockets. The mayor was slowly getting there. Soon he would be able to rule the city without leaving his mansion. It was a good day. Luis's smile was wider than ever.

6

ANDREINA FELT MUCH BETTER THIS MORNING. SHE ATE MOST of her breakfast. A lot had happened in the last week. It was exactly a week since she had been admitted to the hospital. She barely remembered anything of the first two days. She later pieced it together from talking to the nurses, the discharge planner, and now Elva, the social worker.

She was hypoxic and septic when she was brought to the emergency room. She had shaking chills and a temperature of 104. They quickly diagnosed her with severe pneumonia. The bacteria had already spread to her bloodstream. They were worried that it might have gone to her brain. Her final diagnosis was pneumococcal sepsis and bronchopneumonia.

Her condition could have been prevented with a simple vaccine. Her nursing background allowed her full understanding of the details. She knew she was halfway through death's door. Rosa had saved her life by calling 911.

Now it was discharge planning time, arranging follow-up appointments and possible home care. Only problem, she had no home to go to. Elva was exploring every option to get her out of the hospital. Hospitals were expensive. She was not well, but she was stable. They wanted her out as soon as possible. It had already been too long for an uninsured patient.

In a dazed state, Andreina had signed the financial responsibility statement. She had money. She was alive. She would pay the hospital costs. Elva was really nice. Finally, Andreina asked the question.

"How much will it cost?"

"A lot," Elva replied.

"I have some money. I think I can pay for it."

"Without insurance, the cost is even more."

"Why?"

"The insurance companies get a big discount from the hospital."

"I thought individual patients would a get the discount," Andreina replied, thinking clearer than she had for a week.

"Not really. They have prearranged prices."

"Can you kindly give me an idea of a number?"

"They haven't prepared the final bill yet. From people in similar situations, I can make a guess," Elva replied cautiously.

"Please," Andreina pleaded.

"Okay."

Andreina waited.

"Around $100 thousand."

"What?" Andreina almost fell out of the bed. She thought she misheard.

"One hundred thousand American dollars?"

"It is just an estimate," Elva replied, almost embarrassed.

Not in her wildest dreams did Andreina think seven days of hospitalization would cost that much. She thought $10,000 tops. Going at about a thousand dollars a day was her high estimate. Even if it were twenty thousand, she had planned on paying the bill. As her confusion cleared, she managed, "Why so much?"

"I know it is a lot. The discharge planner should have explained some of this."

"She didn't."

"I will try. I know it doesn't make much sense to someone coming from another country."

Andreina waited.

"The total is from emergency room costs, ICU costs, physician costs, radiology costs, procedure costs, supplies cost, and a lot of other things."

"I see."

Elva hastened to provide more detailed explanation as if it would somehow help Andreina. "You had a spinal tap to make sure there was no meningitis. That was after a CT scan of the head. Fortunately, it was negative."

"I know. I was given three antibiotics just in case," Andreina rationalized.

"The antibiotics do not make up a big portion of the cost."

"What does?"

"You spent the first two days in the ICU. You were intubated and had assisted breathing. That costs a lot."

"I see."

"The other big items would be the MRI of the head. You had two different echocardiograms to make sure you didn't have infection of the heart valves. They also did the spinal tap under radiology guidance. Then another CT scan of the abdomen. The one in which they found the mass."

Elva paused to catch her breath. Andreina waited.

"The hospital charges for all of these procedures. They also bill for the doctors who perform them and those who read the scans. The doctors rarely know what is being billed. They usually get a fraction of what the hospital bills for them.

"Sounds complicated," Andreina conceded.

"It is."

Andreina took a deep breath.

"I will try to pay part of the bill. Maybe the rest later."

Elva thought Andreina was very sweet but naïve. Here was this woman who was homeless and near death. Yet she was planning to pay in cash what no one would even would consider. Elva decided to leave it alone.

"It is a lot of money, Andreina. Let's get the other things lined up. Maybe a financial adviser from the hospital can work with you later."

"Yes. Yes."

"So you plan on going back to the motel?"

"Yes. At least for the next two weeks."

"We made an appointment in the HIV clinic for you. They would probably start you on HIV medications as soon as your condition stabilizes."

"Thanks."

Andreina waited. Nothing from Elva. She prompted.

"The biopsy?"

Elva knew, but she sidestepped. "What about it?"

"Have they scheduled it?"

Elva was hurting inside. She knew it wouldn't happen. An AIDS patient without insurance, in the present environment. It wasn't scheduled on purpose. The system would find any reason to postpone it. It just wasn't worth it.

Some anxiety crept into Andreina's voice. "The doctor came in this morning. He said the mass in my abdomen could be an infection or cancer."

Elva nodded.

"He said that there is no way to know for sure unless I get the biopsy. He told me he was thinking infection since my T cell count was only forty. He said they will do the biopsy as an outpatient. Then they will start treatment. As soon as they know what it is."

"I am sure he did, dear."

This was the part of the job Elva disliked most. Medicine was a business these days. She had to stretch the truth on her employer's behalf. She finally admitted it to herself. She had to lie on her employer's behalf.

"When they see you in the clinic, they can refer you for the biopsy," Elva said cautiously.

Andreina's face fell. She knew what it meant. Another road that she was unable to navigate. Her optimism from the last couple of days quickly drained away.

Elva couldn't bear to look at her.

"You have my card?" she asked.

The barely audible response came. "Yes."

"Call me anytime," Elva offered. "Even if it is late at night."

Elva felt tears welling up in her eyes. She quickly walked out of the room. She didn't want to lose control in front of Andreina. She had been in this position far too often. The curse of a medical social worker's profession.

✝

Paul's normally quiet house was even quieter tonight. He had had a long day in the clinic. He was sitting in front the TV. He placed it on mute. The images flashed. His brain hardly registered any of it. Paul kept thinking about his conversation in the parking lot with Felipe that morning.

It had gone around and around in his head all day. It wove itself in a knot on his drive home. Now he had the mother of all headaches. He felt like screaming. Karissa was in the adjacent room, doing her nails. He didn't want to alarm her. He kept it inside, yet again.

Felipe was right, of course. Life as he knew it was coming to an end. He had to face that reality. Whether it was one week or one month. The last few years in Washington, DC, would soon be behind him. First, he had to stay alive.

The medical director was surprised when Paul requested emergency leave. He granted it without prying. Paul had never made such a request. His supervisor knew it must have been something urgent.

Paul had an appointment with the plastic surgeon the following morning. It was scheduled for 8:00 a.m. He was anxious. With the scent of Karissa's nail polish filtering into his brain, he closed his eyes. He tried to bring his subconscious fears into the forefront. He hoped to garner some insight into his anxiety.

He eventually concluded that he wasn't anxious about the procedure itself. Removal of the dagger would be a good thing. His anxiety was caused by the inevitability of facing the recollection. The deep, buried memory of having no control. The pain that was inflicted. It took a massive amount of his strength to push the memory away. It wouldn't stay away.

Karissa had not offered to go with him. He hadn't asked her either. For reasons unknown him, Paul found it hard to ask for her help. Rather ironic, he thought. As a physician, people sought his help every day. He provided it without hesitation. Yet, he had shunned asking those close to him for help. He knew he wasn't unique in this issue among physicians.

His imprisonment in Caracas had worsened the issue. He didn't want to ever feel helpless and have no control again. Despite his unique insight, he remained a victim to his past. He took a deep breath. He urged the 3 percent of his brain to override the unconscious majority.

"Karissa?"

"Yes?"

"Do you have plans for tomorrow?" Paul asked.

"No."

Paul waited. Nothing.

"Why?" Karissa urged.

"Well, you know, I have the surgery tomorrow," Paul started.

"Yes."

An awkward silence ensued. This time, Karissa didn't break it.

Another test of his willpower, Paul began, "If you are not busy ..."

"Yes?"

"I would like you to ... to come with me," Paul stuttered.

"I would be glad to."

"Thanks," Paul replied feebly, relief creeping into his voice.

Another long pause.

Finally Karissa spoke up. "Why didn't you ask earlier?"

Paul didn't answer immediately. He responded in a measured voice. "I was hoping you would offer."

"Idiot," Karissa said. She was hot with emotion.

Paul didn't answer.

Karissa quickly regained her composure. Her response was calm. "And here I was thinking that you didn't want me to go with you. That you wanted to face your demons alone," Karissa said.

"No, quite the opposite," he said softly.

"Idiot, again."

"I want you to be there," Paul said in a much firmer tone.

"I want to be there. I was waiting for you to ask."

Things were getting complicated, Paul thought. They both wanted the same thing but couldn't communicate. They couldn't read minds. The stress was taking a toll on both of them. He was extremely apprehensive.

She walked over and took his hands. He looked her in the eyes. She was silent. He noticed her eyes getting wet. This wasn't easy for her. Despite his life cascading out of control, she had stuck with him.

"I need your support, Karissa."

She nodded.

"I need it more than ever."

There was a soft look in her eyes. He would have liked her to say something. Her looks said it. "I love you, Paul."

She squeezed his hands. He would take it. It was all she could give for now. One day, he hoped, the words would come. They had to escape this wretched situation first.

7

THE HOSPITAL ARRANGED FOR ANDREINA TO TAKE A CAB back to the motel. A plastic bag with pills was all she had to show for her ordeal of the past week. She was tired and weak but cautiously optimistic. Her fever and chills were gone. She didn't have to pay the cabbie, but she was her usual polite self. The driver engaged in friendly conversation.

As soon as she was dropped off, she went to the front desk. She asked for her room key. The receptionist told her that the room was taken. Panicking on the inside but trying to remain calm, she asked for the manager. She recognized him from her previous stay. Mr. Herman Turner. He calmly explained that they didn't know when she was coming back, so they rented her room out.

"Where are my things?" she finally blurted out.

"In storage," Herman replied.

"Can you take me to it?"

"Will you be staying with us?" Herman asked.

"Yes," she said, her anxiety continuing to rise

"I will have the attendant bring it up to your room," he said.

"How will you be paying?" the receptionist asked.

"What?" Andreina wasn't sure she understood.

"Credit or cash," the receptionist asked.

"I will pay you when I get my things."

"Ma'am, I cannot give you a room until you give me a credit card. If you are paying with cash, I need a deposit."

"How much?"

"Two hundred dollars."

"Okay, as soon as I get my things, I will pay."

Herman Turner stepped in. He was trying to follow Andreina's line of thinking. He also knew she was a very good customer and had paid with cash the last time. "Come with me. I will get your things."

"Thanks." The gratitude showed in her eyes.

Andreina followed him to the elevator. They rode one level down to the basement. He took out a key and unlocked a fenced, storage cage. In addition to an assorted variety of items, there were several suitcases. Andreina quickly recognized hers. Two large, red suitcases.

"What room?"

"Room 322," she confirmed.

The manager grabbed both cases. Her name and room number were clearly tagged.

"Here," Herman said, placing it next to her.

Andreina couldn't hold back any longer. She opened the first suitcases, right there. She pushes her clothes aside and reached for the bottom zipper in the corner. She knew before she unzipped it. It was flat.

The money was gone.

She exhaled sharply and moved to the next case. The manager was watching with interest. This time she threw her personal items out of the suitcase. In a panic, she unzipped the false bottom in full view of the manager.

Empty!

All her money was gone.

"Someone stole my money," she gasped.

Herman did not know what to say. Clearly, she was missing something.

"Careful, Ms. Andreina. We don't want to make rash accusations."

"I am telling the truth," she pleaded.

"I didn't say you weren't."

"All my money is gone," she repeated.

Finally he spoke up. "How much money?"

"Fifty thousand dollars," she said.

He looked at her in disbelief.

Andreina nodded her head. "Yes!"

"Nobody carries around that much money."

"Please believe me," she implored. "I brought it from another country."

Herman Turner stared at her. He shook his head.

"It is everything I have," Andreina wailed.

Andreina was hysterical. In an effort to plead her case, she ripped open both suitcases. She showed him the false bottoms. Herman knew that she had lost money. He doubted it was near that amount. He remained calm. His mind searched for solutions.

Herman Turner wasn't new to this job. He knew he should call the police. That could paint his business in a bad light. Let alone shed suspicion on his employees. Maybe even him. He thought the cops could possibly bring charges against Andreina. For smuggling money or something like that. Deep down, Herman was a good man. He weighed his options. Andreina appeared so naïve and honest.

"I will call the police," Herman said finally.

She nodded. She was still holding out some hope.

"What do I do now?" she implored

Herman Turner didn't answer.

"I have no money to pay for the room," she pleaded.

"I will give you a room for one night. Until you get in touch with your family and friends."

"The police?"

"The police will take a couple of hours. They will consider this as a non-emergency. You can wait in the room for them."

Hours later, two policemen came. They took a report and made lot of notes. They told her they would get back to her later. Andreina knew that they did not believe her story. Their expressions said it all. She doubted she would ever hear from them.

Andreina wept silently in her room. Her world had now fully collapsed. She had no family. No friends. She had been diagnosed with AIDS. She had no money. And she had nowhere to go.

She didn't sleep that night. When daylight came, her problems were still the same. Nothing had changed. She was no closer to answers. The tears came again.

It was midmorning before she moved. She reached into the bag with pills. She didn't feel like taking any. She hadn't eaten since the left the hospital. Her fingers found a card. It was for Elva. The social worker at the hospital. She had told her to call if she needed anything.

She stared at it. She played with the edges. An hour later, she mustered all the strength she could. She went down to the lobby. She asked to use the phone. She called Elva.

✝

With each passing day, Felipe got more concerned. The days appeared to drag. February 28 was still two weeks away. That was his deadline. He planned to make his move on February 27. He had almost all the information they promised. Enough to mortally wound his own cartel. Yet he couldn't shed the nervous, uneasy feeling. Inwardly, he didn't believe he would live through it.

Paul and Karissa's chances were even less, he thought. They were defenseless. They didn't belong to his world. They had no idea what the Medellin boys were capable of. They benefitted from the protection of Felipe and his men. Soon, they would be alone.

Felipe asked himself the same question over and over again. *Why did he agree to it?* He knew he had made a deal with the devil. He didn't have to. He had ridden his luck over the years. He had been very careful. He knew it didn't guarantee anything. Yet he could have continued life the way it was. He had chosen not just to rock the boat. He was trying to sink it.

At first, Felipe convinced himself that he did it for Paul. In some small way, to repay Paul. To alleviate his guilt for torturing him back in Venezuela. When Felipe got to know Paul, he discovered Paul was a good man. An innocent man. A good and caring doctor. So he was doing this to save Paul and his wife.

Felipe was no psychologist. But he knew that was only part of the truth. He himself hadn't decided to join the cartel. He was dragged into

248

it by Ramon. Over the years, he had caused enough death and destruction. Collateral damage, they called it.

Felipe wanted out too. For himself. He was so close to the finish line, he could almost touch it. Yet he had the feeling that something would go wrong. He would falter just before the end. Just like that last car he stole.

Felipe remained restless. Later that evening, he cruised past Paul's house. He recognized the vehicle of his men on watch. They knew his car. He saw Paul's car in the driveway. He decided to go in. It was a spur-of-the-moment decision, but it must have been bubbling under his conscious brain.

Paul greeted him at the door.

"Come in, Felipe."

"Sorry I didn't call."

"It's okay."

"Can we talk?"

"Sure."

Paul went to the fridge and brought out two Red Stripe lagers. Felipe took one and smiled.

"I promise to get done before I finish this," Felipe said guiltily.

"Take your time. Glad for the company."

"You must be bored," Felipe said lightly.

"Been home since the surgery."

"How did that go?" Felipe asked.

"Great."

"Laser?"

"A combination of laser and plastic surgery."

Felipe nodded.

"They can do magic with laser these days," Paul continued.

"I know," Felipe said. "Healing?"

"Just some lingering pain. I should be good by next week."

Felipe nodded. He had drifted off to something else. Paul was perceptive.

"What's bothering you, Felipe?" Paul asked.

Felipe was slow to respond, but he answered indirectly.

"Paul, I think we should bring forward the date."

"Why?"

"Lots of things happening in the cartels," Felipe said vaguely.

"February 28 is only two weeks away. I want to be at work for the last two weeks," Paul replied.

"It's better to do this earlier," Felipe said.

"I have lots of loose ends to tie up," Paul protested.

"I understand, Paul. But things have gotten nasty recently. There has been a lot of revenge killings last month. Lots of rookie killings. Men who have been with the cartels for a few months are executing others. They don't even know the rules of the game. They are just pulling the trigger. It's a dangerous time."

"So what's new?"

"It's bad, Paul. Really bad. Worse than it has been in years."

Paul didn't respond.

"Bottom line is I don't think we are safe," Felipe stated flatly.

Paul digested this and then asked. "What do you suggest?"

"Every extra day is a big risk."

"And?"

"We should move up the date," Felipe said.

"By how much?"

"A week," Felipe said.

"So we move next week?"

"Yes."

"Do you have everything ready?" Paul asked.

"Yes."

Silence.

"Well, almost. I need the location of two warehouses in Long Island. I should have it this week. That's about it."

"What should I do?" Paul asked.

Felipe had been planning this for months.

"Paul, listen carefully."

"I am listening."

"You need to follow my instructions to the letter."

"Go ahead."

"The business side is already taken care of. I will leave the info in a PO box. I plan to call Jimmy late that day. I will give them the bank account numbers. As soon as the money is deposited, I will tell them the number of the PO box and the exact location."

"Where is it?"

"Don't ask that question, Paul."

"Why not?"

"It is better if you don't know."

"Okay, what do I do?"

"You go to work and do everything you normally do. One day I will contact you. First thing you do is to find an excuse and have Karissa meet you at work."

"Okay."

"There will be a rented car parked close to yours at work. On the other side of the dumpster. The key will be under the mat in *your* car, driver's side. In the glove compartment of the rental, there will be an address in Florida. I want you and Karissa to leave your clinic as if you are going home. Then get on 95 South and drive all night. I will meet you at that location."

"Where in Florida?"

"Paul, please don't ask. It is South Florida. You should get there before midday the next day."

"And?"

"That's it for now, Paul."

Silence again.

"I know you didn't ask. The bank account numbers will be with the directions in the rental. I asked the money to be split in two accounts. Twenty-five million apiece. I will transfer the five million to you that we agreed upon."

"No, that's fine."

"I insist, Paul. It is two of you and one of me. I gave you my word."

Paul waited. Nothing else from Felipe.

"And when we get to Florida?"

"Paul, you have to trust me. The less you know the better. I have it covered. I will have multiple passports for you and Karissa. We are all leaving the country the same day. Separately. You will buy the airline tickets with cash. I will have the cash."

"Anything else?"

"Yes."

"What?"

"Do *not* take anything with you. Not even wedding pictures. Don't tell Karissa where you are going until she gets in the rental. *Please*."

"Felipe, you know that will be tough."

"It is for the best. Just this time, Paul. Her life is at stake."

Again, another pause.

"Okay, you can take your wedding ring," Felipe said, with a weak attempt at a smile.

"This house?"

"Again, Paul, please promise me that you won't take anything. Anything that is missing will raise suspicion that you planned to leave."

Paul nodded.

"It will be destroyed. Burnt to the ground. Professionally done."

"You?"

"I won't be here. My men will do it."

8

FROM ANY COWORKER'S POINT OF VIEW, IT WAS A ROUTINE Friday for Paul. He had had the same schedule for two years. On Friday mornings, he went to the hospice for terminally ill AIDS patients. In the afternoon, he took care of patients at his clinic. He knew today was his last Friday at the hospice. Yet he couldn't share that knowledge.

Paul pledged to give all his hospice patients an extra hug today. He knew that none of them would be alive in six months, barring a miracle. He bore loss after loss silently. He carried a heavy load. The common burden of all those who worked with AIDS at the time.

Paul parked his car on the side street. The Max Curtis House was located on Thirteenth Street in NW Washington, DC. It was a converted old building that housed between eight and twelve patients. They all had AIDS. Paul saw them weekly. Holiday or not, he didn't miss any week.

Most of his time was spent talking to them. Giving them his company and encouraging words. He prescribed comfort medicines whenever he could. In a few cases, he sent them to the hospital for blood transfusions. He considered this a comfort measure as it relieved their shortness of breath and extreme tiredness.

Most of the patients housed at the Max Curtis House had nowhere to go. Some had no family. Many were discarded by their families. The fear of contracting AIDS by family members often won out. They frequently dumped a sick member at the hospital. Then they refused to accept them back in the house.

In addition to illness, the residents here carried a heavy mental burden. Paul knew some of them from before. The ones who were cared for by his AIDS clinic. Some he met at the hospice for the first time. Usually transferred from the local hospitals. Frequently, a one-way trip.

Paul headed to the tiny office. Donald Hillebrandt ran a tight ship. He was a Physician Assistant by training. He had devoted most of his life to AIDS care. He leaned heavily on Paul Karan.

"How are you, Dr. Karan?" Donald asked.

"Doing well, thanks."

"Glad to see you."

"What do we have today?" Paul asked in his most cheerful voice.

"Things have been quiet this week. Just one new patient."

"No losses?"

"None since last Friday," Donald answered.

"Great."

"I have all the med refills for you in this folder. You just need to sign the highlighted area," Donald stated.

"You sure make my life easy, Donald."

"I do what I can. Imagine if I had to contact a different doctor for every patient."

"You are too kind."

Donald ignored the compliment. "New medications we have to send in separately. I know you like to order those after rounds."

"Yep. I'll get started."

"Thanks."

"See you back here in a couple of hours."

Paul had made himself a little doctor's bag. In addition to stethoscope, penlight, and other medical tools, he kept a few supplies. Gloves, gauze, syringes, blood tubes, and the like. Often times he would just draw the blood and take it back to the clinic. That way, he saved Donald the trouble of transporting a sick patient to the clinic just to get their hemoglobin checked.

Paul saw the least ill patients first. He knew all of their medical histories. He moved efficiently. He took the time to sit at the bedside of each one. Most of all, he did his utmost to appear unhurried. He knew the limits of what he could do for them. They knew it too. But they eagerly looked forward to his company each week.

He had seen most of the regulars when he glimpsed a patient who looked vaguely familiar. Likely the patient of one of his colleagues from the clinic, he thought. The patient was looking out of the window, facing away from him.

As usual, he fell behind his allotted time. It was midday when he got to the new patient. He picked up the medical chart and walked over. He pulled up a chair. He wanted to make a connection first. There was time enough to get into the complicated medical issues.

Paul stared at the new patient's face. He knew he had seen her somewhere before. He drew a blank. He couldn't come up with a name. She got up and looked at him in a strange way. She didn't speak. She continued to stare at him. Tears welled up in her eyes. Slowly they began streaming down her face. She started to move toward him. She stumbled and fell. He caught her before she hit the floor.

He knew she wasn't local. She looked different from the other patients.

"Paul." A hoarse voice escaped her thin, cracked lips.

It hit him like a ton of bricks.

"Andreina!"

9

LUIS ALVAREZ USUALLY GOT WHAT HE WANTED. OF RECENT
times, he always got what he wanted. He had money. Lots of it. Money brought
power. Now, he was working on his status. Skillfully and methodically.

His name was being etched relentlessly into the fabric of Cucuta. It was
everywhere. Luis Alvarez started with several large billboards. Schools, a
stadium, and a park had followed. He considered that just the beginning.
Money bought a lot around here.

Tonight his mood was sour. He summoned Benito, his younger brother,
to his quarters. When Benito arrived, he waved his two female companions
away. They disappeared into the vast expanse of the upper level of his castle.

"My brother!" Luis exclaimed.

Benito waited. Luis wanted something.

"Good to see you, little one."

"What can I do for you, big brother?"

Luis ignored the underlying sarcasm. "I have a job for you. One that
only you can do."

Benito waited. He knew what was coming.

"Nobody must know."

Benito waited.

Luis waited him out.

"What is it?" Benito finally asked.

"I want you to get rid of Munoz," Luis stated flatly.

"Mark?" Benito asked incredulously.

"Which Munoz do you think I was talking about?" Luis replied tartly.

"You've known Mark for years."

"So?"

"He is like family," protested Benito.

"Little brother, nobody disrespects Luis. Remember!"

256

"What did he do?"

"He is stealing from me."

"What?"

"I believe he is stealing my money."

"You have evidence?"

"I pay him very well. He has become a greedy pig."

Benito knew this was a useless argument. Luis had already made up his mind.

"When?"

"Tonight," Luis said.

"He is out?"

"No. He is at home."

"How do you know?"

"I spoke to him an hour ago."

"The man has five kids!" Benito protested one last time.

"The kids will be taken care of."

Benito decided to play Luis's game. "What else did he do, brother?"

Luis answered without hesitation.

"Last week, he was at the club with one of my women."

Benito understood. He knew how Luis's mind worked. As far as Luis was concerned, Mark Munoz had crossed the line. Mark had disrespected Luis. Many people would have seen him at the club. Now he must pay. Didn't matter that Luis had a new woman each week.

"I see," Benito said.

"I want Munoz gone by morning. *Comprende*, brother?"

"Understood."

Luis got up and patted Benito on the back.

Benito took a deep breath and headed out. He knew he would have to break the promise he had made to himself tonight. This is what he had become. A cold-blooded killer. He would have to use the drugs tonight. The same drugs he sold. In an effort to bury his conscience and guilt. The last bit of it that remained.

Just tonight, he promised himself.

10

PAUL GOT THROUGH HIS AFTERNOON CLINIC IN A DAZE. HE tried focusing, but his mind kept returning to the hospice. He promised Andreina that he would return after work. His heart was thumping as he pulled up outside the Max Curtis House.

Andreina was waiting. She had recovered somewhat from her shock. Her hair was combed back. It was still long and dark. She had even put a bit of makeup on. He hadn't recognized her that morning because of her weight loss. She was thin and drained. It had been years since he last saw her. She had recognized him right away.

Paul sat next to her. He pulled up his chair close. He didn't know what to say. Where to start. He had so many questions. They all seemed unimportant now. He touched her leg in a caring way. Her eyes fused with his. He saw a world of caring coming from her. He just hoped his gaze reflected the same.

"Paul?"

"Yes?"

"I have thought of you every day."

Paul didn't speak.

"Every day since you left Caracas."

"That is very sweet of you."

Andreina appeared to be absorbing his words. Then she began slowly again.

"How is Karissa?"

"She is well."

Another pause. Then she resumed.

"My last wish in life was to see you."

Paul waited.

"After I got to Washington … I didn't want to see you anymore."

She choked up. With much effort, she kept herself together.

"I have thought a lot about you too," Paul said.

"Really?"

"Yes."

"Did you think you would ever see me again?" Andreina asked.

"Honestly?"

She nodded.

"No," Paul replied.

"Are you glad to see me, Paul?"

"I am very happy to see you."

Neither of them wanted to go back. The silence was not awkward. However, the void was compelling them to fill it.

Finally, Andreina broke it. "Ramon is dead."

"I know," Paul said.

"Felipe?"

"Yes, he fills me in on these things."

She nodded again.

"You are still with them?" she asked.

It was a statement more than a question.

"I have no choice," Paul said.

"I know. I knew they wouldn't leave you alone."

"You were right," Paul agreed.

"They kill anybody who tries to get away."

Paul didn't know what to say. He looked at the floor. He was trapped between shame and guilt. He wanted to tell her, but he knew he shouldn't. He couldn't hold it back. He wouldn't give her any details, he promised himself.

"Felipe has been good to me," he started.

"Me too," Andreina said.

"One day, Andreina."

She waited.

"One day, I will break out of this."

She looked at him as if he weren't there. Her eyes appeared distant.

"I promise," Paul repeated.

She squeezed his hand tightly.

A few moments later, she said, "I believe you. I believe you, Paul."

He looked at her to gauge her conviction. Her eyes were earnest. She made it clear in her next statement.

"You did it before, Paul. You can do it again."

"Thank you, Andreina."

"You are the only one who I believe can do it."

Paul squeezed her hand. "Your support means a lot to me."

The fountain outside the hospice gurgled gently. The water ran smoothly down a statue. A hidden pump pulled it up, and it flowed down again. And again. It would continue until someone flipped the switch. They listened to the sound of the water. It was relaxing.

Andreina remained quiet for a while. Then she spoke again.

"I have AIDS," she said bluntly.

Paul wanted to say, *I know.* He couldn't bring himself to it. He couldn't decide on the right words. He didn't want to be insensitive. Yet he wanted to acknowledge what she said.

"I've read your chart," he finally said.

It still came out wrong. The conversation stopped. The joys of being a doctor, he thought. She didn't hold it against him.

"So you know I was in the hospital?"

"Yes."

"With pneumonia?"

"There is a discharge summary on your chart."

She waited.

"Donald got it from the hospital. It's here for every patient. That way, I know what to do."

"I understand."

"Thanks."

"They told me a doctor came here every week."

Paul nodded.

"I never dreamt it would be you."

"I come here every Friday morning," Paul said.

"Life is strange," Andreina said softly.

"Yes, it is."

"I had given up hope of seeing you," Andreina continued.

Paul didn't know how to respond. Involuntarily, he sidestepped.

"How long since you have been in DC?" Paul asked.

"Four weeks," she answered.

"A lot has happened in that time," Paul said. He was thinking about her eventful hospital stay.

"Yes. A lot," Andreina agreed.

She didn't tell him about the money. She didn't tell him that she was destitute and homeless. That the social worker, Elva, had placed her here. It wasn't important anymore.

She was just happy to have found him. He had put aside everything to come to spend time with her. That was priceless. She would enjoy it.

He appeared to understand her illness. She was accepting. He wasn't quite yet. Maybe it was still too fresh for him, she thought.

"I will die here," she said.

"No you won't."

"Paul, my time has come."

"Not yet," he insisted. He wasn't thinking clearly.

"I have made my peace," Andreina said, as calm as ever.

"I reviewed your chart, Andreina. Your T cell count is still good. I will try to get you on some new medications. We can still fight this thing," he pleaded.

She looked at him with a smile. Her voice was unruffled. "For how long, Paul?"

He didn't answer. He didn't know the answer. She didn't want to go back. She didn't want to get her hopes up again. Just to have them stamped out one more time. She wasn't going to fight this fight again.

"I don't want to do anything, Paul."

He shook his head.

"Will you at least think about it?" he insisted.

She studied him carefully.

"I will," she said.

Paul fidgeted. He knew it was late and he should go. He didn't want to leave her alone.

She helped him out. "I know you have to go."

He nodded.

"I understand," Andreina said.

"I can come on Sunday afternoon to see you," he offered.

She smiled. "That would be nice."

He got up. She joined him.

"Paul, will you allow me to say something?"

He looked closely at her.

"Something very personal?"

"Anything, Andreina."

Andreina closed the two steps between them. She held both of his shoulders. She looked up at him. "Please do not say anything."

He nodded.

She leaned her head against his chest and neck. Almost inaudibly she spoke.

"I love you, Paul."

✝

Jimmy Martinez didn't like the waiting game. Every day, he was getting more impatient and irritated. He had too many eggs in one basket. They had bought Tomas. They had bought Paul and Felipe. Their next move was totally dependent on Felipe. He had to proceed with caution, he reminded himself.

Jimmy pulled out his cell phone. Steve Johnson had just come out of a meeting. It was county government business. Johnson was impatient throughout the meeting. He didn't need any money from the job. It was just a front. A front and good connections. Next time, he would come up with a better excuse to skip it. His cell phone buzzed.

"Didn't I tell you not to call me here?" Johnson snapped.

"Relax, Johnson. It's a disposable cell phone. It can't be traced," Martinez replied.

"Couldn't it wait for later?"

"No."

Johnson offered no response.

"Did you confirm it?" Martinez asked.

"Yes it was him."

"Positive?"

"The police identified the body as Tomas. The Cali boys got him first."

"Great," Martinez said with disgust. "Now we are left with the doctor and Felipe."

"Looks like it," Johnson replied.

"That's not my worry." Martinez was still hot.

"Well, we didn't pay him too much," Johnson consoled.

"Beside the point," Martinez hissed.

Johnson waited.

"The real problem is how much he spilled. How much he squealed before he croaked," Martinez said.

"Maybe, he didn't," Johnson said.

"Look, Johnson, I wasn't born yesterday."

Johnson didn't contradict him. Instead he changed topics.

"The doctor and Felipe will come through," Johnson reassured him.

"If not?"

"We will eliminate them."

"That's the easy part, Johnson. But we still need the intel."

"Stay calm, Jimmy. We will get it."

"We have to take this thing out from the root," Martinez ranted.

Johnson didn't reply.

"You know what would happen if we killed them?" Martinez asked. "Nothing would change. The underlings will just step up."

Johnson sidestepped. "Do you think they will flee?"

"Sure, they will," Martinez said.

"Should we pick them off before?"

"Do nothing until we get the info," Martinez cautioned.

"After?"

"DC is your territory. Your call."

"I don't like loose ends."

"If you want, you can take them out. Again, not before we get everything!"

"I am not stupid, Jimmy."

"If I were you, I wouldn't put too much effort into it."

"Why?"

"They can't hurt us by themselves. Plus, that doctor is smart."

"Book smart maybe," Johnson mumbled.

"He survived a long time outside his world, Steve."

"That is because of Felipe."

"That too. Felipe is a veteran."

"I know."

"Steve, a friendly bet?"

"What?"

"I bet they'll be long gone before we get the goods."

"You're on. A hundred grand I pick them off before they flee."

11

IT WAS AROUND 2:00 A.M. SUNDAY MORNING WHEN PAUL'S
home phone rang. He wasn't on call this weekend. His initial thought was
Felipe. Who else would disturb him at this time?

It wasn't Felipe. It was Donald Hillebrandt.

"Can I speak to Dr. Karan, please?"

His formal voice already told Paul that all was not well.

"This is Paul Karan."

"Paul, I need your help."

"Yes?"

"I am at the Max Curtis home. One of the residents passed away."

Paul had heard this many times in the past. They rarely called him in
the middle of the night, as the deaths were expected. He usually found
out from Donald the next morning.

"Okay?"

"The police are here. They want to take the body."

Paul held his breath but didn't ask for a name. There were several very
ill patients at the hospice. Donald would give him the details soon enough.

"Why?"

"Well, there isn't a doctor of record. So unless someone is willing to
sign the death certificate, it would be a coroner's case."

"Who is it, Donald?"

"Well, you only saw her once. The new patient. Andreina."

Paul felt his insides churn. His heart was thumping in his chest. The
pit of his stomach tightened. His fingers got cold. His worse fears had
been realized. He temporarily lost his voice.

"Paul?"

"I am here."

"Are you comfortable doing it?"

"I will be right over. I should be there in about thirty minutes."

"The police?"

"Tell the police I will pronounce her. If they can't wait, let them know I will take care of it."

Paul's calm voice concealed his turmoil. Many years of training made him that way. It was a lie to his true self. His voice was a direct contradiction to his emotions. He hung up the phone. Slowly and deliberately, he reached for his clothes.

Traffic was sparse at this hour. He got there in under thirty minutes. His brain was in a loop. He couldn't get out of it. He had seen Andreina just thirty-six hours earlier. She was doing relatively well. He was planning to visit her later today. What happened? This was not an expected death.

Donald was waiting for him. One police officer was still present. The rest had left when Donald told them Dr. Karan would assume responsibility. They were glad to. They had more important things to do than dealing with the death of an AIDS patient. Especially on a late Saturday night.

Donald filled Paul in on the details. Andreina had had lunch with the other residents. Everything was fine according to them. They didn't see her for dinner. One of the residents got concerned and went to look for her around midnight. She couldn't rouse Andreina. They called Donald.

Donald came over immediately. He found her dead. He didn't bother to call 911. He thought she had been dead for more than an hour.

Paul stool in the lobby with Donald. He processed everything in silence. He finally made up his mind and headed to the room. He took a deep breath. He opened the door and went in.

There she was, lying on the bed. A smile on her thin face. Calm and peaceful. Just like she was on Friday evening. She had some makeup on.

Paul reached over and felt for a pulse. The doctor in him was on autopilot. None in the wrist. He moved his hands to her neck. None in her neck. No need for a stethoscope. She wasn't breathing. She had moved on to another world. Hopefully one that was better for her. This one had not been particularly kind to her, he thought.

Paul opened the drawer of her bedside dresser. He saw her medication bottles. One of them was completely empty. It was a sedative that had been given to her in the hospital. He connected the dots. He didn't say anything to anyone. Not even Donald.

He made up his mind, right there. He didn't want her body to be mutilated by an autopsy. It was the least he could do. Nobody would question a death certificate with cause of death as AIDS and pneumonia. He would be stating the truth. Just not the present truth.

Paul held Andreina's hand. It was still warm. He stood there for two full minutes, staring at her face. He lightly stroked the side of her cheek. Then he bent over and kissed her forehead.

He stepped out of the room and nodded to Donald. He was waiting just outside the door.

"I will sign the death certificate as the physician of record."

"Thanks," Donald replied.

"They can take the body," Paul said in an even voice.

Without another word, Paul headed to his car. He closed the door and sat there. Then he allowed himself to cry. Gently at first. Then the floodgates opened.

Paul sobbed and wailed. Out of sight from everyone. He felt his pain by himself. He didn't know how to share it. He didn't know how to explain it.

Like so many other doctors before him, he suffered alone. He had been sent to war without any protection. They didn't teach this in medical school.

✝

It was getting light in the sky when Paul finally got home. He went into the house but didn't go upstairs. He sat on the couch and stared at the wall. He was thinking about everything, but he was thinking about nothing. A calmness had come over him. In the midst of his tumultuous feelings, an odd tranquility surfaced.

He wasn't sure how long he sat there before he heard footsteps. Karissa came down the stairs and sat next to him. She knew something was really wrong. She placed her hand on his knee without saying a word. He didn't speak either. He had told her he was going to the hospital when he had left hours earlier.

Eventually, she asked, "Everything okay?"

He shook his head, indicating no.

"You can talk to me," she said encouragingly.

He didn't answer. He wasn't sure what to say.

She didn't pry.

Then it came out suddenly.

"Andreina is dead," he said.

She didn't answer right away. She wasn't expecting that. She didn't know how to respond.

After some time, Karissa said, "I am sorry to hear that."

"Me too."

"In Caracas?" Karissa asked.

"No. She was here."

"Where?"

"Here, in DC."

"How long?"

"Not sure. I saw her only once."

"When?"

"Friday."

Karissa looked at him strangely.

"Is that why to you had to leave in the middle of the night?"

"Yes."

"She was a patient of yours?" Karissa stated more than asked.

"Sort of. I saw her at the AIDS hospice this week."

"She had AIDS?"

"Unfortunately, yes."

Karissa gave him a long look. One he wasn't sure how to interpret. She didn't ask him anything. However, he felt obliged to respond.

"I am not infected with HIV, Karissa."

She remained silent.

"I have had four negative HIV tests in the last two years. Two with routine physicals. One when I was stuck with a needle, drawing blood from an AIDS patient. Another one for the life insurance physical," Paul explained.

She still didn't answer. He wasn't sure if he was speaking for his benefit or hers. It all came out unexpectedly.

Karissa just sat next to him. She kept her hand on his leg. She sat there for long time.

Karissa finally spoke. "I am not worried about that, Paul."

"What?"

"I am not worried that you have HIV."

Paul didn't answer.

"I am worried about *you*."

"What are you worried about?"

"Exactly that, Paul. You don't even know."

"Know what?"

"This has been going on for so long that it has become you. It is consuming you, Paul. Every day, Felipe this, Felipe that! Late-night meetings. Strangers coming to the house at all hours in the night. AIDS patients every day. You keep most of it to yourself. This is too much for anybody to handle!"

Paul didn't say anything. He wasn't sure if the stress was overwhelming her.

"It is hard for me to remember the happy-go-lucky Paul. The one that I met years ago. The one that is buried somewhere inside of you."

He knew she was correct. He had lost perspective of his own life. She sat with him for a while longer. Then she squeezed his leg and got up. She went upstairs without saying another word.

Paul didn't know what to do. He reflected on what Karissa had just said. His brain was getting scrambled again. He picked up his coat and walked out on the deck.

✝

Paul sat in one of the deck chairs. The early morning was cold. The sun climbed slowly above the horizon. He stared at the trees. They appeared lifeless. He knew they would be filled with thick green leaves in two months. He hoped that he too could regenerate one more time.

Paul sat on the deck for hours—immobile but fully awake. The sun had reached high in the sky before Paul moved. He became aware that his fingers were freezing. He eventually got up and went inside.

He picked up the phone and called Felipe.

"Andreina is dead," Paul stated flatly.

"I am sorry to hear that," Felipe replied with genuine compassion in his voice.

"Did you know she was in DC?" Paul asked.

"No, I didn't."

"You don't seem surprised."

"I knew she had left Caracas. I didn't know where she went," Felipe said.

"Her death?"

"People there told me she wasn't looking well."

"And you didn't tell me?"

"Since Ramon's death, nobody was too concerned with her."

"I see," Paul said sharply.

"Sorry. I didn't mean it that way, Paul."

Felipe was getting defensive. Paul picked up on it. Paul was still angry. Felipe was not to blame.

Paul took a moment and collected his thoughts.

"Felipe, I would like us to postpone everything."

"Can't."

"Just for a week or two."

"Why?"

"Andreina has no one here. I would to like make the funeral arrangements. I want to have a service for her."

"Paul, I understand your feelings."

"But?"

"We can't."

"Why?" It was Paul's turn.

"Paul, I beg you. We have to go next week."

"Why?"

"It is getting really dangerous, Paul. They killed Tomas the day before yesterday. Every extra day is a huge risk."

Paul didn't have the energy to argue. He knew Felipe was right. Death was final. He would leave one more body in the freezer. He would pretend that life went on as usual.

Paul had done this hundreds of times with his patients. He never attended any funerals. He never knew the real reason until now. He couldn't handle it. It was his warped way of protecting himself.

Paul also knew the hospice would have a small funeral for Andreina. They usually did for their unclaimed residents. He doubted there would be a dozen people present. He hoped that Donald would be present. He conceded one last time.

"Okay. We stick to your plan."

271

12

"Good morning, Rick."

"Good morning, Doc."

"How are we doing today?"

Paul was cheerful with his patients as always. He was seeing his last patient for the morning session. It was just past noon on Wednesday. Rick didn't correct his doctor on the time of the day.

"Much better. The nausea is gone. My appetite has improved," Rick said.

"Great!"

Paul felt his phone vibrate. He looked at the number. It was Felipe. He excused himself and stepped out of the exam room.

"Today," Felipe said.

"What?"

"Today is the day."

"Just like that?"

"The rental will be parked next to your car," Felipe stated.

"Really?"

"Yes, Paul."

"You could have warned me."

"The only reason I am calling is to give you time to get Karissa."

"I am in the middle of patients," Paul protested.

"See you tomorrow, Paul."

The phone went dead.

Paul was in a daze. He struggled to get through the afternoon session of the clinic. His heart rate stayed above a hundred the entire time. He told no one anything. He pretended that it was business as usual. He knew it was the last time he would be seeing these patients. The same was true for his colleagues and coworkers.

He called Karissa during a break between patients. He convinced her to join him for an impromptu dinner. They would go to a place near work. She didn't need much convincing. However, his subsequent requests puzzled her. He had asked her not to drive his work place. He insisted she park at the Silver Spring Metro Station then use the Red Line to meet him at work in DC.

At five thirty, Paul left the clinic with Karissa. He stayed until most of the staff had left. He headed directly to the rental. Karissa's bewilderment resurfaced.

"What's going on, Paul?"

"Hop in."

"Where are going?"

"We are going for a drive. I'll explain along the way."

"A long drive?"

"Yes."

"Overnight?"

"Yes."

'I didn't bring anything with me."

"That's okay. You can get some stuff later."

"Where?"

"Florida."

She looked at him as if he were crazy.

"Are you out of your mind?" she asked.

Paul didn't answer. Instead, he pulled onto Fourteenth Street. He headed north out of DC. He snaked along Georgia Avenue. Traffic was heavy as rush hour was in full flow.

Paul was noticeably jumpy. He saw a black Ford Taurus in his rearview mirror. When he saw the same car a mile later, he thought he was being followed. He pulled into a gas station. Fortunately, the car passed him. His heart dropped down a few beats.

From Georgia Avenue, he took Piney Branch Road. He continued on to New Hampshire Avenue north. He exited on to 495. Then he made his way to 95 South.

Paul drove for a couple of hours. The traffic leaving the DC Beltway was, not unexpectedly, heavy. It was well after dark before he pulled off at an exit north of Richmond, Virginia. In a McDonald's parking lot, he finally took out the directions from the glove compartment. The address was in Loxahatchee, Florida.

There were clear, concise directions—all told, just over a thousand miles. It was simple enough. Take 95 South all the way to Palm Beach, Florida. Exit on Northlake Blvd. Make a left on Pratt Whitney Road and a left on Sixty-Eighth Street. The house number was 14296.

A note from Felipe was included. There were three simple instructions.

Don't call.

Use cash for everything, even gas.

I will meet you there.

A roll of twenty-dollar bills was included. Maybe six or seven hundred dollars. Paul didn't count it. Felipe thought of everything.

Finally, he gave Karissa the full explanation. She listened without interruption. Life as they knew it was over. They were going to make a break for freedom. He was confident that they would make it out alive. He sounded more confident than he felt. He knew the odds were against them. He couldn't leave her behind, he explained. They would get to her as soon as he and Felipe disappeared. He apologized once more to Karissa.

Karissa understood. She protested at first. Mainly about having to leave her precious things in the house. Then she became quiet and thoughtful. She insisted that she wanted to be with Paul. For better or for worse, she would travel the path. He had her full support, she reassured him.

"I want you to take a nap," Paul said.

"Why?"

"I need your help driving. We have to get there by midday tomorrow."

She nodded. She squeezed his hand. It was silent consent and reassurance. Paul appreciated the support. It boosted his optimism.

It was around three in the morning. They were well into South Carolina. The roads were empty except for an occasional truck. They were making good time.

Paul's mind began to drift. He was on his second stint of driving. Karissa had dozed off. The monotony of the drive and the lack of conversation allowed his brain to wander. It went into a loop. Try as he might, he couldn't get it unstuck.

It kept returning to Monday afternoon in the church. The church in Anacostia in South East, DC. He was living the experience all over again. His brain had taken a battering. So much had happened in the last week. Now his thoughts were punishing him. Repeatedly.

The night after Andreina's death, he had a call from a coworker. His administrative assistant's teenage son, Tyrone, had been killed in a motor vehicle accident. He had known the boy's mother, Gloria, for years. She took care of the office and its many daily demands, allowing Paul more time with patients. She exemplified kindness and doing for others.

The funeral service was on Monday afternoon. For reasons unclear to him, Paul decided to go. He didn't think it through. He thought it was because he couldn't be there for Andreina. He had shunned all his patients' funerals over the years. Too busy and not really expected to attend was the reason he gave himself. He knew that wasn't the whole truth. He had been protecting himself all along.

Tyrone was not a patient of his. He was the son of a close coworker. Paul thought he would be safe. That he wouldn't be opening his emotional vault. He couldn't have been more wrong.

The coffin was already present when Paul got to the church. Most of the clinic staff was there. Gloria was like family to everyone. Even with Gloria's family and friends, the back section of the large church was unoccupied. Paul sat in the fifth or sixth row. He sat next to two of the clinic's medical clerks.

Paul listened to the minister welcoming those present and saying a prayer. Then he explained something about the Lord having a plan for everyone. He continued on, saying a special plan must have been there for

Tyrone. The boy was only sixteen. The atmosphere was heavy and thick with grief. His voice bounced over the walls and just hung there.

Then the singing began. It made a soundtrack for his thoughts. Paul stared at the walls. He stared at the high ceiling. Soon he didn't hear the words. Or the songs. The melody swirled in the air and settled over him.

The pain of mourning was palpable. The grief was alive and real. As the harmonious voices rose, Paul felt weightless. His body lifted off the pew. It rose upward. Halfway to the high ceiling, it stopped. Then it suspended itself there.

One by one, his patients appeared before him. Many of them surrounded him. From a comfortable distance. Looking at him from the walls of the church. Staring at his face as if they were alive. Not angry with him. Nor were they scary. They just smiled at him.

They wanted to connect with him one more time. To thank him. To let him know that they were not mad at him. Even though he had failed them. The more than two hundred who had died under his care. The majority under the age of thirty. With every one of them, he had tried everything. And he had failed. The weight of which he carried every day. The burden, he thought, he would carry to his own grave.

They were asking him. They were pleading with him. To give up of some of the burden. That they would be happy to share the load with him. They were his angels of help.

Paul imagined how each of them would have had funeral services. Their loved ones, family, and friends would have been present. But the one whom they had trusted with their life was not there. The one whom they had trusted for the months and years before their final service was absent. He didn't show up for the last goodbye.

Him. Dr. Paul Karan.

He had been missing in action. Every time.

The guilt came in waves. The torture was intolerable. As the singing continued, Paul felt his head tighten. He couldn't describe the feelings. It was not just grief. It was sadness and grief, despair, and guilt all rolled into one.

He now understood why he came to Tyrone's funeral service. It was to live what he hadn't lived with all his patients. The only chapter he didn't live with them.

Karyn was one of the medical clerks who sat next to Paul. She was heavyset and always pleasant to be around. Paul didn't know she could sing. But sing, she could. As her voice reached a feverous pitch, everyone was mesmerized. It rose and fell. It was touching and haunting. It was spellbinding and hypnotizing. It was compelling and transfixing. All at the same time.

When she carried a high note to fruition, Paul felt his brain would explode. He wanted to get up and run. Run far away from the church. Into oblivion. Into the cavernous hole he had created in himself. The one place he had partitioned off from his patients. And die there. But he stayed. This time, he forced himself to stay. He would stay until the end.

When Karyn finished, Paul found himself still seated. He was clutching the wooden pew. His fingernails were white. Slowly he exhaled. Bit by bit, his breathing returned to normal. It was an experience that he knew right there he would never forget. One that would stay with him for the rest of his life. However long he lived.

Karissa stirred next to him. She peered over.

"Are you sleepy, honey?" she asked.

"No."

"Do you want me to take over?"

"In another hour. Thanks."

Momentarily, it brought him back to the present. A few minutes later, Karissa dozed off again. It was the wee hours of the morning. The long road ahead was empty. Even the occasional truck was sparser now. He had no company.

Soon after, the loop replayed itself.

And then again.

13

PAUL AND KARISSA MADE GOOD TIME. JUST BEFORE 11:00 a.m., Paul pulled off Pratt Whitney Road and onto Sixty-Eighth Street. The houses were well spaced. Each property was at least two acres. House number 14296 was on the right side at the end of the street. The street dead-ended onto the bank of a drainage canal.

The house looked abandoned. An old pickup truck was parked under a small shed. Paul turned into the driveway. He pulled up next to the pickup truck.

Karissa looked around nervously. Before Paul could get out of the vehicle, the side door opened. Felipe peeked out. He motioned for them to come in.

Felipe greeted them each with a big hug.

"You made it," he said, sounding rather elated.

"We did," Paul answered. "So did you."

"Our luck has been good so far," Felipe replied, keeping the conversation very general.

Karissa glanced around the house. It was a one-level house. The doors of the rooms facing the living room were closed. There was no sign of other occupants.

Felipe answered her unspoken question. "No one is here. We are alone."

Paul didn't bother to ask Felipe about the house. Felipe appeared to have a myriad of resources. Whilst Paul was attending to patients, Felipe had been very busy.

Felipe picked up a laptop that was sitting on a table. He handed it to Paul.

"Please check to see if your money has been deposited," Felipe said.

"And if it's not?"

Felipe sidestepped the question. "Mine is already there."

"We can't take back the information," Paul answered.

"Wrong."

"What?"

"I gave them only about one quarter of it. The rest will be given tonight. When all the money has been transferred."

"How do you plan to do that?"

"Paul, I told you not to worry about these things. If you really want to know, I will tell you this time. Today is the last day I will be seeing you."

"I am curious."

"First, I don't trust the Medellin guys. They would back out of a deal if they could. Then they will kill you. Money is all that matters to them. They won't shell out fifty million if they don't have to."

Paul waited.

"I left some of the information in a PO box. It wasn't accessible till 8:00 a.m. this morning. I detailed the instructions to deposit our money in the listed accounts. After we verify that the money is there, I will send the details of the second PO box. That will be sent after close of business today."

"Where is it?"

"The documents are already there. It is in a US postal facility in Wheaton. I personally placed them there. They won't have access to it until tomorrow morning. By that time, we will not be in this country."

Paul nodded. He wasn't sure whether to say thanks. He was sure of one thing. He could not have pulled this off without Felipe. He just didn't have the background to.

Felipe pointed to his laptop again. Paul got working. He remembered his account number. He had chosen it carefully. After a few security questions, he logged in. *The money was already deposited.*

"It's there," Paul said.

"Good," Felipe said.

"So does this mean they have gotten the first package?" Paul asked.

279

Felipe switched on the TV. It was on CNN.

"Look," he said.

Paul and Karissa saw live pictures of a huge fire. It was in Berkeley Springs, West Virginia. Under the picture was captioned, Cement Plant.

They looked at Felipe questioningly.

"That was in the first package," he said.

Felipe saw puzzled faces. He provided them with the explanation.

"That is an abandoned cement plant. It was one of our storage facilities. It is off Route 70, about ninety minutes from DC. They have already acted on the intelligence we provided. They must have already had it on their radar. We just provided the confirmation."

"They move quickly," Paul said.

"They do. They will try to wipe out the competition in the next few days. Before Luis gets time to move stuff around."

Karissa was fidgeting. A lot of this sounded like Greek to her. She didn't know what to do. Her discomfort came through. She finally spoke up. "What do we do now?"

"Can you kindly give me your purse?" Felipe asked.

"What for?"

"I am sure Paul explained that after today, you will no longer be Karissa Karan."

She stared at Felipe blankly.

Paul nodded gently in her direction. She handed over her pocketbook. Paul provided his wallet.

Felipe flipped the switch of the fireplace. He removed the cash. He then tossed the purse and wallet into the fire. Credits cards, ID cards, and other identifying document went up in smoke.

Paul felt a sadness creeping through him. Karissa felt it too. The reality was sinking in. The identity of Paul and Karissa Karan was being eliminated. In front their very eyes.

Felipe was now in full control. Paul was in the unaccustomed role of being the dependent. He was sure that Felipe had the next moves planned.

"Mind sharing what we do next?"

Paul tried to appear conversational. He was anxious on the inside. His stomach churned, and he felt his heart racing.

"I'll tell you what I can."

Paul and Karissa held their collective breaths and waited.

"First, you both need some rest. It has been a long ride," Felipe said. He paused.

"This afternoon, we drive to nearby Wellington. We'll do some shopping. Suitcases, clothes, and other personal items that you might need. We will leave the rental in the back of a Wal-Mart parking lot. They will take a couple of days to find it. That will give us enough time."

He paused again. He then spoke slowly.

"I have arranged a ride. It will take you to Miami Airport. I will meet you in a parking garage next to the terminal. At exactly 7:00 p.m. It should be dark by then. I will have all your passports and cash. It will be the last time you will be seeing me."

They both stared at Felipe as if they were seeing him for the first time."

"The rest is up to you. You and God."

Paul exhaled. He squeezed Karissa's hand. This chapter was coming to an end. But he couldn't relax just yet. He couldn't sleep either.

✝

The driver didn't speak to them. He wore dark sunglasses. Much darker than the tinted windows of the car. He was all business.

He appeared to know the area well. He moved through the late-afternoon traffic decisively. They headed south on the freeway. At fifteen minutes to seven, he pulled into a covered parking lot. It was opposite the American Airlines terminal. He parked at the far end of the garage.

He sat there and waited. Paul and Karissa didn't know what to say. The silence became uncomfortable. The tension rose. Ten minutes appeared like an hour. At exactly three minutes before seven, he turned and faced them.

"Wait in the car," he said.

"Okay," Paul croaked.

"Felipe will be here shortly."

The precision in which he moved indicated to Paul that he was no layman. His English was slightly accented. He was tall and well muscled. This was a seasoned professional, Paul thought.

He must have sensed their apprehension. He glanced over his shoulder.

"Felipe is a friend of mine," he said.

He opened the driver's side door and got out before they could respond. He disappeared into the darkness. Paul and Karissa were like fish out of water. They just sat and waited.

Seven o'clock came and went. No sign of Felipe.

Five minutes later, a figure emerged from the shadows. He approached the car. He opened the door to the driver's seat and got in. It was Felipe.

"Sorry about that," he said.

"Good to see you, Felipe," Paul said.

"I couldn't risk coming with you. Too many people here know me."

This was not the Felipe that Paul knew over the years. Maybe he wasn't looking for this Felipe. Maybe he liked the image of Felipe as a friend, he thought. He preferred the Felipe having a beer in his house in Silver Spring.

This was a confident, professional, self-assured, highly complex man. One who had survived for years just below the top rung of a major drug cartel. One who had shielded Paul and Karissa with his life.

"We got here okay," Paul mumbled.

"I want both of you to listen carefully."

Paul nodded. He wasn't sure if Felipe saw him in the dark.

"I have three passports for each of you. They are all man and wife. They have the same last name. Pick one and use it to get on a flight tonight. Before midnight."

"Okay," Paul muttered.

"Hide the other two. Make sure you memorize the name you are using."

"Where do we go?" Karissa asked. Her voice reeked of apprehension.

Felipe's tone softened. He sometimes forgot that she had been dragged into this world. A world of which she knew nothing.

"Doc is a very resourceful man. I know he has some ideas. He had been thinking about this for a while."

"Any suggestions, Felipe?" Paul asked.

"This airport has many options. I don't want to know your destination. In case I get caught."

For once, Paul appreciated Felipe calling him "doc." It meant that they were still close. It felt almost endearing.

"Buy all tickets with cash. Cross the Atlantic at least once," Felipe instructed.

"Thanks, Felipe. You think of everything."

"I try."

They were silent for a moment.

"Things will still come up, Paul. You will have to work them out on your own."

"I am sure," Paul said.

"Doc, I have confidence in you. I wouldn't have done this if I didn't think you had a chance. You can pull this off."

"Thanks."

They were silent again.

Paul spoke first. "Anything else?"

"Yes. One thing," Felipe replied.

They waited.

"Paul, *please* do not practice medicine. Any kind of medicine. For at least the next two years. Doesn't matter where you go."

"Why do you think I would?"

"I know you. You will be tempted to help people. But that would make it easier for them to find you."

"Two years is a long time."

"Well, at least a year and a half. I think they will stop looking for you all after about a year. It all depends on if they eliminate Luis. If they don't, both Luis and Medellin might find you quite attractive."

"I see."

"I don't need to say this, but I will. Do not attempt to contact your family. Under no circumstances."

"I understand."

"I don't like this goodbye thing, Paul. But it is time."

Felipe reached over and squeezed Karissa's shoulder. He then got out of the car. Paul got out. The two men embraced. There were no words.

Felipe quickly faded in the darkness. Paul watched him go. It was hard to believe that he wouldn't see Felipe again. He owed his life and Karissa's life to him. But more than his being his protector, Felipe was the only one who knew. The only one who knew the entirety of Paul's double life.

Felipe was his only real friend.

†

Paul just stood there. He remained motionless for a couple of minutes. He didn't know what to do. Finally, he opened the door of the car.

"Let's go," he said to Karissa.

Karissa got out of the car. Her movements were measured. They took their luggage out of the trunk. One suitcase apiece and a carry-on bag. They headed for the terminal. The wheels in Paul's head were turning swiftly. Much faster than those of the suitcases.

Paul and Karissa headed for the elevated walkway that connected the garage and the terminal building. As they were leaving the garage, he heard footsteps. Paul stopped and looked at Karissa. She nodded. She had heard it too.

He looked around. He saw no one in the poorly lit garage. With the shadows and the parked SUVs, hiding places were plentiful.

They continued walking. The footsteps resumed. They stopped again. Silence.

Paul quickened his walk. Karissa kept pace at his side. He was sure they were being followed. His nervousness was contagious. Karissa glanced furtively from side to side.

They entered the terminal building. It was teeming with people. They should be safe here, he thought. Paul looked back suddenly. He glimpsed a face. The person quickly ducked behind a crowd of people.

"The bathroom," he whispered to Karissa.

The male and female restrooms faced each other. Paul dashed into the men's room. Karissa disappeared into the women's. The unspoken plan was to regroup after a few minutes.

The restroom was huge. Paul got into a stall at the far end. He locked the door.

Twenty feet away, a man was using the urinals. Paul heard the jiggle of his belt. Then the water from the sink. Finally the hand drier. Then silence. From the sequence sounds, he knew the man had left.

Paul put the lid down. He sat on the seat. He heard the footsteps. The same deliberate ones he had heard earlier. He pulled his feet up so it wouldn't be seen under the door. He held his breath and waited.

The footsteps came closer. He suddenly realized that his luggage was resting on the floor. It would be visible under the door. He was trapped.

Paul was unarmed. He was defenseless. A sitting duck. He saw the large black shoes of a man. He saw black trousers. Through the tiny crack in the door, he tried to see a face. No luck. He froze, awaiting his fate.

Suddenly there was a lot of commotion. A group of teenage soccer players invaded the bathroom. They must have been travelling as a team. At least ten came into the restroom. They saved Paul. For the moment anyway.

He prayed that they would stay for a while. They were in no hurry. But eventually they all left. Other people came and left the restroom. Paul just sat there. For how long he wasn't sure.

He started to worry about Karissa. He tried to reassure himself that she was safe. A man entering a busy, public female restroom would attract attention, he reasoned. But it didn't relieve his distress. Nothing was beyond these guys. He decided to get up and find her.

He was about to make his move when he heard footsteps again. This time they were quicker. They came straight to his stall. His heart stopped.

A gentle tap on the door. He wasn't expecting that.

Then a vaguely familiar voice said. "You can come out."

Paul hesitated.

"It's safe," the voice continued.

He knew the voice. Paul cautiously opened the door.

Staring at him was their driver. The one who had picked them up them from Loxahatchee. The same one who had left them in the car to wait from Felipe.

He looked at Paul. Paul looked at him.

"I took care of him," the driver said.

Paul didn't know what to say. He was trying to decide between a bodyguard and a guardian angel.

"Thanks," Paul muttered.

The driver nodded.

"A friend of Felipe is a friend of mine."

With that, he turned and disappeared once again. Out of the restroom and into the crowded airport terminal. Paul had a feeling they were being guarded. They would be watched until they boarded a plane.

His respect for Felipe grew. There was no chance that the driver's appearance was random.

✝

When Paul finally emerged from the restroom, Karissa was waiting patiently.

"What took you so long?" she asked worriedly.

Paul relayed the events to her. Her anxiety changed to relief when he told her that the threat was removed by their driver. She didn't ask how. He didn't know how. She didn't want to know.

"We should get going," Paul reminded her.

The departure monitor for American Airlines was full as usual. Flights to pretty much any part of the world were listed. Paul read through the destinations from Miami. He deliberated over their choices. Felipe had indirectly guided them. The three passports he gave them were Canadian,

German, and English. He started toward the American Airlines ticket counter.

"Where are we heading?" Karissa whispered.

"Right now, Brazil."

"Brazil?"

"More specifically, Sao Paulo."

"Are we going to stay there?"

"No. Just a short trip."

Paul took out the passports and gave her the Canadian one.

"For now, we are Canadians," he said.

She looked at him nervously. He tried to smile. Karissa noticed the effort was strained. She appreciated it anyway.

"Think they will notice my accent?" she asked.

"Doubt it, but try to speak as little as possible," Paul replied.

"Suits me fine."

"How so?"

"You are the one who usually does most of the talking."

He was happy with her little dig. Her head was clearing. She was closer to baseline. That meant a more level head. That they could use right now.

They got tickets without any hiccups. To Sao Paulo and retuning to Toronto in a week. They were Canadian tourists going to Brazil for a week. No one really cared. Least of all the ticketing agent.

Paul held Karissa's hand as they headed for the gate. The flight was due to leave at 11:00 p.m. It was listed as eight and half hours. Nonstop. He knew they would get there by 7:00 a.m. The usual thirty-minute over-estimate, just in case.

He was anxious for them to get on the airplane as soon as possible. He could smell it. The first big step to freedom was a closed gate away. Paul glanced around nervously. There was still an hour before boarding time.

The hour felt like a week. Several times, he saw Felipe heading for another gate. Except it wasn't Felipe. Just another man with a similar build and skin color. Several times, he saw their driver. Or so he thought. Paul's mind was playing tricks with him.

Karissa leaned on his shoulder. He could feel the tension in her. She was trying her best to stay calm. It was impossible for either of them. The clock ticked slowly.

The gate agent suddenly appeared behind an empty desk. There was a clutter of activity. Mercifully, the call to board came.

The doorway to the big bird opened. It beckoned invitingly.

Paul and Karissa got up from their seats. Paul was sure that he saw two men staring at them. They were conversing in low tones. They sat in the adjacent gate area. Paul looked away. He made a mental note of their faces. His heart thumped again.

Paul quickly joined the line. Karissa was right in front of him. The gate agent was in no hurry. He took his time inspecting every passenger's documents.

Paul bit his lower lip nervously. Departure time was still forty minutes away.

✝

It was after seven the next morning when they touched down at Sao Paulo International Airport. An hour later, Paul and Karissa left the airport in a taxi. He expected their stay in Sao Paulo to be short.

"Where to?" the taxi driver asked, in accented English. He didn't conceal his surprise when Paul told him their destination. Paul asked to be dropped off at any large shopping mall.

The driver took his time getting there. In the end, he left with a huge smile. He was well compensated.

A couple of hours later and another taxi ride, they checked into an inexpensive hotel. Paul unhooked the smoke detector and took out the battery. Using a cigarette lighter, he burnt both Canadian passports. He flushed the remnants down the toilet.

Paul and Karissa's attempt to sleep was less than successful. He kept hearing noises. He kept seeing the faces of the men at the airport. He eventually got up and stared out of the window.

A meal at the hotel's restaurant used up another hour. A new set of clothes, a switch of bags, and they were off to the airport again.

Paul bought two tickets on Lufthansa to Frankfurt, Germany. They were now Germans. It was going to be another long night of travel. He hoped they could sleep tonight. He took the liberty to buy business-class tickets this time.

He was trying to put distance between them and Washington, DC. Felipe had recommended crossing the Atlantic. He must have had his reasons.

Paul wasn't exactly sure but could venture a guess. The tentacles of the cartels were not as deep in Europe. Not yet, anyway.

14

THE DC FIRE DEPARTMENT WAS NOT SURPRISED WHEN THEY learned of the fire. They were *stunned*. They were shocked. They were numb. They responded in a daze.

The call came at twenty minutes after midnight. It was the third major fire in the city in less than twelve hours. Six in the Metro area since early morning.

The serial arsonist was on the loose, the news cried. The first fire occurred just before dawn that morning. It was a house in Montgomery County just off New Hampshire Avenue. The home of a doctor and his wife.

They had been reported missing. He was last seen leaving work with his wife two days earlier. He had spoken to no one about leaving. He was expected at work the next morning. The news alleged that they had been kidnapped.

Felipe's men did a thorough job with Paul's house. In absentia, his instructions had been carried out to a tee. No investigation was ever going to find any evidence. Certainly not anything linking the house to narco trafficking.

Three hours later, that same day, the men from Medellin got their information. Jimmy Martinez himself gave the orders. Eliminate and destroy. Do it quickly. Do it before they could retreat. Martinez's men moved in swiftly.

As the fire trucks raced to the scene, the DC fire chief called the police chief. Their fourth conversation in as many hours.

"On my way," Police Chief Leonard grunted.

"Will see you there."

"Remember, nothing to the press," Chief Leonard cautioned.

It was a day from hell. The fire department staff was at breaking point. No one had gone home from the previous morning. Many of the staff has been on duty for more than twenty-four hours. A few were finally getting ready to go home. Now this.

All the fires were in residential homes. One in Northeast and two in Southeast. This one was on Twenty-First Street, NE. Two blocks away from Benning Road and less than half a mile from RFK Stadium.

By the time the fire trucks got there, the blaze was twenty-five feet in the air. There was no hope of saving the house. The many fire trucks worked on saving the nearby homes.

The TV trucks got there minutes after the fire engines. Pictures went live on all the TV stations. The orange flames reaching into the night sky. The numerous fire trucks spraying water high in the air. It made for great TV. The television stations were happy.

Chief Leonard once again said a prayer. He prayed no one was inside. He doubted his prayers would come through. The odds were against it. He knew it was inevitable. Months ago, his deputy had told him that this was a shady house.

Chief Leonard decided to hold off on any public briefing. At least until he discussed it with the mayor. He knew he couldn't keep the press at bay for much longer. If he didn't tell them something soon, they would figure it out. Then they would run with even worse scenarios.

He was informed that newsmen were already waiting outside the medical examiner's building. Waiting to see if bodies would be brought in. There was no way to hide it.

As Leonard stared at the smoke rising into the night sky, his brain went over it again. These were professionals. He doubted anyone would ever be caught. Ten bodies had been found after the two fires in DC. Four in the first fire and six in the second. They were all burnt beyond recognition. They had all been handcuffed. Hands behind their backs. That much survived the fire. Their charred remains would provide more information.

The crime scenes had been cordoned off. Leonard was pretty certain they were executed before the buildings were set on fire. Men who were alive didn't stay around to get burnt to death. In time, the medical examiner would find the evidence. Now his job was to get the remnants of the bodies to the morgue. Without an entourage of cameras following them.

The Montgomery County Police bought him a few hours. They had a press conference earlier that night. They had categorically stated that no human remains were found in the Silver Spring house. The doctor and his wife were not inside at the time of the fire. Chief Leonard was not that lucky.

Leonard knew this was drug related. All three of the houses were owned by some corporation in Miami. They had occasionally been under the radar of his men. No one had ever pinned any crimes directly to them. Neighbors never met the owners. They reported people came and went.

He was certain it was cocaine related. He was correct. Too many people were dead. The aftermath would be messy. A late siren brought him back to the present.

Leonard already knew this was going to cost him his job. Whether it was a few weeks or a few months, it was a matter of time. In the end, it was up to the mayor. For now, he would continue to work diligently.

He knew he couldn't win this one. It was the nature of the beast. Working under public scrutiny was part of this job. There was nowhere to hide.

15

PAUL AND KARISSA SAT AT A WINDOW TABLE IN THE SMALL café. It was at the edge of the Market Square in Mainz. It was their first trip to Germany. Paul was beginning to let go. Just a little bit. He hoped the same was true for Karissa. Washington, DC, was a long way away. He hoped it stayed that way.

They had just completed a tour of the Mainz cathedral. A thousand years of history helped to put things into perspective. They were just a dot in time. Even though, they were the present.

As Paul and Karissa wandered through the cathedral, they journeyed back in time. The dim lighting played a big part in that journey. They stared in awe at the walls. Each archbishop for a thousand years was detailed there. Walls that had immortalized these men.

Monarchs were crowned in this cathedral. This old city on the banks of the Rhine was immortal in itself. It had survived the Thirty Years' War. It had survived two World Wars. It rebuilt itself after the Second World War. It was a symbol of resiliency. Some reason for optimism, Paul thought.

Two days earlier, they had come through Frankfurt. The extremely busy airport, with automation at every turn, made it easier. Their German passports allowed them quick entry. Since, they had switched hotels twice. He had destroyed their German passports.

Paul and Karissa Karan had now become Anthony Charles and Elizabeth Charles. English citizens. Language compatibility would attract the least attention, Paul reasoned. They chose this for their final identity.

The commonness of their name gave them a lot of leeway. Paul was practicing calling himself Tony. Karissa was working on Liz. As Paul contemplated their evolving plan, a wind picked up outside. It was still quite cold in Mainz at this time of the year.

Karissa sipped a cup of the City Roast. Paul opted for a local brew. In another week, he planned to shed their nomadic nature. He hoped they would settle in one place. They needed some luck. Just this time, he prayed their luck would hold.

The plan was to travel through Europe by rail. Gradually making their way to Paris. And then to London. From there, they would travel to their final destination. Money was not an issue. Time wasn't either. Paul didn't think a bit of sightseeing would hurt.

Yet Paul couldn't shed the apprehension. They were still on the run. He hadn't been able to escape their circumstances. He had heard about the serial arsonist in DC. The airports terminals carried CNN International. He looked it up on the *Washington Post* online.

Their house in Silver Spring was gone. All their possessions were gone. Forever. He knew the fires in the DC metro area were not random.

A lot was happening on the East Coast. The consequences of his actions were swift. DC wasn't the only city affected. The same thing was happening in Philadelphia. The cities had not yet connected the dots. A cartel was being systematically eliminated.

Paul felt personally responsible for some of the carnage. He agonized over the loss of so many lives. He had provided the ammunition for this. He and Felipe. This was the inevitable fallout, he reasoned. In his zest to get out, he hadn't really thought this far.

He looked at Karissa without really seeing her. He wished he could share his thoughts. He didn't know how to explain them. It was bad guys who were meeting their end, he rationalized.

Paul knew that wasn't quite the whole truth. He himself had not chosen this path. It had been imposed on him ever so gradually. The tentacles had been sunk into many of them, as they had been into Felipe, many years earlier.

He hoped Felipe was alive and well. He could only hope. He had no way of knowing. No double life anymore. It was a huge change. One he had yet to come to terms with. Just like becoming Anthony Charles.

Karissa tapped his hand gently. She brought him back to the present.

"Can we go for a walk?" she asked gently.

Paul nodded. It was a good idea. It might calm him.

"Sure, honey."

It reminded him of why he had chosen this course of action. He was not alone. The beginnings of a smile formed around his lips.

"I am glad we left DC," Karissa said.

"Me too."

The wind coming off the river was cold. Cold and rejuvenating. He held Karissa's hand tightly as they headed away from the square.

16

THE BATTLE FOR CUCUTA STARTED WELL BEFORE THE FIRST shot was fired. That much Police Chief Rafael knew. He had his sources. He could smell the impending bloodbath.

Chief Rafael hoped the carnage would be over quickly. If Luis Alvarez was eliminated, the city would be better off. Some good might even result from it, he thought. He had his doubts. Invariably, the vacuum would be filled. Another cartel would move in. It was just a matter of time.

Chief Rafael had been reliably informed that the men from Medellin were coming. The next day, they moved in big numbers. They didn't try to hide their presence. They took up many rooms at the top hotels. They drank at the fancy bars and clubs that night. Money flowed freely. Alcohol flowed. Business was good for those they patronized. Including the strippers and prostitutes.

An anonymous note was placed on Rafael's desk during the day. Handwritten. It simply said, "*Stay out of IT.*" He wasn't surprised. He didn't even need the warning.

His deductions were correct. The obvious questions were, who placed it there and what *IT* was. The first one was easy. Two of his five deputies were close friends of Luis Alvarez. They had access to the cartel and his office. He was sure it was one of them. *IT* was what was going to happen next. The big wolf had moved in to eliminate its competition. And to expand its territory. An old-fashioned drug war.

The chief's suspicion was confirmed early next day. Neither of the deputies reported for work. A few calls and a visit by a squad car later verified the predictable. Both men had been murdered in their homes overnight. No one saw anything. Rafael knew that was not the whole truth. Anyone who saw anything was too afraid to talk. That was how it was going to be going forward.

Rafael decided he was really going to try to stay out of *it* as much as possible. He didn't want to lose good men in the battle of cartels. Still, he had to keep the order in the city. Fortunately for him, most of Luis's facilities were located outside the city limits. Outside of his jurisdiction. He wasn't obligated to send men there. He could defend that stance.

The entire day was quiet. It was the calm before the storm. Rafael knew better than to relax. The Medellin men were out of sight. It meant only one thing. They were resting for later.

Rafael held a meeting with some of his senior officers. He brought them up to date. He shared everything he knew. Including the fact that both deputies killed worked for Luis Alvarez.

Chief Rafael's biggest worry was the future of his city. In many ways, dealing with the known was easier than dealing with the unknown. He knew about Luis and his operations. It was stable and contained. He had little idea of what would come after.

If Medellin replaced Alvarez, it could be anarchy. He hoped fervently that they would accomplish their mission and go. If they stayed on, it was going to be another bloody chapter.

Judging from their vivid past, it could really bad for the city and him. His sources had told him that Cali would be the lesser of the two evils. But Cali's recent history suggested that they weren't going to be much different.

┼

Luis Alvarez had prepared for this day. It was the reason he had constructed his mansion as a castle. That castle was the only building on a twenty-five square mile property. Built on the top of a hill, it was only accessible by a single road. The entrance was heavily guarded.

Luis paid his guards well. They were not under any illusions about what was expected of them. They would guard him with their lives.

The mansion had an outer and inner perimeter. The outer wall was ten feet high with barbed wire on the top. That alone was not insurmountable. However, the wire on top of the fence was electrified. A break in the circuit would be instantly detected by the guards.

If you were lucky enough to get over it, the second perimeter was a twelve-foot stone wall. It was a hundred yards from the mansion. There was no chance anyone could get over the first perimeter and make it to the second wall a mile away. They would be hunted down by the guards with time to spare. Luis had spent many millions on his security.

The outpost for the guards was at the outer perimeter. The guardhouse was huge. It was well stocked with semiautomatic rifles, machine guns, and grenades. No one had ever dared to get past them. Every vehicle entering the compound was searched from side to side and top to bottom.

That the place was impregnable was no secret. How impregnable was only understood by the men who worked for Luis. Two of them had recently defected to Medellin. They couldn't resist the huge monetary payoff. It was they who helped to craft the final plans.

At 10:00 p.m., the first of the Medellin troops moved in. They used the public access road to get in the general area. A mile from Luis's guardhouse was a small sentinel hut. Two guards were stationed there to give a heads-up on anything suspicious. They never knew what hit them.

Deftly and silently, they were executed. The Medellin men hung their bodies upside down from the nearby trees. It was a warning to outsiders. No interference.

When one of the guards at the main outpost called the sentinel hut, he got no response. He tried again a few minutes later. Nothing. He informed his supervisor. A former military man named Hector. Hector immediately placed them on high alert. He was ready for this. He was expecting a break in the electrified fence any moment now.

Hector's men were excitable. They were armed to the teeth with military grade assault weapons. They had all-terrain vehicles at their disposal. Equipped with night vision goggles, they were *looking* for a fight. Like hunters before a big hunt, they were energized. This would be like picking off sitting ducks for them. Anyone who dared to scale the perimeter would pay the full price.

They waited. Nothing. No alarm sounded. There was no break in the fence.

Then they heard a strange whirring noise. Hector immediately recognized it. It took a few moments for the others to comprehend.

Helicopters.

Two helicopters, designed to carry four, were stuffed with Medellin men. Eight each from the Medellin cartel. The pilots made good on their deal. They deposited their human cargo close to the inner perimeter. The Medellin men quickly took up positions in a thicket of trees. They waited.

As usual, Luis Alvarez was in the top floor of his mansion. He was angry. He had just received the news that three of his processing plants had been destroyed. Benito tried to calm him. They still had ten other functional plants, Benito reminded him. Benito promised to personally have them reconstructed.

News came from the guardhouse that they were expecting a break-in. Luis wasn't worried. He knew it was just a matter of time before Hector's army overpowered any intruders.

A few minutes later, Luis heard the sound of the helicopters. His senses heightened. He had to admit it was a daring and brazen plan. He was glad there were only two choppers. Hector would take care of them, he reassured himself.

Hector's men charged up the hill in their vehicles. Weapons drawn, they closed in on the on the drop-off point. The battle began. Gunfire sprayed the wooded area, chopping branches from the trees. The invaders returned fire.

Protected by the trees, the sixteen men fought like a company of soldiers. Hector and his troops couldn't get close enough for grenades. The battle was unrelenting. Waves of intense gunfire shattered the normally quiet countryside. One of the vehicles caught fire. A few of Hector's men fell. Hector's army took their hits and pressed forward.

Hector's men slowly gained ground. But he had underestimated the scale of the attack. Twenty minutes after Hector and his men came charging up the hill, the second phase began. He had been outfoxed.

The commander of the Medellin men, Andres, took charge. Hector had left just four men at the guardhouse. With a hundred men at his disposal, Andres moved in. They blasted through the front entrance like a sledgehammer through a glass wall.

They charged up the road to the inner perimeter. Hector saw that they were baited. The helicopter idea was ingenious. But it was not the main event. Bravely, Hector tried to redirect his men to the main entrance. They still had the advantage of armed vehicles. But they were greatly outnumbered.

The battle raged for a full hour. Periods of silence were punctuated by extended periods of gunfire. Andres lost some men. Hector lost most of his men. Eventually Hector's small army was overwhelmed. Andres and his men methodically moved forward. They breached the inner perimeter.

Hector's men had put up stiff resistance. In the end, the numbers won. The last few of Hector's men fled on foot. Hector turned the gun on himself. Andres continued on to the mansion.

"Time to make a move," Luis said.

"In a minute," Benito replied.

They had witnessed the gunfire from the castle. Luis knew it was time to quit. He wanted to live and fight another day. Benito was still young.

"Let's go," Luis said, with authority in his voice.

"What about them?" Benito motioned in the direction of the two women who were sharing Luis's quarters that week.

"*Putas!*"

†

Luis darted into his vast bedroom. He punched a few numbers and opened a safe. He stuffed a couple of guns in his waistband. He took a key from the safe and headed into a large walk-in closet. Benito was right behind him.

A full-sized door made up the back wall of the closet. It was completely concealed by a panel. Luis pressed a switch, and the panel slid away. He unlocked the door.

The door led to a narrow flight of stairs. Luis stepped through. Benito followed. They locked the door behind them. It was their escape exit. It had been designed specifically for this purpose. They began their descent.

The stairs were steep and winding. It was well lit. They disappeared into the bowels of the mansion. The exit route eventually flattened out. It led to a narrow tunnel. They moved as quickly as they could in the small space.

The tunnel was all of three miles long. It weaved its way well beyond the outer perimeter. It ended unobtrusively in the cellar of a small farmhouse. Their path to the outside world.

Luis and Benito made good progress. They were now completely insulated from the noise and battle that raged around and above them. Another hour, and the tunnel would take them to safety. They hoped.

Andres and his men stormed the mansion. With resistance now futile, most of Luis's men gave up the battle. They tried to flee. Many were killed. The looting began. Andres let his men roam. The troops needed to be fed. They took whatever they wanted. But they all knew Andres's orders. They should be out by 2:00 a.m.

The intelligence from the defectors of Luis's camp was excellent. Not only did Andres know where Luis and Benito lived, he knew of the alleged tunnels of escape. Accompanied by four of his senior men, Andres headed for the upper level of the mansion. They blasted through any doors that got in their way.

As Andres entered Luis's quarters, he wasn't surprised. Not at the luxury. Nor at the emptiness of the quarters. There was no sign of Luis or Benito. He had expected as much. After a quick search, Andres found the concealed door.

He didn't waste any time. He made a decision. He didn't want to be ambushed fighting in some enclosed space. Capturing Luis was not the main goal. He stuck to his mission.

All four of his men carried backpacks. They were loaded with C-4.

Andres looked at the time. It was 1:45 a.m. Time to get moving. His men placed the backpacks in strategic locations. They quickly headed out. He saw most of his men exiting the mansion. They were on the same page.

Andres stood four hundred yards away and stared at the mansion. The detonator was in his hand. He waited until 2:05 a.m. He gave his men the benefit of five minutes.

He pressed the button on the timer.

Sixty seconds.

He waited.

Sixty seconds seemed like a long time.

The ground under him shook. The earth shivered. Multiple explosions rocked the mansion.

Debris flew high in the air. Wreckage catapulted in all directions. Two sides of the mansion came crumbling down. The explosion was heard all the way to Cucuta.

Then silence.

Andres calculated that the tunnels would collapse with the explosion. It should trap any occupants. He had no way of knowing the outcome. Only time would tell whether Luis would resurface.

For now, his job was done. He turned his back on what was left of the mansion. He headed out. His bosses would be pleased. Now it was time to enjoy the fruits of their labor.

17

ANTHONY AND ELIZABETH CHARLES SAT IN THE FRONT OF the small ferry. The warm air on their faces felt good. The sound of the waves was comforting. The newest chapter of their lives had begun.

Paul signed the lease for the modest house just this morning. He wanted to buy it but decided to wait. There would be lots of time in the future. As he reflected on the last few months, he knew this ferry was going to be their main connection to the outside world.

The ferry ride from Kingston, St. Vincent, to Bequia was under an hour. They got off at St. Elizabeth. A representative from the travel agency met them. He drove them to the small house.

The house was nestled on the hillside, a hundred yards from the beach. A winding coastal road took them to it. The area was outside the reaches of the fancy touristy destinations, a few miles away. From the house, a path had been carved to the gravel and sandy beach.

After a lot of deliberation, Paul and Karissa had decided on this island of four thousand people. Paul had considered the more remote and private Isla A Quatre, off the coast of Bequia. That it was expensive was not a barrier. The isolation, he reasoned, would be difficult.

Two weeks ago, they were in Mainz, Germany. Two days ago, they boarded a flight from London to Barbados. A LIAT airplane brought them to St Vincent. Today, the ferry to Bequia.

Paul and Karissa stepped out on small patio of the single-level house. She took his hand. They just stood there. Words were not needed. Washington, DC, might as well be a million miles away.

The wind coming off the sea was refreshing. The view of the beach was beautiful. The tip of waves in the distance was calming. The continually changing shape was idyllically enhancing.

Paul put his arm around her waist. He looked out in the distance. He said a silent prayer. He prayed that they could put it all behind them. A lot had happened on the way from San Fernando to here.

He knew he would never be able to forget. He hoped that Karissa could. He would try to push it into the crevices of his brain. Deep into the inner recesses of his memory.

The cry of a seagull nudged them back to the present.